I0651170

Phlip Freneau

Poems relating to the American Revolution

Phlip Freneau

Poems relating to the American Revolution

ISBN/EAN: 9783743305151

Manufactured in Europe, USA, Canada, Australia, Japa

Cover: Foto ©Andreas Hilbeck / pixelio.de

Manufactured and distributed by brebook publishing software
(www.brebook.com)

Phlip Freneau

Poems relating to the American Revolution

POEMS

RELATING TO THE

AMERICAN REVOLUTION

BY

PHILIP FRENEAU.

WITH AN INTRODUCTORY MEMOIR AND NOTES.

BY

EVERT A. DUYCKINCK.

NEW YORK:

W. J. WIDDLETON, PUBLISHER.

M.DCCC.LXV

CONTENTS.

Winter

But, are no joys to the cold months assign'd?
Has winter nothing to delight the mind?
No friendly sun that beams a distant ray? —
No social snows that light us on our way? —
Yes, these are joys that May all clouds deny,
The child of Boreas and a frozen sky.

Happy with innocence may indulge an hour.
The modest beverage of the sober power
Happy, with love to share every care)
Happy with sense and not an hour to share.)

Philip Saunders

PHILIP FRENEAU.

———◆———

PHILIP FRENEAU, the popular poet of the days of the Revolution, who cheered the hearts of the citizens by his ready rhymes in behalf of the good caufe, and oppofition to its foes, while patriots were ftruggling for independence, was born in Frankfort Street, in the City of New York, January 2, 1752. The family was of French Huguenot defcent, his firft anceftors in America having taken refuge in this country, with many other moft eftimable emigrants to our fhores, from the religious and civil perfecutions confequent upon that unhappy policy, fo injurious to the true wealth of France, the Revocation, by Louis XIV., of the Edict of Nantes. Thefe refugees came in confiderable numbers, a peaceful, intelligent, induftrious population, and their fimple virtues are to this day the pride of their defcendants. The Freneaus were of this wholefome ftock; they were good citizens of New York,

and their names are cherished in the records of the St.
Esprit Church, the "Old French Church," the quaint
place of worship in Pine Street, still remembered by our
citizens, though the impulse of trade has, since its removal
from that spot, a second time driven the wandering house of
worship to a new locality.

Andrew Freneau, the grandfather of Philip Freneau,
was a shipping-merchant in the City of New York, of high
repute among the inhabitants. Some interesting notices of
his standing and liberal hospitality are recorded in that interesting volume, the "Memoirs of the Huguenot Family
of the Fontaines." John Fontaine, a traveller from France,
visited New York in 1716, on purposes of business and ob-
servation. Immediately upon his arrival he called upon
Andrew Freneau, at his home, where he met with a cordial
reception, and was much with him during his stay in the
city, at the Coffee House, at the French Club, and at
Church.* Andrew Freneau resided, at the time of his
death, in Pearl Street, near Hanover Square. He left two
sons, born in New York, Pierre and Andrew, who pursued
the business of wine-merchants in the city, and were engaged
in the Bordeaux and Madeira trade. Pierre was the father

---

* "Memoirs of a Huguenot Family," by Ann Maury, 296–310.

of Philip, the poet of the Revolution, and of Peter Freneau, who became hardly lefs diftinguifhed in South Carolina. Andrew Freneau, the uncle of Philip, married a daughter of Bifhop Provooft. Pierre, the father of the poet, bought an eftate of a thoufand acres at Mount Pleafant, New Jerfey, a family inheritance which his fon afterwards occupied, and where he wrote many of his poems. Both the father and grandfather of Philip Freneau are buried in a vault in Trinity Churchyard, New York, by the fide of their family relations.

Of the boyhood of Philip Freneau we know little, but we may infer from the pofition of his family, and his fubfequent attainments, that he was well inftructed at the fchools of the city, for we find him in 1767 a ftudent at the College of New Jerfey, at Princeton, where he graduated with credit, after the ufual four years' courfe, in 1771. He began early the practice of verfification; for, in his fophomore year, at the age of feventeen, he compofed a rhymed poem of decided promife, entitled "The Poetical Hiftory of the Prophet Jonah," which appears at the head of the firft general collection of his "Poems." Other compofitions, in various metres, on claffical and hiftorical themes, preferved in the fame volume, were written during his collegiate courfe. It was a creditable year for the inftitution when he graduated; for in his class were James Madison, the future President; Hugh Henry Brackenridge, the celebrated Judge, and author of "Modern Chivalry;" besides others of note in the annals of America, among whom we may mention the father of the venerable Rev. Dr. Gardiner Spring, Samuel Spring, who became a chaplain of the Revolutionary army, was with Arnold at the attack of Quebec, in 1775, and in that disastrous affair carried in his arms the wounded Aaron Burr from the field. The commencement exercises at Nassau Hall that year, 1771, were of unusual interest. It was in the Presidency of that eminent patriot, John Witherspoon, who, though born in Scotland, was proving himself, by his enlightened sagacity and devotion to freedom, an "American of the Americans." The political independence of the country, though not yet formally proclaimed, was ripening, in Massachusetts and elsewhere, to its great declaration and invincible resolve. The young patriots of Princeton, on a spot destined to become memorable in the struggle, were already animated by the kindling promise of the future. Brackenridge and Freneau had already developed a taste for poetry, and they united, for their commencement exercise, in the composition of a dialogue, *A Poem on the Rising Glory of America*, which they pronounced together, founding, in animated blank verse, the achievements of colonization in the paſt and the viſionary grandeur of empire hereafter. This joint poem was publiſhed in Philadelphia in 1772, with the well-known motto from Seneca, the Roman tragic writer, afterwards adopted by Irving on the title-page of the "Life of Columbus." The portion written by Freneau opens the preſent collection—the prelude to his poems of the Revolution.

The next information we have of Freneau is gathered from the dates of the poems which he contributed to the journals publiſhed by Hugh Gaine and Anderſon, in New York, in 1775. They exhibit his intereſt in the important military affairs of the year at Boſton, and will be found re-produced in the preſent volume. In a poem of this year, "Mac Sniggen," a ſatire on ſome hoſtile poetaſter, he ex-preſſes a deſire to croſs the Atlantic :—

> "Long have I ſat on this diſaſt'rous ſhore,
> And, ſighing, ſought to gain a paſſage o'er
> To Europe's towns, where, as our travellers ſay,
> Poets may flouriſh, or perhaps they may;"—

an inclination for foreign travel which was gratified, in 1776, by a voyage to the Weſt Indies, where he appears to have remained ſome time, in a mercantile capacity, viſiting Jamaica and the Daniſh iſland, Santa Cruz. Several of his

moft ftriking poems, as the "Houfe of Night," and the
"Beauties of Santa Cruz," were written on thefe vifits.

In 1779, Freneau was engaged as a leading contributor
to *The United States Magazine : A Repofitory of Hiftory,
Politics, and Literature,* edited by his college friend and fel-
low-patriot, Hugh Henry Brackenridge, and publifhed by
Francis Bailey, in Philadelphia.   It was iffued monthly from
January to December, when its difcontinuance was announced "until an eftablifhed peace and a fixed value of the
money fhall render it convenient or poffible to take it up
again."   The volume forms a moft interefting memorial, in
its literary as well as hiftorical matter, of this important year
of the war.   Freneau wrote much for it, in profe and verfe,
and with equal fpirit in both.*   Here at firft appeared the
two poems written in the Weft Indies, already alluded to,
and two of the poems, "King George III.'s Soliloquy,"
and the fpirited "Dialogue between his Britannic Majefty
and Mr. Fox," reprinted in this volume.   In comparing

---

* It is ftated in Allibone's Dictionary, that Freneau edited this magazine.
That his relation to the work was that of a contributor, appears from a note to a
poetical imitation of the 137th Pfalm, in the September number.   The poem is
figned by Freneau, and dated at Monmouth, N. J.   The note is to the author's
name :—"A young gentleman to whom, in the courfe of this work, we are
greatly indebted,"—an acknowledgment which would hardly be made in fuch
terms if Freneau had been the editor.   Befides, it is diftinctly ftated in the
Biography of Brackenridge, by his fon, that the magazine was edited by the
author of "Modern Chivalry."

thefe with the poems as they appear in the later editions, we find numerous important additions and changes, fhowing the care and fkill which the poet beftowed upon his productions. The "Houfe of Night," in the Magazine, is comprifed in feventy-three ftanzas; in the fubfequent collection of the author's poems it was extended to one hundred and thirty-fix, and the fifty-two ftanzas of the poem on "Santa Cruz," to one hundred and nine; and various alterations occur. The laft-mentioned poem in the Magazine is prefaced by an interefting profe defcription of the ifland. In it occurs this noticeable teftimony of the author on the fubject of negro flavery :—

"The only difagreeable circumftance attending this ifland," fays he, "which it has in common with the reft, is the cruel and deteftable flavery of the negroes. 'If you have tears to fhed, prepare to fhed them now.' A defcription of the flavery they endure would be too irkfome and unpleafant to me; and, to thofe who have not beheld it, would be incredible. Sufficient be it to fay, that no clafs of mankind in the known world undergo fo complete a fervitude as the common negroes in the Weft Indies. It cafts a fhade over the native charms of the country; it blots out the beauties of the eternal fpring which Providence has there ordained to reign; and amidft all the profufion of bounties which nature has scattered—the brightness of the heaven, the mildness of the air, and the luxuriancy of the vegetable kingdom—it leaves me melancholy and disconsolate, convinced that there is no pleasure in this world without its share of pain.   And thus the earth, which, were it not for the lust of pride and dominion, might be an earthly paradise, is, by the ambition and overbearing nature of mankind, rendered an eternal scene of desolation, woe, and horror; the weak goes to the wall, while the strong prevails; and after our ambitious frenzy has turned the world upside down, we are contented with a narrow spot, and leave our follies and cruelties to be acted over again, by every succeeding generation."

Freneau has also recorded his detestation of the cruelties of West India slavery in verse, in the poem, a terrific picture of slave life, addressed " To Sir Toby, a Sugar-Planter in the interior parts of Jamaica :"—

> " If there exists a HELL—the case is clear—
> Sir Toby's slaves enjoy that portion here."

In another poem, " On the Emigration to America, and Peopling the Western Country," published in his volume of 1795, Freneau comes nearer home in the declaration of his opinions on this subject, when he writes : —

"O come the time and hafte the aay,
  When man fhall man no longer crufh
When reafon fhall enforce her fway,
  Nor thefe fair regions raife our blufh,
Where ftill the African complains,
And mourns his yet unbroken chains."

In after life, when the poet himfelf, under the mild fyf-
tem of Northern fervitude, became the owner of flaves in
New Jerfey, he uniformly treated them with kindnefs, manu-
mitted them in advance of the Emancipation Act in the
State, and fupported on the farm thofe of them who were
not able to take care of themfelves. One of thefe, a veteran mammy, proud of having opened the door in her day
to General Wafhington, and been addrefled by him in a
word or two on that important occafion, long furvived the
poet.

In the year following the publication of the Magazine,
Freneau, having embarked as paffenger in a merchant veffel
from Philadelphia, on another voyage to the Weft Indies,
was captured with the crew by a Britifh cruifer off the
Capes of the Delaware, and carried with the prize to New
York. There he was confined on his arrival in the *Scorpion*, one of the hulks lying in the harbour ufed as prifon-
fhips. The cruel treatment which he experienced on board,

with the aggravated horrors of foul air and other privations, speedily threw him into a fever, when he was transferred to the hofpital-fhip *Hunter*, which proved fimply an exchange of one fpecies of fuffering for another more aggravated. How long Freneau was confined in this hideous prifon we are not informed, nor by what influences he gained his difcharge. He carried with him, however, on his efcape, a burning memory of the feverities and indignities he had endured, which he gave expreffion to in one of the moft characteriftic of his poetical productions, "*The Britifh Prifon-Ship*," which was publifhed by Francis Bailey, in Philadelphia, in 1771. This poem, originally divided into four cantos, was fubfequently recaft by the author in the form in which it appears in the prefent volume, with the title, "Cantos from a Prifon-Ship." The picturefque incidents of the voyage, which is defcribed; the animated action of the capture; the melancholy circumftances of the prifon-fhip contrafted with the happy fcenery of the fhore; the ftern terrors of the hofpital, with the fatirical humour expended upon the defcription of the Heffian Doctor, are all in Freneau's beft manner.

Freneau now became a frequent contributor of patriotic odes and occafional poems, celebrating the incidents of the war, to *The Freeman's Journal* of Philadelphia. Here

many of the poems in the prefent volume, including the
humorous verfes on Rivington and his "Royal Gazette,"
were firft publifhed. Literature, however, was not then
a profitable occupation; and Government, which had ex-
haufted its refources in keeping an army in the field, had
fcant opportunity of rewarding its champions. The poet,
looking to other means of fubfiftence, returned to his fea-
faring and mercantile habits, and became known by his
voyages to the Weft Indies as Captain Freneau. He ftill,
however, kept up the ufe of the pen. In 1783, befides his
poetical contributions to the newfpapers, including feveral
New Years' Addreffes, written for the carriers of the Philadelphia journals, a fpecies of rhyming for which he had
great facility, we find him publifhing in that city a tranfla-
tion of the travels of M. Abbé Robin, the chaplain of Count
Rochambeau, giving an account of the progrefs of the
French army from Newport to Yorktown. In 1784, Freneau is at the Ifland of Jamaica, writing a poetical defcription of Port Royal.

The firft collection of his poetical writings which he
made, entitled "*The Poems of Philip Freneau, written chiefly*
during the late War," was publifhed by Francis Bailey, "at
Yorick's Head in Market ftreet," Philadelphia, in 1786.
It is prefaced by a brief "Advertifement," figned by the

publisher, in which he states that the pieces now collected had been left in his hands by the author more than a year previously, with permission to publish them whenever he thought proper. "A considerable number of the performances," he adds, "as many will recollect, have appeared at different times in newspapers (particularly *The Freeman's Journal*), and other periodical publications in the different States of America, during the late war, and since; and, from the avidity and pleasure with which they generally appear to have been read by persons of the best taste, the Printer now the more readily gives them to the world in their present form (without troubling the reader with any affected apologies for their supposed or real imperfections), in hopes they will afford a high degree of satisfaction to the lovers of poetical wit and elegance of expression."

The success of this volume led to the publication, by Mr. Bailey, of another collection of Freneau's writings in 1788. It is entitled, "*The Miscellaneous Works of Mr. Philip Freneau, containing his Essays and Additional Poems.*" A number of the poems were printed from manuscript. "Some few of the pieces," the publisher announced, "have heretofore appeared in American newspapers; but, through a fatality not unusually attending publications of that kind, are now, perhaps, forgotten; and, at any time, may possi-

bly never have been feen, or attended to, but by very few."
The volume, as not uncommon even with works of very
limited extent, in that early period of the nation, was publifhed by fubfcription. The Honorable David Rittenhoufe,
Mathew Carey, and John Parke, A. M., of Horatian ce-
lebrity, were among the fubfcribers in Philadelphia; New
York furnifhed, among others of note, De Witt Clinton,
Edward Livingfton, Colonel Marinus Willet, and John
Pintard, who took two copies; Maryland fent fome thirty;
but the largeft number was contributed by South Carolina,
that State fupplying two hundred and fifty, or more than half
the entire lift. Captain Freneau was well known and highly
appreciated at Charlefton, which he frequently vifited in the
courfe of his mercantile adventures to the Weft Indies, and
where his younger brother Peter, who fubfequently edited a
political journal in that city, and was in intimate correfpondence with Prefident Jefferfon, was already eftablifhed as
an influential citizen.

The "Effays" and "Tales," in this collection, difplay
the author's tafte and ingenuity. They cover a wide range
of fubjects, moral, humorous, and fatirical; and, like the
kindred productions of Franklin and Francis Hopkinfon,
thefe fketches of manners and fociety are remarkably neat
in execution. The formal parts of literature were, in the

days of our author, more attended to than at prefent, at leaft in thefe occafional compofitions. The writer who appeared in print before the public, in that age of ceremonial coftume, felt it incumbent upon himfelf to pay fome regard to the drefs in which he clothed his thoughts. Freneau had, befide, a true author's inftinct in regard to the fmall proprieties of expreffion. He would polifh and refine at every opportunity, as the ftudied improvement of particular paffages in the fucceffive editions of his writings bears witnefs. The " Tracts and Effays," by Mr. Robert Slender, the name under which Freneau frequently wrote, are, in fact, quite pleafant reading at this day; they are enlivened with various happy inventions, and reflect, in a genial vein of humour, the habits and opinions of our forefathers at a period which will always be peculiarly interefting to the genuine American.

After feveral years fpent in voyaging, we find Freneau again in active literary employment in 1791, as editor of the *Daily Advertifer*, a journal printed in New York, the fuperintendence of which he prefently exchanged for that of the *National Gazette* at Philadelphia, the firft number of which appeared under his direction in October of the year juft mentioned. He was employed at the fame time by Jefferfon, the Secretary of State,—the feat of government being now removed to Philadelphia,—as tranflating clerk in the

State Department, with a falary of two hundred and fifty dollars a year. It was a time of fierce political excitement, when the newly framed Conftitution, not yet fully eftab-lifhed in its working, was expofed to the fierce criticifm of its adverfaries ; while popular opinion was greatly excited by the rifing tumult of ideas generated in the French Revolu-tion. In this ftrife of parties Freneau was an active partifan of the new French ideas, was a fupporter of Genet, the minifter who fought to entangle the country in the great European ftruggle, and, as might be expected, was an un-fparing affailant of the policy of Wafhington, whofe charac-ter he had heretofore eulogized. Wafhington was annoyed, and Hamilton attacked Jefferfon for his official fupport of the troublefome editor. Jefferfon replied that he had be-friended Freneau, as a man of genius ; but that he had never written for his paper. It is unqueftionably true, how-ever, that Freneau's political writings, at this time, had Jef-ferfon's warmeft fympathy.

The *Gazette* came to an end with its fecond volume and fecond year, in 1793, after which Freneau became, as ne had been before, a refident of New Jerfey. He had ftill, however, an inclination to editorial life, and we accordingly find him, in the fpring of 1795, publifhing at Mount Plea-fant, near Middletown Point, a new journal, entitled *The*

Jersey Chronicle. A copy of this journal is preserved in the library of the New York Historical Society. The first number was dated May 2; it was issued weekly and continued for a year, when it was arrested by that frequent malady of such undertakings, want of support. This *Chronicle* is quite a curious affair. It was printed by the author himself, who had mustered a medley of types for the purpose. The first number was of the humble dimensions of eight small quarto pages, of seven inches by eight. But it bore a brave motto, from the editor's favourite Horace :—

> "Inter sylvas Academi quærere verum,"

and loftily proposed to review the foreign and domestic politics of the times, and "mark the general character of the age and country." The spirited little journal was presently somewhat enlarged, but typographically, at least, it always appeared of a somewhat sickly constitution.

The office types, however, were well employed in printing, this year, 1795, a new and comprehensive edition of the author's poems, in an octavo volume of four hundred and fifty-six pages, of the title-page of which we present a close imitation :—

P O E M S

WRITTEN BETWEEN THE YEARS 1768 & 1794,

B Y

PHILIP FRENEAU,

O F

N E W   J E R S E Y.

A NEW EDITION, REVISED and CORRECTED by the
AUTHOR; Including a confiderable number of
PIECES never before PUBLISHED.

Audax inde cohors ftellis e pluribus unum
Ardua pyramidos tollit ad aftra caput.

M O N M O U T H
[N. J.]

P R I N T E D
At the Preſs of the AUTHOR, at MOUNT-PLEASANT, near
MIDDLETOWN-POINT : M.DCC.XCV : and, of
—AMERICAN INDEPENDENCE—
XIX.

The explanation of the ſtars in the title will be found in the concluding poem of the preſent volume, entitled " The Pyramid of the Fifteen American States." In this collection Freneau revived his poem on the Priſon-Ship, and reprinted at length his humorous animadverſions on Rivington and Gaine; all of which, with the other Revolutionary poems, have been transferred to the preſent volume.

One more newſpaper venture concludes the liſt of Freneau's undertakings of this deſcription. In 1797 he edited, at New York, a miſcellaneous periodical, entitled *The Time-Piece and Literary Companion.* It was printed in quarto form, appeared three times a week; and, beſides his editorſhip, Freneau was aſſociated with a partner in its printing and publication. As uſual, his part was well done, the journal being well arranged, judiciouſly filled with a variety of matter, ſpirited and entertaining; in faᴄt, what its title promiſed, an agreeable companion to an intelligent reader. This, at leaſt, was its charaᴄter while in charge of Freneau. He appears to have left it during the year, after which it languiſhed and died.

In 1799, Freneau publiſhed at Philadelphia, "printed for the author," a thin octavo volume, entitled, " *Letters on Various Intereſting and Important Subjeᴄts ; many of which have appeared in the Aurora. Correᴄted and much en-*

larged. By Robert Slender, O. S. M.," with the motto
from Pope :—

> " Worth makes the man, and want of it the fellow ;
>   The reft is all but leather or prunella."

Freneau, of whofe occupations we have now no particular account, appears to have refided in New Jerfey, doubtlefs often vifiting New York, and certainly keeping alive his poetical faculty, by his habit of penning occafional verfes on topics fuggefted by the day. In 1809 he publifhed a new collection, the fourth, of his writings, which he entitled, *" Poems Written and Publifhed during the American Revolutionary War, and now Republifhed from the Original Manufcripts ; interfperfed with Tranflations from the Ancients, and other pieces not heretofore in print."* The title-page alfo bore the motto—

> " —— Juftly to record the deeds of fame,
>   A mufe from heaven fhould touch the foul with flame ;
>   Some powerful fpirit, in fuperior lays,
>   Should tell the conflicts of the ftormy days."

The tranflations " from the ancients," are the third Elegy of the firft book of Ovid's " Triftia," and the paffage of Lucretius, in the fixth book of his poem, in which he defcribes the great plague at Athens. The felection fhows

that Freneau had not altogether loſt the early inſtruction in
the claſſics which he had received at Naſſau Hall.   The
collection in which theſe poems appeared was publiſhed in
two duodecimo volumes, at Philadelphia, "from the preſs
of Lydia R. Bailey."

Freneau lived to commemorate the incidents of the ſec-
ond war with Great Britain, in 1812.   He wrote various
poems celebrating the naval actions of Hull, Macdonough,
Porter, and others, which ſtirred the ſoul of the old Revolutionary warrior.   His traditionary hatred of England ſurvives in theſe and other compoſitions which he publiſhed in
New York, in 1815, in two ſmall volumes, from the preſs
of David Longworth, entitled, "*A Collection of Poems on
American Affairs and a Variety of other Subjects, written between the years 1797 and the preſent time.*"

> "Then England come!—a ſenſe of wrong requires
>   To meet with thirteen ſtars your thouſand fires:
>   Through theſe ſtern times the conflict to maintain,
>   Or drown them, with your commerce, in the main."

Theſe volumes received a genial notice in the *Analectic
Magazine*, from the pen of Mr. Gulian C. Verplanck.
Deprecating the ſeverity of criticiſm towards poems of an
occaſional character, the writer remarks: "He depicts land

battles and naval fights with much animation and gay col-
ouring; and being himfelf a fon of old Neptune, he is never
at a lofs for appropriate circumftance and expreffive diction,
when the fcene lies at sea.   *   *   *   His martial and political ballads are free from bombaft and affectation, and
often have an arch fimplicity in their manner that renders
them very poignant and ftriking.   If the ballads and fongs
of Dibdin have cheered the fpirits and incited the valour of
the Britifh tars, the ftrains of Freneau, in like manner, are
calculated to impart patriotic impulfes to the hearts of his
countrymen, and their effect in this way fhould be taken as
the teft of their merit, without entering into a very nice ex-
amination of the rhyme or the reafon.   For our own part,
we have no inclination to dwell on his defects; we had
much rather—

> ' With full applaufe, in honour to his age,
>   Difmifs the veteran poet from the ftage;
>   Crown his laft exit with diftinguifhed praife,
>   And kindly hide his baldnefs with the bays.' "*

After witneffing and chronicling in his verfe the conflicts
of two wars, Freneau had yet many years of life before him.
They were moftly paffed in rural retirement, at the home

* "Analectic Magazine," v. 518.

where he had been long fettled, near Monmouth, New Jerfey. He occafionally vifited New York, keeping up his
acquaintance with the Democratic leaders, with whom he
had been affociated in the political ftruggles of the paft, and
honoured by the friends of literature in the city, who never
failed to appreciate the merits of the veteran finger of the
Revolution. His appearance and converfation at this time
have been graphically defcribed by the late Dr. John W.
Francis, in whom the genius and hiftory of Freneau excited the warmeft intereft. " I had," fays he, " when very
young, read the poetry of Freneau, and as we inftinctively
become attached to the writers who firft captivate our
imaginations, it was with much zeft that I formed a perfonal acquaintance with the Revolutionary bard. He was
at that time about feventy-fix years old, when he firft intro-
duced himfelf to me in my library. I gave him an earneft
welcome. He was fomewhat below the ordinary height;
in perfon thin, yet mufcular; with a firm ftep, though a little
inclined to ftoop; his countenance wore traces of care, yet
lightened with intelligence as he fpoke; he was mild in
enunciation, neither rapid nor flow, but clear, diftinct, and
emphatic. His forehead was rather beyond the medium
elevation; his eyes a dark gray, occupying a focket deeper
than common; his hair muft have once been beautiful; it

was now thinned and of an iron gray. He was free of all ambitious difplays; his habitual expreffion was penfive. His drefs might have paffed for that of a farmer. New York, the city of his birth, was his moft interefting theme; his collegiate career with Madifon, next. His ftory of many of his occafional poems was quite romantic. As he had at command types and a printing-prefs, when an incident of moment in the Revolution occurred, he would retire for compofition, or find fhelter under the fhade of fome tree, indite his lyrics, repair to the prefs, fet up his types, and iffue his productions. There was no difficulty in verfification with him. I told him what I had heard Jeffrey, the Scotch Reviewer, fay of his writings, that the time would arrive when his poetry, like that of Hudibras, would command a commentator like Grey.

"It is remarkable how tenacioufly Freneau preferved the acquifitions of his early claffical ftudies, notwithftanding he had for many years, in the after portion of his life, been occupied in purfuits fo entirely alien to books. There is no portrait of the patriot Freneau; he always firmly declined the painter's art, and would brook no ' counterfeit prefentment.' "*

* A fketch contributed by Dr. Francis to the "Cyclopædia of American Literature," i. 333, 334.

John Pintard, in a biographical notice of Freneau, alfo celebrates his mental accomplifhments: "He was," fays he, "a man of great reading and extenfive acquirements; few were more thoroughly verfed in claffical literature, and fewer ftill, who knew as much about the early hiftory of our country, the organization of the government, and the rife and progrefs of parties."*

The averfion of the poet to fitting for his portrait, noticed by Dr. Francis, was one of his peculiarities, for which it is not eafy to fuggeft a fufficient explanation. As an author he was careful of the prefervation of his fame. Certainly the caufe was not to be found in any unfavourable impreffion his likenefs might create, for he was, as accurately defcribed by Dr. Francis, of an interefting appearance in age. In youth he was regarded as handfome. His brother Peter was renowned, in South Carolina, for his perfonal beauty. But, whatever the motive, Freneau refolutely declined to have his portrait painted. He was once waited upon by the artift, Rembrandt Peale, with a requeft for this purpofe, by a body of gentlemen in Philadelphia; but he was inexorable on the fubjeft. On another occafion, the elder Jarvis, with a view of fecuring his likenefs, was fmuggled into a

* New York *Mirror*, Jan. 12, 1833.

corner of the room at a dinner-party, at Dr. Hofack's, to which the poet had been invited; but the latter detected the defign and arrefted its accomplifhment. At this late day, the neglect has been, in a meafure, repaired. The portrait prefixed to this volume has been fketched by an artift, at the fuggeftion and dictates of feveral members of the poet's family, who retain the moft vivid recollection of his perfonal appearance. . It is pronounced by them, a fair reprefentation of the man in the maturity of his phyfical powers, previous to the inroads of old age. His daughter, Mrs. Leadbeater, and his grandfon and adopted fon, Mr. Philip L. Freneau, of this city, to whom we are indebted, in this Memoir, for feveral interefting perfonal particulars, pronounce it a fatisfactory likenefs. Though wanting the authenticity which might have been conferred by a Trumbull or Stuart, the fketch is of undoubted intereft as an embodiment of the recollections and impreffions of his family, who are not likely to be deceived in a matter fo clofely touching the affections. It is, at any rate, all that now can be refcued from the paft. The attempt, under the circumftances, was well worthy of being made, and muft be regarded, with the evidence before us, as reafonably fuccefsful.

Freneau furvived nearly to the completion of his eightieth

year. He died December 18, 1832.* The *Monmouth* (N.
J.) *Inquirer* thus announced his death :—

"Mr. Freneau was in the village, and started, towards
evening, to go home, about two miles. In attempting to
go acrofs he appears to have got loft and mired in a bog
meadow, where his lifelefs corpfe was difcovered yefter-
day morning. Captain Freneau was a ftanch Whig in the
time of the Revolution, a good foldier, and a warm patriot.
The productions of his pen animated his countrymen in
the darkeft days of '76, and the effufions of his mufe

---

* Philip Freneau left a family of four daughters, all of whom, at this prefent
time (1865), are living. The mother of Governor Seymour, of New York
(Mary, the daughter of General Jonathan Forman), was a niece of Mrs. Philip
Freneau, the wife of the poet. The Freneaus, through the fecond marriage of
the poet's mother, are connected with the Kearney family, of New Jerfey. Philip
Freneau married early in life, at about the age of thirty, Mifs Eleanor Forman,
daughter of Samuel Forman, a wealthy citizen of New Jerfey. General Jonathan Forman and Denife Forman, who were much engaged in military affairs in
the State during the Revolution, were her brothers. David Forman, alfo in
military life, was her coufin. This lady, who fhared her hufband's talent for
poetry, correfponding with him, for feveral years before their marriage, in verfe,
was of marked character and intelligence. She was devotedly attached to the
Epifcopal Church, which the family attended, having left the French Church in
the lifetime of the poet's father. Mrs. Freneau furvived her hufband many
years, retaining, in her latter days, much of the perfonal activity of her youth,
and a fund in converfation of the moft interefting memories of the days of the
Revolution. The remains of Mrs. Freneau repofe, with thofe of her hufband, in
the family burial-ground at Mount Pleafant, New Jerfey. A monument to the
poet's memory, within a few years, has been erected on the fpot.

cheered the defponding foldier as he fought the battles of freedom."

The eulogy of the Monmouth journal will remain Freneau's higheft diftinction. He was the popular poet of the Revolution. We have made this fervice the ground of felection of the poems which compofe the prefent volume. For the firft time, all that he himfelf thought worthy of republication of this nature, is here brought together in a fingle volume. The poems have been carefully gathered from the feveral editions, and the author's lateft revifed text has in all cafes been followed. Where changes of any intereft were made by him, the variations have been pointed out in a note.

It is not to be forgotten, however, that Freneau had other claims to attention as a poet, than his literary affociation with the events of the Revolution. He was effentially of a poetic mood, and had many traits of rare excellence in the divine art. His fympathies were with nature and his fellow-men. His mind was warmed into admiration at the beauties of landfcape; his conceptions were imaginative; vifionary fcenes fwarmed before his imagination; and the fame fufceptibility of mind which led him to inveft with intereft the fading fortunes of the Indian, and Nature's prodigality in the luxurious fcenery of the tropics, made him keenly appreciative of the humble ways and manners of his race. The practical Captain Freneau combined humour with fancy, and his Muse, laying aside what Milton termed "her singing robes," could wear with ease the garments of every-day life. The common, once familiar incidents and manners of his time, will be found pleasantly reflected in many a quaint picture in his poems.

"The poems of Philip Freneau," if we may be allowed here to repeat our estimate of his powers, from a sketch written some years ago, "represent his times, the war of wit and verse no less than of sword and stratagem of the Revolution; and he superadds to this material a humorous, homely simplicity peculiarly his own, in which he paints the life of village rustics, with their local manners fresh about them; of days when tavern delights were to be freely spoken of, before temperance societies and Maine laws were thought of, when men went to prison at the summons of inexorable creditors, and when Connecticut deacons rushed out of meeting to arrest and waylay the passing Sunday traveller. When these humours of the day were exhausted, and the impulses of patriotism were gratified in song; when he had paid his respects to Rivington and Hugh Gaine, he solaced himself with remoter themes: in the version of an ode of Horace, a visionary meditation on the antiquities of America, or

a fentimental effufion on the loves of Sappho. Thefe fhow
the fine tact and delicate handling of Freneau, who deferves
much more confideration in this refpect from critics than he
has received. A writer from whom the faftidious Campbell, in his beft day, thought it worth while to borrow an
entire line, is worth looking into. It is from Freneau's
Indian Burying-Ground, the laft image of that fine vifionary
ftanza :—

> ' By midnight moons, o'er moiftening dews,
> In veftments for the chafe array'd,
> The hunter ftill the deer purfues,
> The hunter and the deer—a fhade.'

Campbell has given the line a rich fetting in the ' lovelorn
fantafy' of *O'Conor's Child :—*

> ' Bright as the bow that fpans the ftorm,
> In Erin's yellow vefture clad,
> A fon of light—a lovely form,
> He comes and makes her glad;
> Now on the grafs-green turf he fits,
> His taffell'd horn befide him laid;
> Now o'er the hills in chafe he flits,
> *The hunter and the deer a fhade.'*

" There is alfo a line of Sir Walter Scott which has its

prototype in Freneau. In the introduction to the third canto of *Marmion*, in the apostrophe to the Duke of Brunswick, we read—

> ‘ Lamented chief!—not thine the power
> To fave in that prefumptuous hour,
> When Pruffia hurried to the field,
> And fnatch’d the fpear but left the fhield.’

“ In Freneau’s poem on the heroes of Eutaw, we have this ftanza :—

> ‘ They faw their injur’d country’s woe ;
> The flaming town, the wafted field ;
> Then rufh’d to meet the infulting foe ;
> They took the fpear—but left the fhield.’

“ An anecdote which the late Henry Brevoort was accuftomed to relate of his vifit to Scott, affords affurance that the poet was really indebted to Freneau, and that he would not, on a proper occafion, have hefitated to acknowledge the obligation. Mr. Brevoort was afked by Scott refpecting the authorfhip of certain verfes on the battle of Eutaw, which he had feen in a magazine, and had by heart, and which he knew were American. He was told that they were by Freneau, when he remarked, ‘ The poem is as fine a thing as there is of the kind in the language.’ Scott alfo praifed one of the Indian poems.

"We might add to thefe inftances, that in 1790, Freneau, in his poetical correfpondence between Nanny, the Philadelphia Houfe-keeper, and Nabby, her friend in New York, upon the fubject of the removal of Congrefs to the former city, hit upon fome of the peculiar pleafantry of Moore's Epiftles in verfe, of the prefent century.

"Freneau furprifes us often by his neatnefs of execution and fkill in verfification. He handles a triple-rhymed ftanza in the octofyllabic meafure particularly well. His appreciation of nature is tender and fympathetic,—one of the pure fprings which fed the more boifterous current of his humour when he came out among men, to deal with quackery, pretence, and injuftice. But what is, perhaps, moft worthy of notice in Freneau is his originality, the inftinct with which his genius marked out a path for itfelf, in thofe days when moft writers were languidly leaning upon the old foreign fchool of Pope and Darwin. He was not afraid of home things and incidents. Dealing with facts and realities, and the life around him, wherever he was, his writings have ftill an intereft where the vague expreffions of other poets are forgotten. * * * It is not to be denied, however, that Freneau was fometimes carelefs. He thought and wrote with improvidence. His jefts are fometimes mifdirected; and his verfes are unequal in execution. Yet it is not too much to predict, that, through the genuine nature of some of his productions, and the historic incidents of others, all that he wrote will yet be called for, and find favour in numerous editions."*

This prediction was ventured ten years ago.   It is now in a measure fulfilled, in the demand for the present imprint—the only publication in America of any collection of Freneau's writings since the year 1815, and the first of his Revolutionary Poems since 1809.

* "Cyclopædia of American Literature," I. 327–348.

THE

RISING GLORY OF AMERICA.

Being part of a DIALOGUE, *pronounced on a public occaſion.**

——————— Venient annis
Sæcula ſeris, quibus oceanus
Vincula rerum laxet, et ingens
Pateat tellus, Typhiſque novos
Detegat orbes ; nec ſit terris
Ultima Thule.——————
Seneca, Med. Act. iii. v. 375.

A R G U M E N T.

THE ſubject propoſed——The diſcovery of America by Columbus——A philo-
ſophical enquiry into the origin of the ſavages of America——The firſt planters
from Europe——Cauſes of their migration to America——The difficulties
they encountered from the jealouſy of the natives——Agriculture deſcanted
on——Commerce and navigation——Science——Future proſpects of Britiſh
uſurpation, tyranny, and devaſtation on this ſide the Atlantic——The more
comfortable one of Independence, Liberty, and Peace——Concluſion.

Acaſto.

NOW ſhall the adventurous Muſe attempt a theme
    More new, more noble, and more fluſh of fame
Than all that went before——
Now through the veil of ancient days renew

* N. B. This Poem is a little altered from the original (publiſhed in Philadel
phia, in 1772), ſuch parts being only inſerted here as were written by the author of
this Volume.   A few more modern lines, towards the concluſion, are incorporated
with the reſt, being a ſuppoſed prophetical anticipation of ſubſequent events.

[The circumſtances under which the Poem was compoſed have been noticed
in the Prefatory Memoir of the author.]

I

The period fam'd when firſt Columbus touch'd
Theſe ſhores ſo long unknown—through various toils,
Famine, and death, the hero forc'd his way,
Thro' oceans pregnant with perpetual ſtorms,
And climates hoſtile to advent'rous man.
But why, to prompt your tears, ſhould we reſume
The tale of *Cortez*, furious chief, ordain'd
With Indian blood to dye the ſands, and choak,
Fam'd *Mexico*, thy ſtreams with dead? or why
Once more revive the tale ſo oft rehears'd
Of *Atabilipa*, by thirſt of gold,
(All conquering motive in the human breaſt)
Depriv'd of life, which not *Peru's* rich ore
Nor *Mexico's* vaſt mines could then redeem?
Better theſe northern realms demand our ſong,
Deſign'd by nature for the rural reign,
For agriculture's toil.—No blood we ſhed
For metals buried in a rocky waſte.——
Curs'd be that ore, which brutal makes our race,
And prompts mankind to ſhed a brother's blood!

Eugenio.

——————————— But whence aroſe
That vagrant race who love the ſhady vale,
And chooſe the foreſt for their dark abode?—
For long has this perplext the ſages' ſkill
To inveſtigate.—Tradition lends no aid
To unveil this ſecret to the mortal eye,
When firſt theſe various nations, north and ſouth,

Poſſeſt theſe ſhores, or from what countries came.—
Whether they ſprang from ſome primæval head
In their own lands, like Adam in the eaſt,—
Yet this the ſacred oracles deny,
And reaſon, too, reclaims againſt the thought :
For when the general deluge drown'd the world
Where could their tribes have found ſecurity,
Where find their fate, but in the ghaſtly deep ?—
Unleſs, as others dream, ſome choſen few
High on the Andes 'ſcap'd the general death,
High on the Andes, wrapt in endleſs ſnow,
Where winter in his wildeſt fury reigns,
And ſubtile æther ſcarce our life maintains.
But here philoſophers oppoſe the ſcheme :
This earth, ſay they, nor hills nor mountains knew
Ere yet the univerſal flood prevail'd ;
But when the mighty waters roſe aloft,
Rous'd by the winds, they ſhook their ſolid baſe,
And, in convulſions, tore the delug'd world,
'Till by the winds aſſuag'd, again they fell,
And all their ragged bed expos'd to view.
  PERHAPS, far wandering toward the northern pole,
The ſtreights of Zembla, and the frozen zone,
And where the eaſtern Greenland almoſt joins
America's north point, the hardy tribes
Of baniſh'd Jews, Siberians, Tartars wild
Came over icy mountains, or on floats
Firſt reach'd theſe coaſts, hid from the world beſide.—
And yet another argument more ſtrange,

4

Referv'd for men of deeper thought, and late,
Prefents itfelf to view :—*In Peleg's* days,*
(So fays the Hebrew feer's unerring pen)
This mighty mafs of earth, this folid globe
Was cleft in twain,—" *divided*" eaft and weft,
While ftraight between, the deep Atlantic roll'd.—
And traces indifputable remain
Of this primæval land, now funk and loft.—
The iflands rifing in our eaftern main
Are but fmall fragments of this continent,
Whofe two extremities were Newfoundland
And St. Helena.—One far in the north,
Where fhivering feamen view with ftrange furprize
The guiding pole-ftar glittering o'er their heads ;
The other near the fouthern tropic rears
Its head above the waves—Bermuda's ifles,
Cape Verd, Canary, Britain, and the Azores,
With fam'd Hibernia, are but broken parts
Of fome prodigious wafte, which once fuftain'd
Nations and tribes, of vanifh'd memory,
Forefts, and towns, and beafts of every clafs,
Where navies now explore their briny way.

Leander.

Your fophiftry, Eugenio, makes me fmile :
The roving mind of man delights to dwell
On hidden things, merely becaufe they're hid :

---

* Gen. X. 25.

He thinks his knowledge far beyond all limit,
And boldly fathoms Nature's darkeſt haunts——
But for uncertainties, your broken iſles,
Your northern Tartars, and your wandering Jews,
(The flimſy cobwebs of a ſophiſt's brain)
Hear what the voice of hiſtory proclaims—
The Carthaginians, ere the Roman yoke
Broke their proud ſpirits, and enſlav'd them too,
For navigation were renown'd as much
As haughty Tyre with all her hundred fleets,
Full many a league their vent'rous ſeamen ſail'd
Thro' ſtreight Gibraltar, down the weſtern ſhore
Of Africa, to the Canary iſles :
By them call'd Fortunate ; ſo Flaccus* ſings,
Becauſe eternal ſpring there clothes the fields
And fruits delicious bloom throughout the year.——
From voyaging here, this inference I draw,
Perhaps ſome barque with all her numerous crew
Falling to leeward of her deſtin'd port,
Caught by the eaſtern *Trade*, was hurried on
Before the unceaſing blaſt to Indian iſles,
Brazil, La Plata, or the coaſts more ſouth—
There ſtranded, and unable to return,
Forever from their native ſkies eſtrang'd
Doubtleſs they made theſe virgin climes their own,
And in the courſe of long revolving years
A numerous progeny from theſe aroſe,

* Hor. Epod. 16.

And ſpread throughout the coaſts—thoſe whom we call
Brazilians, Mexicans, Peruvians rich,
The tribes of Chili, Patagon, and thoſe
Who till the ſhores of Amazon's long ſtream.——
When firſt the power of Europe here attain'd
Vaſt empires, kingdoms, cities, palaces
And poliſh'd nations ſtock'd the fertile land.
Who has not heard of Cuſco, Lima, and
The town of Mexico—huge cities form'd
From Europe's architecture ; ere the arms
Of haughty Spain diſturb'd the peaceful ſoil.——
But *here*, amid this northern dark domain
No towns were ſeen to riſe.—No arts were here ;
The tribes unſkill'd to raiſe the lofty maſt,
Or force the daring prow thro' adverſe waves,
Gaz'd on the pregnant ſoil, and crav'd alone
Life from the unaided genius of the ground,—
This indicates they were a different race ;
From whom deſcended, 'tis not ours to ſay—
That power, no doubt, who furniſh'd trees, and plants,
And animals to this vaſt continent,
Spoke into being man among the reſt,——
But what a change is here !—what arts ariſe !
What towns and capitals ! how commerce waves
Her gaudy flags, where ſilence reign'd before !

Acaſto.

Speak, my Eugenio, for I've heard you tell
The diſmal ſtory, and the cauſe that brought

The firſt adventurers to theſe weſtern ſhores;
The glorious cauſe that urg'd our fathers firſt
To viſit climes unknown, and wilder woods
Than e'er Tartarian or Norwegian ſaw,
And with fair culture to adorn a ſoil
That never felt the induſtrious ſwain before.

Eugenio.

All this long ſtory to rehearſe, would tire,
Beſides, the ſun toward the weſt retreats,
Nor can the nobleſt theme retard his ſpeed,
Nor loftieſt verſe—not that which ſang the fall
Of Troy divine, and fierce Achilles' ire.
Yet hear a part :—By perſecution wrong'd,
And ſacerdotal rage, our fathers came
From Europe's hoſtile ſhores to theſe abodes,
Here to enjoy a liberty in *faith*,
Secure from tyranny and baſe controul.
For this they left their country and their friends,
And dar'd the Atlantic wave in queſt of peace;
And found new ſhores, and ſylvan ſettlements,
And men, alike unknowing and unknown.
Hence, by the care of each adventurous *chief*
New governments (their wealth unenvied yet)
Were form'd on liberty and virtue's plan.
Theſe ſearching out uncultivated traɛts
Conceiv'd new plans of towns, and capitals,
And ſpacious provinces—Why ſhould I name
Thee, Penn, the Solon of our weſtern lands;

Sagacious legiſlator, whom the world
Admires, long dead : an infant *colony*,
Nurs'd by thy care, now riſes o'er the reſt
Like that tall Pyramid in Egypt's waſte
O'er all the neighbouring piles, they alſo great.
Why ſhould I name thoſe heroes ſo well known,
Who peopled all the reſt from Canada
To Georgia's fartheſt coaſts, Weſt Florida,
Or Apalachian mountains ?—Yet what ſtreams
Of blood were ſhed! what Indian hoſts were ſlain,
Before the days of peace were quite reſtor'd !

Leander.

Yes, while they overturn'd the rugged ſoil
And ſwept the foreſts from the ſhaded plain
'Midſt dangers, foes, and death, fierce Indian tribes
With vengeful malice arm'd, and black deſign,
Oft murdered, or diſpers'd, theſe colonies—
Encourag'd, too, by Gallia's hoſtile ſons,
A warlike race, who late their arms diſplay'd
At *Quebec*, *Montreal*, and fartheſt coaſts
Of *Labrador*, or *Cape Breton*, where now
The Britiſh ſtandard awes the ſubject hoſt.
Here, thoſe brave chiefs, who, laviſh of their blood,
Fought in Britannia's cauſe, in battle fell !—
What heart but mourns the untimely fate of *Wolfe*
Who, dying, conquer'd !—or what breaſt but beats
To ſhare a fate like his, and die like him !

Acaſto.

But why alone commemorate the dead,
And paſs thoſe glorious heroes by, who yet
Breathe the ſame air, and ſee the light with us ?—
The dead, Leander, are but empty names,
And they who fall to-day the ſame to us
As they who fell ten centuries ago !—
Loſt are they all that ſhin'd on earth before ;
Rome's boldeſt champions in the duſt are laid,
Ajax and great Achilles are no more,
And *Philip's* warlike ſon, an empty ſhade !——
A WASHINGTON among our ſons of fame
We boaſt conſpicuous as the morning ſtar
Among the inferior lights——
To diſtant wilds Virginia ſent him forth—
With her brave ſons he gallantly oppos'd
The bold invaders of his country's rights,
Where wild *Ohio* pours the mazy flood,
And mighty meadows ſkirt his ſubjeɛt ſtreams.—
But now, delighting in his elm tree's ſhade,
Where deep *Potowmac* laves the enchanting ſhore,
He prunes the tender vine, or bids the ſoil
Luxuriant harveſts to the ſun diſplay.——

Behold a different ſcene—not thus employ'd
Were *Cortez*, and *Pizarro*, pride of Spain,
Whom blood and murder only ſatisfy'd,
And all to glut their avarice and ambition !——

Eugenio.

Such is the curfe, Acafto, where the foul
Humane is wanting—but we boaft no feats
Of cruelty like Europe's murdering breed—
Our milder epithet is merciful,
And each American, true hearted, learns
To conquer, and to fpare ; for coward fouls
Alone feek vengeance on a vanquifh'd foe.
Gold, fatal gold, was the alluring bait
To Spain's rapacious tribes—hence rofe the wars
From Chili to the Caribbean fea,
And Montezuma's Mexican domains :
More bleft are we, with whofe unenvied foil
Nature decreed no mingling gold to fhine,
No flaming diamond, precious emerald,
No blufhing fapphire, ruby, chryfolite,
Or jafper red—more noble riches flow
From agriculture, and the induftrious fwain,
Who tills the fertile vale, or mountain's brow,
Content to lead a fafe, a humble life,
Among his native hills, romantic fhades
Such as the mufe of Greece of old did feign,
Allur'd the Olympian gods from chryftal fkies,
Envying fuch lovely fcenes to mortal man.

Leander.

Long has the rural life been juftly fam'd,
And bards of old their pleafing pictures drew

Of flowery meads, and groves, and gliding ftreams;
Hence, old Arcadia—wood-nymphs, fatyrs, fawns;
And hence Elyfium, fancied heaven below!—
Fair agriculture, not unworthy kings,
Once exercis'd the royal hand, or thofe
Whofe virtues rais'd them to the rank of gods.
See, old *Laertes** in his fhepherd weeds
Far from his pompous throne and court auguft,
Digging the grateful foil, where round him rife
Sons of the earth, the tall afpiring oaks,
Or orchards, boafting of more fertile boughs,
Laden with apples red, fweet fcented peach,
Pear, cherry, apricot, or spungy plumb;
While through the glebe the induftrious oxen draw
The earth-inverting plough.—Thofe Romans too,
Fabricius and Camillus, lov'd a life
Of neat fimplicity and ruftic blifs,
And from the noify Forum haftening far,
From bufy camps, and fycophants, and crowns,
'Midft woods and fields fpent the remains of *life*,
Where full enjoyment ftill awaits the wife.

How grateful, to behold the harvefts rife,
And mighty crops adorn the extended plains!—
Fair plenty fmiles throughout, while lowing herds
Stalk o'er the fhrubby hill or graffy mead,
Or at fome fhallow river flake their thirft.——
The *inclofure*, now, fucceeds the fhepherd's care,

* Hom. Odyff. B. 24.

Yet milk-white flocks adorn the well ftock'd farm,
And court the attention of the induftrious fwain—
Their fleece rewards him well; and when the winds
Blow with a keener blaft, and from the north
Pour mingled tempefts through a funlefs fky
(Ice, fleet, and rattling hail) fecure he fits
Warm in his cottage, fearlefs of the ftorm,
Enjoying now the toils of milder moons,
Yet hoping for the fpring.——Such are the joys,
And fuch the toils of thofe whom heaven hath blefs'd
With fouls enamour'd of a country life.

Acafto.

Such are the vifions of the ruftic reign—
But this alone, the fountain of fupport,
Would fcarce employ the varying mind of man;
Each feeks employ, and each a different way:
Strip Commerce of her fail, and men once more
Would be converted into favages—
No nation e'er grew focial and refin'd
'Till Commerce firft had wing'd the adventurous prow,
Or fent the flow-pac'd caravan, afar,
To waft their produce to fome other clime,
And bring the wifh'd exchange—thus came, of old,
Golconda's golden ore, and thus the wealth
Of *Ophir*, to the wifeft of mankind.

Eugenio.

Great is the praife of Commerce, and the men
Deferve our praife, who fpread the undaunted fail,
And traverfe every fea—their dangers great,
Death ftill to combat in the unfeeling gale,
And every billow but a gaping grave :—
There, fkies and waters, wearying on the eye,
For weeks and months no other profpect yield
But barren waftes, unfathom'd depths, where not
The blifsful haunt of human form is feen
To cheer the unfocial horrors of the way——
Yet all thefe bold defigns to Science owe
Their rife and glory——Hail, fair Science ! thou,
Tranfplanted from the eaftern fkies, doft bloom
In thefe bleft regions——Greece and Rome no more
Detain the Mufes on *Cithæron's* brow,
Or old *Olympus,* crown'd with waving woods,
Or *Hæmus'* top, where once was heard the harp,
Sweet *Orpheus'* harp, that gain'd his caufe below,
And pierc'd the heart of Orcus and his bride ;
That hufh'd to filence by its voice divine
Thy melancholy waters, and the gales
O *Hebrus !* that o'er thy fad furface blow.——
No more the maids round Alpheus' waters ftray,
Where he with *Arethufa's* ftream doth mix,
Or where fwift *Tiber* difembogues his waves
Into the Italian fea, fo long unfung ;
Hither they wing their way, the laft the beft

Of countries, where the arts ſhall riſe and grow,
And arms ſhall have their day—even now we boaſt
A *Franklin*, prince of all philoſophy,
A genius piercing as the electric fire,
Bright as the lightning's flaſh, explain'd ſo well
By him, the rival of Britannia's ſage.*—
This is the land of every joyous ſound,
Of liberty and life, ſweet liberty !
Without whoſe aid the nobleſt genius fails,
And Science irretrievably muſt die.

Leander.

But come, Eugenio, ſince we know the paſt——
What hinders to pervade with ſearching eye
The myſtic ſcenes of dark futurity !
Say, ſhall we aſk what empires yet muſt riſe,
What kingdoms, powers and STATES, where now are ſeen
Mere dreary waſtes and awful ſolitude,
Where Melancholy ſits, with eye forlorn,
And time anticipates, when we ſhall ſpread
Dominion from the north, and ſouth, and weſt,
Far from the Atlantic to Pacific ſhores,
And ſhackle half the convex of the main !——
A glorious theme !—but how ſhall mortals dare
To pierce the dark events of future years
And ſcenes unravel, only known to fate ?

* Newton.

Acaſto.

This might we do, if warm'd by that bright coal
Snatch'd from the altar of cherubic fire
Which touch'd Iſaiah's lips—or if the ſpirit
Of Jeremy and Amos, prophets old,
Might ſwell the heaving breaſt——I ſee, I ſee
Freedom's eſtabliſh'd reign; cities, and men,
Numerous as ſands upon the ocean ſhore,
And empires riſing where the ſun deſcends !—
The *Ohio* ſoon ſhall glide by many a town
Of note ; and where the *Miſſiſippi* ſtream,
By foreſts ſhaded, now runs weeping on,
Nations ſhall grow, and STATES not leſs in fame
Than Greece and Rome of old !—we too ſhall boaſt
Our Scipio's, Solon's, Cato's, ſages, chiefs
That in the womb of time yet dormant lie,
Waiting the joyous hour of life and light—— .
O ſnatch me hence, ye muſes, to thoſe days
When through the veil of dark antiquity
Our ſons ſhall hear of us as things remote,
That bloſſom'd in the morn of days——Alas !
How could I weep that we were born ſo ſoon,
Juſt in the dawning of theſe mighty times,
Whoſe ſcenes are panting for eternity !
Diſſentions that ſhall ſwell the trump of fame,
And ruin brooding o'er all monarchy !

Eugenio.

Nor ſhall theſe angry tumults here ſubſide
Nor murders* ceaſe, through all theſe provinces,
Till foreign crowns have vaniſh'd from our view
And dazzle here no more——no more preſume
To awe the ſpirit of fair Liberty—
Vengeance ſhall cut the thread—And Britain, ſure,
Will curſe her fatal obſtinacy for it !
Bent on the ruin of this injur'd country,
She will not liſten to our humble prayers,
Though offer'd with ſubmiſſion :
Like vagabonds, and objects of deſtruction,
Like thoſe whom all mankind are ſworn to hate,
She caſts us off from her protection,
And will invite the nations round about,
Ruſſians and Germans, ſlaves and ſavages,
To come and have a ſhare in our perdition——
O cruel race, O unrelenting Britain, .
Who bloody beaſts will hire to cut our throats,
Who war will wage with prattling innocence,
And baſely murder unoffending women !——
Will ſtab their priſoners when they cry for quarter,
Will burn our towns, and from his lodging turn
The poor inhabitant to ſleep in tempeſts !——
Theſe will be wrongs, indeed, and all ſufficient
To kindle up our ſouls to deeds of horror,

* The maſſacre at Boſton, March 5th, 1770, is here more particularly
glanced at.

And give to every arm the nerves of *Sampſon*—
Theſe are the men that fill the world with ruin,
And every region mourns their greedy ſway——
Nor only for ambition————————
But what are this world's goods, that *they* for them
Should exerciſe perpetual butchery?
What are theſe mighty riches we poſſeſs,
That they ſhould ſend ſo far to plunder them?—
Already have we felt their potent arm—
And ever ſince that inauſpicious day,
When firſt Sir *Francis Bernard*
His cannons planted at the *council door*,
And made the aſſembly room a home for ſtrumpets,
And ſoldiers rank and file—e'er ſince that day
This wretched land, that drinks its children's gore,
Has been a ſcene of tumult and confuſion!—
Are there not evils in the world enough?
Are we ſo happy that they envy us?
Have we not toil'd to ſatisfy their harpies,
King's deputies, that are inſatiable;
Whoſe practice is to incenſe the royal mind
And make us deſpicable in his view?
Have we not all the evils to contend with
That, in this life, mankind are ſubject to,
Pain, ſickneſs, poverty and natural death—
But into every wound that nature gave
They will a dagger plunge, and make them mortal!

2

Leander.

Enough, enough—such difmal fcenes you paint,
I almoft fhudder at the recollection—
What, are they dogs that they would mangle us ?—
Are thefe the men that come with bafe defign
To rob the hive, and kill the induftrious bee !—
To brighter fkies I turn my ravifh'd view,
And fairer profpects from the future draw—
Here independent power fhall hold her fway,
And public virtue warm the patriot breaft :
No traces fhall remain of tyranny,
And laws, a pattern to the world befide,
Be here enacted firft.———

Acafto.

And when a train of rolling years are paft,
(So fung the exil'd feer in Patmos ifle)
A new Jerufalem, fent down from heaven,
Shall grace our happy earth—perhaps this land,
Whofe ample breaft fhall then receive, tho' late,
Myriads of faints, with their immortal king,
To live and reign on earth a thoufand years,
Thence called *Millennium.* Paradife anew
Shall flourifh, by no fecond Adam loft.
No dangerous tree with deadly fruit fhall grow,
No tempting ferpent to allure the foul
From native innocence.——A *Canaan* here,
Another *Canaan* fhall excel the old,

And from a fairer *Pifgah's* top be.feen.
No thiftle here, nor thorn, nor briar fhall fpring,
Earth's curfe before : the lion and the lamb,
In mutual friendfhip link'd, fhall browfe the fhrub,
And timorous deer with foften'd tygers ftray
O'er mead, or lofty hill, or graffy plain :
Another Jordan's ftream fhall glide along,
And Siloah's brook in circling eddies flow :
Groves fhall adorn their verdant banks, on which
The happy people, free from toils and death,
Shall find fecure repofe. No fierce difeafe,
No fevers, flow confumption, ghaftly plague,
(Fate's ancient minifters) again proclaim
Perpetual war with man : fair fruits fhall bloom,
Fair to the eye, and grateful to the tafte ;
Nature's loud ftorms be hufh'd, and feas no more
Rage hoftile to mankind—and, worfe than all,
The fiercer paffions of the human breaft
Shall kindle up to deeds of death no more,
But all fubfide in univerfal peace.——
———————————— Such days the world,
And fuch, AMERICA, thou firft fhalt have,
When ages, yet to come, have run their round,
And future years of blifs alone remain.

[1771.]

TO THE AMERICANS

ON THE RUMOURED APPROACH OF THE HESSIAN FORCES,
WALDECKERS, &c., 1775.

> The blaft of death ! the infernal guns prepare—
> " Rife with the ftorm and all its dangers fhare."

Occafioned by General Gage's Proclamation: That the Provinces were in a
ftate of Rebellion and out of the King's protection.*

R EBELS you are—the Britifh champion cries—
   TRUTH, ftand thou forth!—and tell the wretch, He
   lies :—
Rebels!—and fee this mock imperial *lord*
Already threats *thefe rebels* with the CORD.†

* General Gage's celebrated Proclamation at Bofton, iffued June 12, 1775.
It began: "Whereas the infatuated multitudes, who have long fuffered themfelves to be conducted by certain well-known incendiaries and traitors, in a fatal
progreffion of crimes againft the conftitutional authority of the ftate, have at
length proceeded to avowed rebellion, and the good effects which were expected
to arife from the patience and lenity of the king's government have been often
fruftrated, and are now rendered hopelefs by the influence of the fame evil counfels, it only remains for thofe who are intrufted with the fupreme rule, as well
for the punifhment of the guilty as the protection of the well-affected, to prove
that they do not bear the fword in vain." Frothingham, in his "Siege of Bofton," cites the comment of Mrs. Adams, in a letter dated June 15, 1775, to her
hufband John Adams: "Gage's Proclamation you will receive by this convey-
ance. All the records of time cannot produce a blacker page. Satan, when
driven from the regions of blifs, exhibited not more malice. Surely the father
of lies is fuperfeded. Yet we think it the beft proclamation he could have
iffued."

† General Wafhington, from his head-quarters at Cambridge, on the 11th of

The hour draws nigh, the glafs is almoft run,
When truth will fhine, and ruffians be undone;
When this bafe mifcreant will forbear to fneer,
And curfe his taunts, and bitter infults, *here*.

If to controul the cunning of a knave,
Freedom refpect, and fcorn the name of SLAVE;
If to proteft againft a tyrant's laws,
And arm for vengeance in a righteous caufe
Be deemed REBELLION—'tis a harmlefs thing:
This bug-bear name, like death, *has loft its fting*.

AMERICANS! at freedom's fane adore!
But truft to Britain and her flag, no more:
The *generous genius* of their ifle has fled,
And left a mere impoftor in his ftead.
If conquered, rebels (their Scotch records fhow)
Receive no mercy from the *parent* foe.*

Nay, even the grave, that friendly haunt of peace,
(Where nature gives the woes of man to ceafe)

Auguft, 1775, addreffed Lieutenant-General Gage, afferting, among other com-
plaints: "That the officers engaged in the caufe of liberty and their country, who
by the fortune of war have fallen into your hands, have been thrown indifcrim-
inately into a common gaol appropriated for felons," and threatening retaliation
in like cafes, "exactly by the rule you fhall obferve towards thofe of ours now in
your cuftody." To this Gage replied, on the 13th : "Britons, ever pre-eminent
in mercy, have outgone common examples, and overlooked the criminal in the
captive. Upon thefe principles your prifoners, whofe lives, by the law of the
land, *are deftined to the cord*, have hitherto been treated with care and kind-
ness," &c.

* After the battle of Culloden. See Smollett's Hiftory of England, 1745.
—*Author's Note.*

Vengeance will fearch—and buried corpfes there
Be raifed to feaft the vultures of the air—
Be hanged on gibbets!—fuch a war they wage—
Such are the devils that fwell our fouls with rage!—

If Britain conquers, help us, heaven, to fly :   •
Lend us your wings, ye ravens of the fky ;—
If Britain conquers, we exift no more ;
Thefe lands will redden with their children's gore,
Who, turned to flaves, their fruitlefs toils will moan,
Toils in thefe fields, that once they called their own!

To arms! to arms!—and let the murdering fword
Decide, who beft deferves the HANGMAN'S CORD:
Nor think the hills of Canada too bleak
When defperate Freedom is the prize you feek ;
For *that*, the call of honour bids you go
O'er frozen lakes, and mountains wrapt in snow :
No toils fhould daunt the nervous and the bold,
They fcorn all heat, or wave congealing cold.—

Hafte !—to your tents in iron fetters bring
Thefe SLAVES, that ferve a tyrant, and a king,
So juft, so virtuous is your caufe, I fay,
Hell muft prevail, if Britain gains the day.

EMANCIPATION FROM BRITISH DEPENDENCE.

Libera nos, Domine—Deliver us, O Lord,
Not only from British Dependence, but alfo,

FROM a junto that labour for abfolute power,
    Whofe fchemes difappointed, have made them look four,
From the lords of the council, who fight againft freedom,
Who ftill follow on where delufion fhall lead 'em.

From the group at St. James's that flight our Petitions,
And fools that are waiting for further fubmiffions—
From a nation whofe manners are rough and abrupt,
From fcoundrels and rafcals, whom gold can corrupt.

From pirates fent out by command of the king
To murder and plunder, but never to fwing ;
From *Wallace*, and *Graves*, and *Vipers*, and *Rofes*,*
Whom, if heaven pleafes, we'll give bloody nofes.

---

* Sir James Wallace, Admiral Graves, and Captain Montague were Britifh
naval officers employed on our coaft. The Viper and Rofe were veffels in the
fervice. Lord Dunmore, the laft Royal Governor of Virginia, had recently, in
April, 1775, removed the public ftores from Williamfburg, and, in conjunction
with a party of adherents, fupported by the naval force on the ftation, was making war on the province. William Tryon, the laft Royal Governor of New
York, informed of a refolution of the Continental Congrefs : "That it be recom-
mended to the feveral provincial affemblies in conventions and councils, or com-

From the valiant *Dunmore*, with his crew of banditti,
Who plunder Virginians at *Williamſburg* city,
From hot-headed *Montague*, mighty to ſwear,
The little fat man, with his pretty white hair.

From biſhops in Britain, who butchers are grown,
From ſlaves, that would die for a ſmile from the throne,
From aſſemblies, that vote againſt *Congreſs proceedings*,
(Who now ſee the fruit of their ſtupid miſleadings.)

From *Tryon* the mighty, who flies from our city,
And ſwell'd with importance diſdains the committee :
(But ſince he is pleas'd to proclaim us his foes,
What the devil care we where the devil he goes.)

From the caitiff, lord *North*, who would bind us in chains,
From our noble king Log, with his tooth-full of brains,
Who dreams, and is certain (when taking a nap)
He has conquered our lands, as they lay on his map.

From a kingdom that bullies, and hectors, and ſwears,
I ſend up to heaven my wiſhes and prayers
That we, diſunited, may freemen be ſtill,
And Britain go on—to be damn'd if ſhe will.   [1775.]

mittees of ſafety, to arreſt and ſecure every perſon in their reſpective colonies
whoſe going at large may, in their opinion, endanger the ſafety of the colony or
the liberties of America," diſcerning the ſigns of the times, took refuge on board
the Halifax packet in the harbour, and left the city in the middle of October,
1775.

GENERAL GAGE'S SOLILOQUY.

Scene, BOSTON, befieged by the men of Maffachufetts.*

Written and publifhed in New York, 1775.

> Why, let the ftricken deer go weep,
> The hart, unwounded, play—
> For fome muft *write,* while fome muft *fpeak;*
> So runs the world away!
> *Shakefpeare.*

" **D**ESTRUCTION waits my call—fome demon fay
    Why does deftruction linger on her way!
Charleftown is burnt, and Warren is deceas'd—
Heav'ns! fhall we never be from war releas'd?

* General Thomas Gage, the laft Royal Governor of Maffachufetts, arrived at Bofton as the fucceffor of Governor Hutchinfon in May, 1774. His firft appearance in America was in 1755, as Lieutenant-Colonel in the army of General Braddock. He was with that ill-fated officer at the time of his defeat, bore himfelf confpicuoufly in the battle, and was wounded on the field. A few years later, in 1760, he was Governor of Montreal, and, in 1763, fucceeded General Amherft in command of the Britifh forces in North America. He had married a lady of New Jerfey, and was in good efteem in the colonies for his agreeable manners. Not much, however, fays Irving, was expected from him in his new poft of Governor of Maffachufetts, " by thofe who knew him well." He was narrow-minded, and failed to eftimate at their proper value the new elements of the fituation in which he was placed. He relied upon force for the fuppreffion of the popular fentiment, offended the people by his dictatorial interference, and clofed a year of aggreffion by his celebrated Proclamation of the 12th of June,

Ten years the Greeks befieg'd the walls of Troy,
But when did Grecians their own towns deftroy?
Yes! that's the point—Let thofe who will, fay, No;
If GEORGE and NORTH decree—it muft be fo.

Doubts, black as night, difturb my lov'd repofe—
Men that were once my friends have turn'd my foes—
What if we conquer this *rebellious town.*
Suppofe we burn it, ftorm it, tear it down—
This land's like *Hydra*, cut off but *one* head,
And TEN fhall rife, and dare you in its ftead.
If to fubdue a league or two of coaft
Requires a navy, and fo large a hoft,
How fhall a length of twice feven hundred miles
Be brought to bend to two European ifles?—
And *that*, when all their utmoft ftrength unite,
When twelve* dominions fwear to arm and fight,
When the fame fpirit darts from every eye,
One fix'd refolve to gain their point or die.
As for myfelf—true—I was born to fight

1775, in which he declared martial law, and offered pardon, on fubmiffion, to all
offenders fave Samuel Adams and John Hancock.   He had juft before been
joined by Generals Howe, Clinton, and Burgoyne.   Admiral Graves was in command of the government veffels in the harbour.   The war of the Revolution, commenced at Lexington in April, was now in progrefs.   The battle of Bunker Hill
was the prompt anfwer of the yeomanry of Maffachufetts to the Proclamation.
Wafhington took the field, arriving before Bofton at the beginning of July, and
the fiege of that city, commemorated in the poem, was commenced.   General
Gage continued in command till October, when, leaving Major-General Howe
as his fucceffor, he returned to England.   Howe remained at Bofton till the following March, when he was compelled, by the military operations of Wafhington in the vicinity, to evacuate the city.   Gage died in England in 1788.

* Georgia had not at this time acceded to the Union of the 13 States.

As George commands, let him be wrong or right,
While from his hand I fqueeze the golden prize
I'll afk no queftions, and he'll tell no lies—
But did I fwear, I afk my heart again,
In their bafe projects monarchs to maintain?
Yes—when REBELLION her artillery brings
And aims her arrows at the beft of kings,
I ftand a champion in my monarch's caufe—
The men are *rebels* that refift his laws.

    A VICEROY I—like modern monarchs, ftay
Safe in the town—let others guide the fray:
A life, like mine, is of no common worth:
'Twere wrong, by heaven, that I fhould fally forth!
A random bullet from a RIFLE fent
Might pierce my heart; and ruin NORTH's intent:
Let others combat in the dufty field,
Let petty captains fcorn to live or yield,
I'll fend my fhips to neighbouring ifles, where ftray
Unnumb'red herds, and fteal thofe herds away,
I'll ftrike the women in this town with awe,
And make them tremble at my martial law.

    Should gracious heaven befriend our troops and fleet,
And throw this vaft dominion at my feet,
How would Britannia echo with my fame!
What endlefs honours would await my name!
In every province fhould the traveller fee
Recording marble rais'd, to honour me——
Hard by the lakes, my fovereign lord would grant
A rural empire to fupply my want,

A manor would but poorly ferve my turn,
Lefs than a kingdom from my foul I fcorn !
An ample kingdom round Ontario's lake
By heaven, fhould be the leaft reward I'd take,
There might I reign, unrivall'd and alone,
An ocean and an empire of my own !——
What though the fcribblers and the wits might fay,
He built his pile on vanquifh'd LIBERTY——
Let others meanly dread the flanderous tongue,
While I obey my king, can I do wrong ?—

   Then, to accomplifh all my foul's defire,
Let red-hot bullets fet their towns on fire ;
May heaven, if fo the righteous judgment pafs,
Change earth to fteel, the fky to folid brafs,
Let hofts combin'd, from Europe centring here,
Strike this bafe offspring with alarm and fear ;
Let heaven's broad concave to the center ring,
And blackeft night expand her fable wing,
The infernal powers in dufky combat join,
Wing the fwift ball, or fpring the deadly mine ;
(Since 'tis moft true, tho' fome may think it odd,
The foes of Britain are the foes of God :)
Let bombs, like comets, kindle all the air,
Let cruel famine prompt the orphan's prayer,
And every ill that war or want can bring
Be fhower'd on fubjects that renounce their king.

   What is their plea ?—our fovereign only meant
This people fhould be *tax'd without confent.*
Ten years the court with fecret cunning try'd

To gain this point—the event their hopes bely'd :
How fhould they elfe than fometimes mifs the mark
Who fleep at helm, yet think to fteer the barque ?
NORTH, take advice ; thy lucky genius fhow,
Difpatch Sir JEFFERY* to the *ftates* below.
That gloomy prince, whom mortals *Satan* call,
Muft help us quickly, if he help at all—
You ftrive in vain by force of bribes to tie,
They fee thro' all your fchemes with half an eye,
If open force with fecret bribes *I* join,
The conteft fickens—and the day is mine.

    But hark the trumpet's clangor—hark—ah me !
What means this march of *Wafhington* and *Lee?*
When men, like thefe, fuch diftant marches make,
Fate whifpers fomething—that we can't miftake ;—
When men like thefe defy my martial rule,
Good heaven ! it is no time to play the fool——
Perhaps, they for their country's freedom rife ;
North has, perhaps, deceiv'd me with his lies.—
If George at laft a tyrant fhould be found,
A cruel tyrant, by no fanctions bound,
And I, myfelf, in an unrighteous caufe
Be fent to execute the worft of laws,
How will thofe dead whom I conjur'd to fight—
Who funk in arms to everlafting night,
Whofe blood the conquering foe confpir'd to fpill
At Lexington and Bunker's fatal hill,

---

* Sir Jeffery Amherft, who about this time refufed to act againft the colonial caufe.—*Author's Note.*

Whofe mangled corpfes fcanty graves embrace—
Rife from thofe graves, and curfe me to my face ?—
　　Alas ! that e'er ambition bade me roam,
Or thirft of power forfake my native home—
What fhall I do ?—*there*, crowd the hoftile bands ;
Here, waits a navy to receive commands—
I fpeak the language of my heart—fhall I
Steal off by night, and o'er the ocean fly,
Like a loft man to unknown regions ftray,
And to oblivion leave this ftormy day ?—
Or fhall I to Britannia's fhores again,
And, big with lies, conceal my thoufands flain ?—
　　Yes—to fome diftant clime my courfe I fteer,
To any country rather than be here,
To worlds, where Reafon fcarce exerts her law,
A branch-built cottage, and a bed of ftraw——
Even Scotland's coaft feems charming in my fight,
And frozen *Zembla* yields a ftrange delight.—
But fuch vexations in my bofom burn,
That to thefe fhores I never will return,
'Till fruits and flowers on Greenland's coafts be known,
And frofts are thaw'd in climates once their own.
　　Ye fouls of fire, who burn for chief command,
Come ! take my place in this difaftrous land ;
To wars like thefe I bid a long good night—
Let NORTH and GEORGE themfelves fuch battles fight."

THE MIDNIGHT CONSULTATIONS: OR A TRIP TO BOSTON.

SMALL blifs is theirs, whom Fate's too heavy hand
 Confines through life to fome fmall fpeck of land;
More wretched they, whom heaven infpires to roam,
Yet languifh out their lives, and die at home.

Heaven gave to man this wide extended round,
No climes confine him, and no oceans bound;
Heaven gave him foreft, mountain, vale and plain,
And bade him vanquifh, if he could, the main;
But fordid cares our fhort-liv'd race confine,
Some toil at trades, fome labour in the mine,
The mifer hoards, and guards his fhining ftore,
The fun ftill rifes where he rofe before—
No happier fcenes his earth-born fancy fill
Than one dark valley, or one well-known hill,
To other fhores his mind, untaught to ftray,
Dull and inactive, flumbers life away.

BUT by the aid of yonder glimmering beam
The pole ftar, faithful to my vagrant dream,
Wild regent of my heart! in dreams convey
Where herded *Britons* their bold ranks difplay;
So late the pride of England's fertile foil.
(Her grandeur heighten'd by fucceffive toil)

See, how they ficken in thefe hoftile climes,
Themes for the ftage, and fubjects for our rhimes.
　　WHAT modern poet have the mufes led
To draw the curtain that conceals the *dead?*
What bolder bard to Bofton fhall repair,
To view the peevifh, half-ftarv'd fpectres there ?
　　O thou wrong'd country ! why fuftain thefe ills ?
Why reft thy navies on their native hills ?
See, endlefs forefts fhade the uncultur'd plain,
Defcend, ye forefts, and command the main :
A leafy verdure fhades the mighty maft,
And every oak bends idly to the blaft,
Earth's entrails teem with ftores for your defence,
Defcend, and drag the ftores of war from thence ;
Your fertile foil the flowing fail fupplies,
And Europe's arts in every village rife——
No want is yours—Difdain unmanly fear.
And fwear, *no Tyrant fhall reign mafter here ;*
Know your own ftrength—in rocky deferts bred,
Shall the fierce tiger by the dog be led,
And bear all infults from that fnarling race
Whofe courage lies in impudence of face ?——
No—rather bid the wood's wild native turn,
And from his fide the unfaithful guardian fpurn.
　　Now, pleas'd, I wander to the dome of ftate
Where *Gage* refides, our weftern potentate—
Chief of ten thoufand, all a race of flaves,
Sent to be fhrouded in untimely graves ;
Sent by our angry *Jove,* fent fword in hand

To murder, burn, and ravage through the land—
   You dream of conqueſt—tell me how or whence—
Act like a man, and get you gone from hence ;
A madman ſent you to this hoſtile ſhore
To vanquiſh nations, that ſhall ſpill your gore—
Go fiends, and each in friendly league combin'd
Deſtroy, diſtreſs, and triumph o'er mankind !—
'Tis not our peace this murdering hand reſtrains,
The want of power is made the monſter's chains ;
Compaſſion is a ſtranger to his heart,
Or if it came, he bade the gueſt depart ;
The melting tear, the ſympathiſing groan
Were never yet to *Gage* or *Jefferies** known ;
The ſeas of blood his heart fore-dooms to ſpill
Is but a dying ſerpent's rage to kill,
What power ſhall drive theſe vipers from our ſhore,
Theſe monſters ſwoln with carnage, death, and gore ?
   Twelve was the hour—congenial darkneſs reign'd,
And no bright ſtar a mimic day-light feign'd——
Firſt, GAGE we ſaw—a crimſon chair of ſtate
Receiv'd the honour of his honour's weight,
This man of ſtraw the regal purple bound,
But dullneſs, deepeſt dullneſs, hover'd round.
   Next *Graves*, who wields the trident of the brine,
The tall arch-captain of the embattled line
All gloomy ſate—mumbling of flame and fire,
Balls, cannon, ſhips, and all their damn'd attire ;

* An inhuman butchering Engliſh Judge.—*Author's Note.*
   3

Well pleas'd to live in never ending hum,
But empty as the interior of his drum.

    Hard by, BURGOYNE affumes an ample fpace,
And feem'd to meditate with ftudious face,
As if again he wifh'd our world to fee
Long, dull, dry letters writ to General LEE—
Huge fcrawls of words through endlefs circuits drawn
Unmeaning, as the errand he's upon.—
Is he to conquer—he fubdue our land ?—
This buckram hero, with his lady's hand ?
By Cefars to be vanquifh'd is a curfe,
But by a fcribbling fop—by heaven, is worfe !

    Lord *Piercy* feem'd to fnore—but may the mufe
This ill-tim'd fnoring to the peer excufe ;
Tir'd was the long boy of his toilfome day,
Full fifteen miles he fled—a tedious way,
How fhould he then the dews of Somnus fhun,
Perhaps not ufed to walk, much lefs to run.*

---

* Lord Percy, fubfequently Duke of Northumberland. He was fent by Gage
with a detachment to the fupport of Colonel Smith on the retreat of the latter
from Concord, on the celebrated 19th of May, 1775. He came up with the retreating party in the afternoon, and returned with the fugitives to Bofton. Trumbull, in his " McFingal," celebrates the exploits of the Yankee provincials in this
difaftrous flight, as they

> " Taught Percy fafhionable races,
> And modern modes of Chevy-chaces."

Halleck's allufion to Percy among the Dukes of Northumberland, in his " Aln-
wick Caflle," will be remembered by the reader :—

> " Who, when a younger fon,
> Fought for King George at Lexington,
> A major of dragoons."

Red fac'd as funs, when finking to repofe,
Reclin'd the infernal captain of the ROSE,*
In fame's proud temple aiming for a nich,
With thofe who find her at the cannon's breech;
Skill'd to direct the cannonading fhot,
No Turkifh rover half fo murdering hot,
Pleas'd with bafe vengeance on defencelefs towns,
His heart was malice—but his words were, *Zounds!*

HOWE, vext to fee his ftarving army's doom,
Once more befought the fkies for *elbow room*—
Small was his ftock, and theirs, of heavenly grace,
Yet juft enough to afk a larger *place*.—
He curs'd the brainlefs minifter that plann'd
His bootlefs errand to this hoftile land,
But aw'd by Gage, his burfting wrath recoil'd,
And in his inmoft bofom doubly boil'd.

These, chief of all the tyrant-ferving train,
Exalted fate—the reft (a penfion'd clan,)
A fample of the multitudes that wait,
Pale fons of famine, at perdition's gate,
NORTH's friends down fwarming, (fo our monarch wills)
Hungry as death, from Caledonian hills;
Whofe endlefs numbers if you bid me tell,
(I'll count the atoms of this globe as well)
Knights, captains, 'fquires—a wonder-working band!
Held at fmall wages 'till they gain the land,
Flock'd penfive round—black fpleen affail'd their hearts,

* Captain Wallace.

(The fport of plough boys, with their arms and arts)
And made them doubt (howe'er for vengeance hot)
Whether they were invincible or not.

   Now *Gage up-ftarting* from his cufhion'd feat
Swore thrice, and cry'd—"'Tis nonfenfe to be beat !
Thus to be drubb'd !—pray, warriors, let me know
Which be in fault, myfelf, the fates, or you——
Henceforth let Britain deem her men mere toys—
Gods ! to be frightened thus by country boys ;
Why, if your men had had a mind to fup,
They might have eat that fcare-crow* army up—
Three thoufand to twelve hundred thus to yield,
And twice five hundred ftretch'd upon the field !—
O fhame to Britain, and the Britifh name,
Shame damps my heart, and I muft die with fhame——
Thus to be worfted, thus difgrac'd and beat !—
. You have the knack, Lord Piercy, to retreat,
. The death you 'fcap'd my warmeft blood congeals,
Heaven grant me, too, fo fwift a pair of heels—
In Chevy-Chace, as, doubtlefs, you have read,
Lord Piercy would have fooner died than fled—
Behold the virtues of your houfe decay—
Ah ! how unlike the Piercy of that day !"

   Thus fpoke the great man in difdainful tone
To the gay peer—not meant for him alone—
But ere the tumults of his bofom rife
Thus from his bench the intrepid peer replies :

* School-boy.—Ed. 179 ⁵

" When once the foul has reach'd the Stygian fhore,
My prayer-book fays, it fhall return no more——
When once old Charon hoifts his tar-black'd fail,
And his boat fwims before the infernal gale,
Farewell to all that pleas'd the man above,
Farewell to feats of arms, and joys of love,
Farewell the trade that father *Cain* began,
Farewell to wine, that cheers the heart of man ;
All, all farewell !—the penfive fhade muft go
Where cold *Medufa* turns to ftone below,
Where *Belus'* maids eternal labours ply
To drench the cafk that ftays forever dry,
And *Sifiphus*, with many a weary groan,
Heaves up the mount the ftill recoiling ftone !

" Since, then, this truth no mortal dares deny,
That heroes, kings—and lords, themfelves, muft die,
And yield to *him* who dreads no hoftile fword,
But treats alike the peafant and the lord ;
Since even great George muft in his turn give place
And leave his crown, his Scotchmen, and his lace——
How bleft is he, how prudent is the man
Who keeps aloof from fate—while yet he can ;
One well-aim'd ball can make us all no more
Than fhipwreck'd fcoundrels on that leeward fhore.

" But why, my friends, thefe hard reflections ftill
On Lexington affairs——'tis Bunker's Hill—
O fatal hill !—one glance at thee reftrains
My once warm blood, and chills it in my veins—
May no fweet grafs adorn thy hateful creft

That faw Britannia's braveft troops diftreft—
Or if it does—may fome deftructive gale
The green leaf wither, and the grafs turn pale—
All moifture to your brow may heaven deny,
And God and man deteft you, juft as I——
'Tis Bunker's Hill, this night has brought us here,
Pray queftion him who led your armies there,
Nor dare my courage into queftion call,
Or blame Lord Piercy for the fault of all."

   Howe chanc'd to nod while heathenifh *Piercy* fpoke,
But as his lordfhip ceas'd, his honour 'woke,
(Like thofe whom fermons into fleep betray)
Then rubb'd his eyes, and thus was heard to fay :

   " Shall thofe who never ventur'd from the *town*,
Or their fhips' fides, now pull our glory down ?
We fought our beft—fo God my honour fave—
No Britifh foldiers ever fought fo brave—
Refolv'd I led them to the hoftile lines,
(From this day fam'd where'er great Phœbus fhines)
Firm at their head I took my dangerous ftand,
Marching to death and flaughter, fword in hand,
But wonted Fortune halted on her way,
We fought with madmen, and we loft the day—
Putnam's brave troops, your honours would have fwore
Had robb'd the clouds of half their nitrous ftore,
With my bold veterans ftrew'd the aftonifh'd plain,
For not one mufquet was difcharg'd in vain.—
But, honour'd Gage, why droops thy laurell'd head ?—
Five hundred foes we pack'd off to the dead.——

" Now captains, generals, hear me and attend !
Say, fhall we home for other fuccours fend ?
Shall other navies crofs the ftormy main ?——
They may, but what fhall awe the pride of Spain ?
Still for dominion haughty *Louis* pants—
Ah ! how I tremble at the thoughts of France.—
Shall mighty George, to enforce his injur'd laws,
Tranfport all Ruffia to fupport the caufe ?——
That ally'd empire countlefs fhoals may pour
Numerous as fands that ftrew the Atlantic fhore,
But policy inclines my heart to fear
They'll turn their arms againft us, when they're here—
Come, let's agree—for fomething muft be done
Ere autumn flies, and winter haftens on—
When pinching cold our navy binds in ice,
You'll find 'tis then too late to take advice."

The clock ftrikes *two !*—Gage fmote upon his breaft,
And cry'd,—" What fate determines muft be beft——
But now attend—a counfel I impart
That long has laid the heavieft at my heart——
Three weeks—ye gods !—nay, three long years it feems
Since *roaft-beef* I have touch'd, except in dreams.
In fleep, choice difhes to my view repair,
Waking, I gape and champ the empty air.—
Say, is it juft that I, who rule thefe bands,
Should live on hufks, like rakes in foreign lands ?—
Come let us plan fome projeƈt ere we fleep
And drink deftruƈtion to the rebel fheep.
On neighbouring ifles uncounted cattle ftray,

Fat beeves, and fwine, an ill defended prey—
Thefe are fit vifions for my noon day difh,
Thefe, if my foldiers act as I would wifh,
In one fhort week fhould glad your maws and mine—
On mutton we will fup—on roaft beef dine."

Shouts of applaufe re-echo'd thro' the hall,
And what pleas'd one as furely pleas'd them all,
WALLACE was nam'd to execute the plan,
And thus fheep-ftealing pleas'd them to a man.

Now flumbers ftole upon the great man's eye,
His powder'd foretop nodded from on high,
His lids juft ope'd to find how matters were,
Diffolve, he faid, *and fo diffolv'd ye are*,
Then downward funk to flumbers dark and deep,
Each nerve relaxed—and even his guts afleep.

E P I L O G U E.

WHAT are thefe ftrangers from a foreign ifle,
That we fhould fear their hate, or court their fmile—
Pride fent them here, pride blafted in the bud,
Who if fhe can, will build her throne in blood,
With flaughter'd millions glut her tearlefs eyes,
And bid even virtue fall, that fhe may rife.

What deep offence has fir'd a monarch's rage?
What moon-ftruck madnefs feiz'd the brain of GAGE?
Laughs not the foul when an imprifon'd crew
Affect to pardon thofe they can't fubdue,
Tho' thrice repuls'd, and hemm'd up to their ftations,

Yet iffue pardons, oaths, and proclamations !——
Too long our patient country wears their chains,
Too long our wealth all-grafping Britain drains.
    Why ftill a handmaid to that diftant land ?
Why ftill fubfervient to their proud command ?
Britain the bold, the generous, and the brave
Still treats our country like the meaneft flave,
Her haughty lords already fhare the prey,
Live on our labours, and with fcorn repay——
Rife, fleeper, rife, while yet the power remains,
And bind their nobles and their chiefs in chains :
Bent on deftructive plans, they fcorn our plea,
'Tis our own efforts that muft make us free—
Born to contend, our lives we place at ftake,
And rife to conquerors* by the ftand we make.—
    The time may come when ftrangers rule no more,
Nor cruel mandates vex from Britain's fhore,
When commerce may extend her fhorten'd wing,
And her rich freights from every climate bring.
When mighty towns fhall flourifh free and great,
Vaft their dominion, opulent their ftate,
When one vaft cultivated region teems
From ocean's fide to Miffifippi ftreams,
While each enjoys his vine tree's peaceful fhade,
And even the meaneft has no foe to dread.
    And you, who far from Liberty detain'd,
Wear out exiftence in fome flavifh land—

---

* Grow immortal.—Ed. 1795.

Forfake thofe fhores, a felf-ejected throng,
And arm'd for vengeance, *here* refent the wrong :
Come to our climes, where unchain'd rivers flow,
And loftieft groves, and boundlefs forefts grow,
Here the bleft foil your future care demands ;
Come, fweep the forefts from thefe fhaded lands,
And the kind earth fhall every toil repay,
And harvefts flourifh as the groves decay.

O heav'n-born Peace, renew thy wonted charms—
Far be this rancour, and this din of arms—
To warring lands return, an honour'd gueft,
And blefs our crimfon fhore among the reft—
Long may Britannia rule our hearts again,
Rule as fhe rul'd in George the fecond's reign,
May ages hence her growing grandeur fee,
And fhe be glorious—but ourfelves as free !

[1775.]

AMERICA INDEPENDENT:

AND HER EVERLASTING DELIVERANCE FROM BRITISH TYRANNY AND OPPRESSION.

Firſt publiſhed in Philadelphia, by Mr. Robert Bell, in 1778.

To him who would relate the ſtory right,
A mind ſupreme ſhould dictate, or indite.—
   Yes!—juſtly to record the tale of fame,
A muſe from heaven ſhould touch the ſoul with flame,
Some powerful ſpirit, in ſuperior lays,
Should tell the conflicts of theſe ſtormy days!

'TIS done! and Britain for her madneſs ſighs—
   Take warning, tyrants, and henceforth be wiſe.
If o'er mankind *man* gives you regal ſway,
Take not the rights of human kind away.
   When God from chaos gave this world to be,
Man then he form'd, and form'd him to be free,
In his own image ſtampt the favourite race—
How dar'ſt thou, tyrant, the fair ſtamp deface!
When on mankind you fix your abject chains,
No more the image of that God remains;
O'er a dark ſcene a darker ſhade is drawn,
His work diſhonour'd, and our glory gone!
   When firſt Britannia ſent her hoſtile crew

To thefe far fhores, to ravage and fubdue,
We thought them gods, and almoft feem'd to fay
No ball could pierce them, and no dagger flay—
Heavens! what a blunder—half our fears were vain;
Thefe hoftile *gods* at length have quit the plain,
On neighbouring ifles the ftorm of war they fhun,
Happy, thrice happy, if not quite undone.

  Yet foon, in dread of fome impending woe,
Even from thofe *iflands* shall thefe ruffians go—
This be their doom, in vengeance for the flain,
To pafs their days in poverty and pain;
For fuch bafe triumphs, be it ftill their lot
To triumph only o'er the rebel *Scot;*
And to their infect ifle henceforth confin'd
No longer lord it o'er the human kind.—

  But, by the fates, who ftill prolong their ftay,
And gather vengeance to conclude their day,
Yet, ere they go, the angry Mufe fhall tell
The treafured woes that in her bofom fwell :——

  Proud, fierce, and bold, O Jove! who would not laugh
To fee thefe bullies worfhipping a *calf:*
But they are *flaves* who fpurn at Reafon's rules;
And men, once flaves, are foon transform'd to fools.—

  To recommend what monarchies have done,
They bring for witnefs David and his fon;
How one was brave, the other juft and wife,
And hence our plain Republics they defpife;
But mark how oft, to gratify their pride,
The people fuffer'd, and the people died:

Though one was wife, and one Goliah flew,
Kings are the choicest curfe that man e'er knew!
 Hail, worthy Britain!—how enlarg'd your fame;
How great your glory, terrible your name,
" Queen of the ifles, and emprefs of the main,"——
Heaven grant you all thefe mighty things again;
But first infure the gaping crowd below
That you lefs cruel, and more juft may grow:
If fate, vindictive for the fins of man,
Had favour fhown to your infernal plan,
How would your nation have exulted here,
And fcorn'd the widow's figh, the orphan's tear!
How had your prince, of all bad men the worft,
Laid worth and virtue proftrate in the duft!
A fecond *Sawney** had he fhone to-day,
A world fubdued, and murder but his play.
How had that prince, contemning right or law,
Glutted with blood his foul, voracious maw:
In him we fee the depths of bafenefs join'd,
Whate'er difgrac'd the dregs of human kind;
Cain, Nimrod, Nero—fiends in human guife,
Herod, Domitian—thefe in judgment rife,
And, envious of his deeds, I hear them fay
None but a GEORGE could be more vile than they.
 Swoln tho' he was with wealth, revenge, and pride,
How could he dream that heaven was on his fide—
Did he not fee, when fo decreed by fate,

---

 * Alexander the Great.—*Author's note.*

They plac'd the crown upon his royal pate,
Did he not fee the richeft jewel fall—*
Dire was the omen, and aftonifh'd all—

That gem no more fhall brighten and adorn ;
No more that gem by Britifh kings be worn,
Or fwell to wonted heights of fair renown
The fading glories of their boafted crown.

Yet he to arms, and war, and blood inclin'd,
(A fair-day warrior, with a feeble mind,
Fearlefs, while others meet the fhock of fate,
And dare that death, which clips his thread too . .,
He to the fane (O hypocrite !) did go,
While not an angel there, but was his foe,
There did he kneel, and figh, and fob, and pray,
Yet not to lave his thoufand fins away,
Far other motives fway'd his fpotted foul ;
'Twas not for thofe the fecret forrow ftole
Down his pale cheek—'twas vengeance and defpair
Diffolv'd his eye, and planted forrow there—
How could he hope to bribe the impartial fky
By his bafe prayers, and mean hypocrify—
Heaven ftill is juft, and ftill abhors all crimes,
Not acts like George, the Nero of our times—
What were his prayers—his prayers could be no more
Than a thief's wifhes to recruit his ftore ;
Such prayers could never reach the worlds above ;
They were but curfes in the ear of Jove ;—

* A real event of that day. See the REMEMBRANCER of 1777.—*Author's note.*

You pray'd that conqueſt might your arms attend,
And cruſh that freedom virtue did defend,
That the fierce Indian, rouſing from his reſt,
Might theſe new regions with his flames inveſt,
With ſcalps and tortures aggravate our woe,
And to the infernal world diſmiſs your foe.

　No mines of gold our fertile country yields,
But mighty harveſts crown the loaded fields,
Hence, trading far, we gain'd the golden prize,
Which, though our own, bewitch'd their greedy eyes—
For that they ravag'd India's climes before,
And carried death to Aſia's utmoſt ſhore—
Clive was your envied ſlave, in avarice bold
He mow'd down nations for his dearer gold;
The fatal gold could give no true content,
He mourn'd his murders, and to *Tophet* went.

　Led on by luſt of lucre and renown,
Burgoyne came marching with his thouſands down,
High were his thoughts, and furious his career,
Puff'd with ſelf-confidence and pride ſevere,
Swoln with the idea of his future deeds,
Onward to ruin each advantage leads:
Before his hoſts his heavieſt curſes flew,
And conquer'd worlds roſe hourly to his view:
His wrath, like Jove's, could bear with no controul,
His words beſpoke the miſchief in his ſoul;
To fight was not this General's only trade,
He ſhin'd in writing, and his wit diſplay'd—
To awe the more with titles of command

He told of *forts he rul'd* in Scottifh land ;—
Queen's *colonel* as he was, he did not know
That thorns and *thiftles*, mix'd with honours, grow ;
In Britain's fenate tho' he held a place,
All did not fave him from one long difgrace,
One ftroke of fortune that convinc'd them all
That we could conquer, and *lieutenants* fall.

　Foe to the rights of man, proud plunderer, fay
Had conqueft crown'd you on that mighty day
When you, to GATES, with forrow, rage, and fhame
Refign'd your conquefts, honours, arms, and fame,
When at his feet Britannia's wreathes you threw,
And the fun ficken'd at a fight fo new ;
Had you been victor—what a wafte of woe !
What fouls had vanifh'd to where fouls do go !
What dire diftress had mark'd your fatal way,
What deaths on deaths difgrac'd that difmal day !

　Can laurels flourifh in a foil of blood,
Or on thofe laurels can fair honours bud—
Curs'd be that wretch who murder makes his trade,
Curs'd be all wars that e'er ambition made !

　What murdering Tory now relieves your grief,
Or plans new conquefts for his favourite chief ;
Defigns ftill dark employ that ruffian race,
Beafts of your choofing, and our own difgrace.
So vile a crew the world ne'er faw before,
And grant, ye pitying heavens, it may no more :
If ghofts from hell infeft our poifon'd air,
Thofe ghofts have enter'd their bafe bodies here,

Murder and blood is ftill their dear delight—
Scream round their roofs, ye ravens of the night !
Whenc'er they wed, may demons, and defpair,
And grief and woe, and blackeft night be there ;
Fiends leagu'd from hell the nuptial lamp difplay,
Swift to perdition light them on their way,
Round the wide world their devilifh fquadrons chafe,
To find no realm, that grants one refting place.
 Far to the north, on Scotland's utmoft end
An ifle there lies, the haunt of every fiend,
No fhepherds there attend their bleating flocks
But wither'd witches rove among the rocks ;
Shrouded in ice, the blafted mountains fhow
Their cloven heads, to daunt the feas below ;
The lamp of heaven in his diurnal race
There fcarcely deigns to unveil his radiant face,
Or if one day he circling treads the fky
He views this ifland with an angry eye,
Or ambient fogs their broad, moift wings expand,
Damp his bright ray, and cloud the infernal land ;
The blackening winds inceffant ftorms prolong,
Dull as their night, and dreary as my fong ;
When ftormy winds and gales refufe to blow,
Then from the dark fky drives the unpitying fnow ;
When drifting fnows from iron clouds forbear,
Then down the hailftones rattle through the air—
There fcreeching owls, and fcreaming vultures reft
And not a tree adorns its barren breaft ;
No peace, no reft, the elements beftow,

4

But feas forever rage, and ftorms forever blow.

   There, Loyals, there ; with loyal hearts retire
There pitch your tents, and kindle *there* your fire ;
There defert Nature will her ftings difplay,
And fierceft hunger on your vitals prey,
And with yourfelves let *John Burgoyne* retire
To reign the monarch, whom your hearts admire.

   Britain, at laft to arreft your lawlefs hand,
Rifes the genius of a generous land,
Our injur'd rights bright Gallia's prince defends,
And from this hour that prince and we are friends,
Feuds, long up-held, are vanifh'd from our view.
Once we were foes—but for the fake of you—
Britain, afpiring Britain, now muft bend—
Can fhe at once with France and us contend,
When we alone, remote from foreign aid,
Her armies captur'd, and diftrefs'd her trade—
Britain and we no more in combat join,
No more, as once, in every fea combine ;
Dead is that friendfhip which did mutual burn,
Fled is the fceptre, never to return ;
By fea and land, perpetual foes we meet,
Our caufe more honeft, and our hearts as great ;
Loft are thefe regions to Britannia's reign,
Nor fhall thefe ftrangers of their lofs complain,
Since all, that *here* with greedy eyes they view,
From our own toil, to wealth and empire grew :——

   Our hearts are ravifh'd from our former queen
Far as the ocean God hath plac'd between,

They ſtrive in vain to join this mighty maſs,
Torn by convulſions from its native place
As well might men to flaming *Hecla* join
The huge high *Alps* or towering *Appennine;*
In vain they ſend their half-commiſſioned tribe
And whom they cannot conquer ſtrive to bribe;
Their pride and madneſs burſt our union chain,
Nor ſhall the unwieldy maſs unite again.

Nor think that France ſuſtains our cauſe alone;
With gratitude her helping hand we own.
But hear, ye nations—Truth herſelf can ſay
We bore the heat and danger of the day:
She calmly view'd the tumult from afar,
We brav'd each inſult, and ſuſtain'd the war:
Oft drove the foe, or forc'd their hoſts to yield,
Or left them, more than once, a dear bought field—
'Twas then, at laſt on Jerſey plains diſtreſt,
We ſwore to ſeek the mountains of the weſt,
There a free empire for our ſeed obtain,
A terror to the ſlaves that might remain.*

* "In this dark day of peril to the cauſe and to himſelf (at the cloſe of 1776) Waſhington remained firm and undaunted. In caſting about for ſome ſtronghold where he might make a deſperate ſtand for the liberties of his country, his thoughts reverted to the mountain regions of his early campaigns. General Mercer was at hand, who had ſhared his perils among thoſe mountains, and his preſence may have contributed to bring them to his mind. 'What think you,' ſaid Waſhington, 'if we ſhould retreat to the back parts of Pennſylvania, would the Pennſylvanians ſupport us?' 'If the lower counties give up, the back counties will do the ſame,' was the diſcouraging reply. 'We muſt then retire to Auguſta County, in Virginia,' ſaid Waſhington. 'Numbers will repair to us for ſafety, and we will try a predatory war. If overpowered, we muſt croſs the Alleghanies.' Such was the indomitable ſpirit, riſing under difficulties and buoyant

Peace you demand, and vainly wifh to find
Old leagues renew'd, and ftrength once more combin'd—
Yet fhall not all your bafe diffembling art
Deceive the tortures of a bleeding heart—
Yet fhall not all your mingled prayers that rife,
Wafh out your crimes, or bribe the avenging fkies;
Full many a corpfe lies mouldering on the plain
That ne'er fhall fee its little brood again:
See, yonder lies, all breathlefs, cold, and pale,
Drench'd in her gore, *Lavinia* of the vale;
The cruel Indian feiz'd her life away,
As the next morn began her bridal day!—
This *deed* alone our juft revenge would claim,
Did not ten thoufand more your fons defame.*

Return'd, a captive, to my native fhore,
How chang'd I find thofe fcenes that pleas'd before!
How chang'd thofe groves where fancy lov'd to ftray,
When fpring's young bloffoms bloom'd along the way:
From every eye diftils the frequent tear,
From every mouth fome doleful tale I hear!
Some mourn a father, brother, hufband, friend:
Some mourn, imprifon'd in their native land,

in the darkeft moment, that kept our tempeft-toft caufe from foundering."—
IRVING's *Life of Wafhington*, II., p. 448.

* An allufion to Mifs Jane McCrea, whofe murder by a party of Burgoyne's
Indians, in the vicinity of Fort Edward, was one of the tragic incidents of the
war, which, with the feeling of horror it created, called forth alfo much romantic fympathy. Barlow has a poetic verfion of " Lucinda's Fate" in the fixth
book of the Columbiad. Wafhington Irving has told the ftory in his fimple,
effective way, with fome circumftances derived from a niece of Mifs McCrea, in
the third volume of his " Life of Wafhington."

In fickly fhips what numerous hofts confin'd
At once their lives and liberties refign'd :
In dreary dungeons woeful fcenes have pafs'd,
Long in the hiftorian's page the tale will laft,
As long as fpring renews the flowery wood,
As long as breezes curl the yielding flood :—
Some fent to India's fickly climes, afar,
To dig, with flaves, for buried diamonds there,
There left to ficken in a land of woe
Where o'er fcorch'd hills infernal breezes blow,
Whofe every blaft fome dire contagion brings,
Fevers or death on its deftructive wings,
'Till fate relenting, its laft arrows drew,
Brought death to them, and infamy to you.

Pefts of mankind! remembrance fhall recall
And paint thefe horrors to the view of all ;
Heaven has not turn'd to its own works a foe
Nor left to monfters thefe fair realms below,
Elfe had your arms more wafteful vengeance fpread,
And thefe gay plains been dy'd a deeper red.——

O'er Britain's ifle a thoufand woes impend,
Too weak to conquer, govern, or defend,
To liberty fhe holds pretended claim—
The fubftance we enjoy, and they the name ;
Her prince, furrounded by a hoft of flaves,
Still claims dominion o'er the vagrant waves :
Such be his claims o'er all the world befide,—
An empty nothing—madnefs, rage, and pride.

From Europe's realms fair freedom has retir'd,

And even in Britain has the fpark expir'd—
Sigh for the change your haughty empire feels,
Sigh for the doom that no difguife conceals!
Freedom no more fhall *Albion's* cliffs survey;
Corruption there has centred all her fway,
Freedom difdains her honeft head to rear,
Or herd with nobles, kings, or princes there;
She fhuns their gilded fpires, and domes of ftate,
Refolv'd, O Virtue, at thy fhrine to wait;
'Midft favage woods and wilds fhe dares to ftray,
And bids uncultur'd nature bloom more gay.

　　She is that glorious and immortal fun,
Without whofe ray this world would be undone,
A mere dull chaos, funk in deepeft night,
An 'abject fomething, void of form and light,
Of reptiles, worft in rank, the dire abode,
Perpetual mifchief, and the dragon's brood.

　　Let Turks and Ruffians glut their fields with blood,
Again let Britain dye the Atlantic flood,
Let all the eaft adore the fanguine wreathe
And gain new glories from the trade of death—
America! the works of peace be thine,
Thus fhalt thou gain a triumph more divine—
To thee belongs a fecond golden reign,
Thine is the empire o'er a peaceful main;
Protect the rights of human kind below,
Crufh the proud tyrant who becomes their foe,
And future times fhall own our ftruggles bleft,
And future years enjoy perpetual reft.

Americans ! revenge your country's wrongs ;
To you the honour of this deed belongs,
Your arms did once this finking land fuftain,
And fav'd thofe climes where Freedom yet muft reign—
Your bleeding foil this ardent tafk demands,
Expel yon' thieves from thefe polluted lands,
Expect no peace till haughty Britain yields,
'Till humbled Britons quit your ravag'd fields—
Still to the charge that routed foe returns,
The war ftill rages, and the battle burns—
No dull debates, or tedious counfels know,
But rufh, at once, embodied, on your foe ;—
With hell-born fpite a feven years war they wage,
The pirate *Goodrich*, and the ruffian *Gage*.
Your injur'd country groans while yet they ftay,
Attend her groans, and force their hofts away ;
Your mighty wrongs the tragic mufe fhall trace,
Your gallant deeds fhall fire a future race ;
To you may kings and potentates appeal,
You may the doom of jarring nations feal ;
A glorious empire rifes, bright and new !
Firm be its bafis, and muft reft on you—
Fame o'er the mighty *pile* expands her wings,
Remote from princes, bifhops, lords, and kings,
Thofe fancied gods, who, fam'd through every fhore,
Mankind have fafhion'd, and, like fools, adore.——
Here yet fhall heaven the joys of peace beftow,
While thro' our foil the ftreams of plenty flow,
And o'er the main we fpread the trading fail,
Wafting the produce of the rural vale.

ALLIANCE.*

A S Neptune trac'd the azure main,
    That own'd fo late proud Britain's reign,
A floating pile approach'd his car,
The fcene of terror, and of war.

* The "Alliance" was built at Salifbury, Maffachufetts, and launched about the time of the Treaty with France, in 1778, a circumftance from which her name was derived. "She was," says Cooper, "the favourite fhip of the American Navy, and, it might be added, of the American nation, during the war of the Revolution; filling fome fuch fpace in the public mind, as has fince been occupied by her more celebrated fucceffor, the Conftitution. She was a beautiful and an exceedingly faft fhip, but was rendered lefs efficient than fhe might otherwife have proved, by the miftake of placing her under the command of a French officer, who had entered the fervice with a view to pay a compliment to the new allies of the republic." This was Captain Landais, with whom Lafayette embarked in the frigate on her firft voyage from Bofton to Breft, in January, 1779. She had a motley crew, including fome wrecked Britifh failors, volunteers from Britifh prifoners, and a few French feamen. The refult was a deeply laid plan for a mutiny at fea, which was revealed at the laft moment by an American failor on board, to whom it had been communicated. By the energy of the officers and paffengers the ringleaders were feized and the danger averted. The Alliance was fubfequently added by Dr. Franklin, in Paris, to the fquadron placed at the difpofal of Commodore Paul Jones, and, under the management of her captain, Landais, bore no creditable part in the memorable engagement with the Serapis. Captain Landais was fufpended for his conduct on this occafion, though he was allowed to return with the veffel to America in 1780. On the paffage he was depofed from the command on the charge of infanity, and was, foon after

As nearer ftill the monarch drew,
(Her ftarry flag difplay'd to view)
He afk'd a Triton of his train
" What flag was this that rode the main—

" A fhip of fuch a gallant mien .
" This many a day I have not feen,
" To no mean power can fhe belong,
" So fwift, fo warlike, ftout, and ftrong.

" See how fhe mounts the foaming wave —
" Where other fhips would find a grave,
" Majeftic, aweful, and ferene,   '
" She walks the ocean, like its queen."—

" Great monarch of the hoary deep,
" Whofe trident awes the waves to fleep,
(Reply'd a Triton of his train)
" This fhip, that ftems the weftern main,

" To thofe new, rifing *States* belongs,
" Who, in refentment of their wrongs,

landing, difcharged from the Navy. The Alliance, on this voyage, brought a
large quantity of arms and ammunition for the United States. Captain John
Barry fucceeded Landais in command of the Alliance. He carried Colonel Laurens in her to France early in 1781, and, in a fubfequent cruife that year, victo-
rioufly encountered on the Atlantic the Britifh veffels Atalanta and Trepaffy. In
the following year, Barry gained other laurels in command of the Alliance in the
Weft Indies. After the peace this renowned frigate was fold, and converted into
an Indiaman. " Her wreck," fays Cooper, in 1839, " ftill lies on the ifland oppofite to Philadelphia."

" Oppofe proud Britain's tyrant fway,
" And combat her, by land and fea.

" This pile, of fuch fuperior fame,
" From their ftrict *union* takes her name,
" For them fhe cleaves the briny tide,
" While terror marches by her fide.

" When fhe unfurls her flowing fails,
" Undaunted by the fierceft gales,
" In dreadful pomp, fhe ploughs the main,
" While adverfe tempefts rage in vain.

" When fhe difplays her gloomy *tier*,
" The boldeft Britons freeze with fear,
" And, owning her fuperior might,
" Seek their beft fafety in their flight.

" But, when fhe pours the dreadful blaze,
" And thunder from her cannon plays,
" The burfting flafh that wings the ball,
" Compells thofe foes to *ftrike*, or fall.

" Though fhe, with her triumphant crew,
" Might to their fate all foes purfue,
" Yet, faithful to the land that bore,
" She ftays, to guard her native fhore.

" Though fhe might make the cruifers groan
' That fail beneath the torrid zone,

" She kindly lends a nearer aid,
" Annoys them here, and guards the trade.

" Now, traverſing the eaſtern main,
" She greets the ſhores of France and Spain ;
" Her gallant flag, diſplay'd to view,
" Invites the old world to the new.

" This taſk achiev'd, behold her go
" To ſeas congeal'd with ice and ſnow,
" To either tropic, and the *line*,
" Where ſuns with endleſs fervour ſhine.

" Not, Argo, in thy womb was found
" Such hearts of braſs, as here abound ;
" They for their golden fleece did fly,
" Theſe ſail—to vanquiſh tyranny."——

[1778.]

CAPTAIN NICHOLAS BIDDLE,

Commander of the Randolph Frigate, blown up near Barbadoes.

W HAT diſtant thunders rend the ſkies,
  What clouds of ſmoke in columns riſe,
 What means this dreadful roar !
Is from his baſe *Veſuvius* thrown,
Is ſky-topt *Atlas* tumbled down,
  Or *Etna's* ſelf no more !

---

* Nicholas Biddle, deſcended from an old colonial family of Weſt Jerſey, was born in Philadelphia, in 1750. He had been a ſeaman from his boyhood, and, at one time, was rated as midſhipman on board a Britiſh ſloop-of-war. "It is a ſingular fact," ſays Cooper, in his Naval Hiſtory, "in the life of this remarkable young man, that he entered on board one of the veſſels ſent towards the north pole, under the Honourable Captain Phipps, where he found Nelſon, a volunteer like himſelf. Both were made cockſwains by the Commodore." This was in 1773; two years later, young Biddle, foreſeeing the troubles at hand in his native country, returned to America, took part in the ſtruggle of the colonies, and was early employed in the ſervice of Congreſs. He was employed on the eaſtern coaſt, and when the Randolph, 32, was launched at Philadelphia, in 1776, he was made her commander. He ſailed in her on her firſt cruiſe early the next year, put into Charleſton, and, ſailing again out of that port, captured four Jamaica-men, with which he returned to the city. There he was detained for ſome months by the enemy's blockade. The South Carolinians, " pleaſed with his

Shock after fhock torments my ear ;
And lo ! two hoftile fhips appear,
    Red lightnings round them glow :
The *Yarmouth* boafts of fixty-four,
The *Randolph* thirty-two—no more—
    And will fhe fight this foe !

zeal and deportment," fitted out for him four fmall veffels, which he took out with the Randolph on a cruife, in the enfuing fpring of 1778. On the 7th of March he encountered, to the eaftward of Barbadoes, the Britifh fhip Yarmouth, 64, Captain Vincent. An action was fought at clofe quarters, which was maintained with vigour for twenty minutes, when the Randolph blew up. "The two fhips were fo near at the time," fays Cooper, in his narrative of the affair, derived from a publifhed letter of Captain Vincent, "that many fragments of the wreck ftruck the Yarmouth; and, among other things, an American enfign, rolled up, was blown in upon her forecaftle. This flag was not even finged." The Yarmouth, after this, left the fpot, and gave chafe to two of the veffels in Captain Biddle's company. Returning feveral days after to the place, Captain Biddle picked up four men furviving of the crew of the Randolph, who had faved themfelves on a fragment of the wreck. "In the action with the Yarmouth," fays Cooper, "Captain Biddle was feverely wounded in the thigh, and he is faid to have been feated in a chair, with the furgeon examining his hurt, when his fhip blew up. His death occurred at the early age of twenty-feven, and he died unmarried, though engaged at the time to a lady in Charlefton. His lofs was greatly regretted in the midft of the excitement and viciffitudes of a revolution, and can fcarcely be appreciated by thofe who do not underftand the influence that fuch a character can produce on a fmall and infant fervice."

Freneau, with patriotic or poetic licenfe, reprefents his hero falling at the point of victory—an affumption hardly juftified in face of the fuperiority of the enemy, and Captain Vincent's report of but five men killed and twelve wounded in the engagement. Captain Biddle, however, undoubtedly acted with great gallantry in fteadily working his fhip in fuch an unequal conteft; and although, in the words of Cooper, "victory was almoft hopelefs, even had all his veffels behaved equally well with his own fhip, we find it difficult, under the circumftances, to fuppofe that this gallant feaman did not actually contemplate carrying his powerful antagonift, moft probably by boarding."

A memoir of Captain Biddle, with a portrait, will be found in *The Port Folio* for October, 1809.

The Randolph foon on Stygian ftreams
Shall coaft along the land of dreams,
    The iflands of the dead!
But fate, that parts them on the deep,
Shall fave the Briton yet to weep
    His days of victory fled.*

Say, who commands that difmal blaze,
Where yonder ftarry ftreamer plays;
    Does *Mars* with *Jove* engage!
'Tis Biddle wings thofe angry fires,
Biddle, whofe bofom *Jove* infpires
    With more than mortal rage.

Tremendous flafh!—and hark, the ball
Drives through old Yarmouth, flames and all:
    Her braveft fons expire;
Did Mars himfelf approach fo nigh,
Even Mars, without difgrace, might fly
    The Randolph's fiercer fire.

The Briton views his mangled crew,
" And fhall we ftrike to *thirty-two*
    (Said Hector, ftain'd with gore)
" Shall Britain's flag to *thefe* defcend—

* We give this ftanza as it appears in the author's third edition of 1809. It
is entirely omitted in the fecond edition of 1795. In the firft, of 1786, the concluding lines read:—
        Shall fave the Briton, ftill to weep
        His ancient honours fled.

" Rife, and the glorious conflict end,
   " Britons, I afk no more!"

He fpoke—they charg'd their cannon round,
Again the vaulted heavens refound,
   The Randolph bore it all,
Then fix'd her pointed cannons true—
Away the unwieldy vengeance flew;
   Britain, thy warriors fall.

The Yarmouth faw, with dire difmay,
Her wounded hull, fhrouds fhot away,
   Her boldeft heroes dead—
She faw amidft her floating flain
The conquering *Randolph* ftem the main—
   She faw, fhe turn'd—and fled!

That hour, bleft chief, had fhe been thine,
Dear *Biddle*, had the powers divine
   Been kind as thou wert brave;
But fate, who doom'd thee to expire,
Prepar'd an arrow, tipt with fire,
   And mark'd a wat'ry grave.

And in that hour, when conqueft came,
Wing'd at his fhip a pointed flame,
   That not even *he* could fhun—
The battle ceas'd, the Yarmouth fled,

> The burſting Randolph ruin ſpread,
> And left her taſk undone.*

---

* As publiſhed in the edition of 1786, the laſt three lines of this ſtanza read :—

> The conqueſt ceas'd, the Yarmouth fled,
> The burſting Randolph ruin ſpread,
> And loſt what honour won.

In the edition of 1795, "honour," in the laſt line, is changed to "courage." We print the ſtanza from the author's reviſed edition of 1809. The date of the action is erroneouſly given, 1776, in the title of the poem in the edition of 1786 (reprinted in England in 1861), and in the Philadelphia edition of 1809.

GEORGE THE THIRD'S SOLILOQUY.

WHAT mean thefe dreams, and hideous forms that rife
    Night after night, tormenting to my eyes—
No real foes thefe horrid fhapes can be,
But thrice as much they vex and torture me.
    How curs'd is he,—how doubly curs'd am I—
Who lives in pain, and yet who dares not die;
To him no joy this world of Nature brings,
In vain the wild rofe blooms, the daify fprings.
Is this a prelude to fome new difgrace,
Some baleful omen to my name and race !—
It may be fo—ere mighty Cefar died,
Prefaging Nature felt his doom, and figh'd ;
A bellowing voice through midnight groves was heard,
And threatening ghofts at dufk of eve appear'd—
Ere Brutus fell, to adverfe fates a prey,
His evil genius met him on the way,
And fo may mine !—but who would yield fo foon
A prize, fome luckier hour may make my own ?—
Shame feize my crown, ere fuch a deed be mine—
No—to the laft my fquadrons fhall combine,
And flay my foes, while foes remain to flay,
Or *heaven* fhall grant me one fuccefsful day.
  5

Is there a robber clofe in Newgate hemm'd,
Is there a cut-throat, fetter'd and condemn'd?
Hafte, loyal flaves, to George's ftandard come,
Attend his lectures when you hear the drum;
Your chains I break—for better days prepare,
Come out, my friends, from prifon and from care,
Far to the weft I plan your defperate fway,
There 'tis no fin to ravage, burn, and flay;
There, without fear, your bloody aims purfue,
And fhow mankind what Englifh thieves can do.

That day, when firft I mounted to the throne,
I fwore to let all foreign foes alone.
Through love of peace to terms did I advance,
And made, they fay, a fhameful league with France.
But different fcenes rife horrid to my view,
I charg'd my hofts to plunder and fubdue—
At firft, indeed, I thought fhort wars to wage,
And fent fome jail-birds to be led by *Gage*,
For 'twas but right, that thofe we mark'd for flaves
Should be reduc'd by cowards, fools, and knaves:
Awhile, directed by his feeble hand,
Thofe *troops* were kick'd and pelted through the land,
Or ftarv'd in Bofton, curs'd the unlucky hour
They left their dungeons for that fatal fhore.

France aids them now, a defperate game I play,
And hoftile Spain will do the fame, they fay;
My armies vanquifh'd, and my heroes fled,
My people murmuring, and my commerce dead,
My fhatter'd navy pelted, bruis'd, and clubb'd,

By Dutchmen bullied, and by Frenchmen drubb'd,
My name abhorr'd, my nation in difgrace,
How fhould I act in fuch a mournful cafe !
My hopes and joys are vanifh'd with my coin,
My ruin'd army, and my loft Burgoyne !
What fhall I do—confefs my labours vain,
Or whet my tufks, and to the charge again !
But where's my force—my choiceft troops are fled,
Some thoufands crippled, and a myriad dead—
If I were own'd the boldeft of mankind,
And hell with all her flames infpir'd my mind,
Could I at once with Spain and France contend,
And fight the *rebels*, on the world's green end ?——
The pangs of *parting* I can ne'er endure,
Yet *part* we muft, and part to meet no more !
Oh, blaft this *Congrefs*, blaft each upftart STATE,
On whofe commands ten thoufand captains wait ;
From various climes that dire *Affembly* came,
True to their truft, as hoftile to my fame ;
'Tis thefe, ah thefe, have ruin'd half my fway,
Difgrac'd my arms, and led my flaves aftray—
Curs'd be the day, when firft I faw the fun,
Curs'd be the hour, when I thefe wars begun :
The fiends of darknefs then poffefs'd my mind,
And powers unfriendly to the human kind.
To wafting grief, and fullen rage a prey,
To *Scotland's* utmoft verge I'll take my way,
There with eternal ftorms due concert keep,
And while the billows rage, as fiercely weep—

Ye highland lads, my rugged fate bemoan,
Affift me with one fympathizing groan;
For late I find the nations are my foes,
I muft fubmit, and that with bloody nofe,
Or, like our James, fly bafely from the ftate,
Or fhare, what ftill is worfe—old *Charles's* fate.

    [1779.]

A DIALOGUE BETWEEN GEORGE AND FOX.

[Suppofed to have paffed about the time of the approach of the combined fleets of France and Spain to the Britifh coafts, Auguft, 1779.]

GOOD CHARLY Fox, your counfel I implore,
   Still George the third, but potent George no more.
By NORTH conducted to the brink of fate,
I mourn my folly and my pride, too late :
The promifes he made, when once we met
In Kew's gay fhades, I never fhall forget ;
That at my feet the weftern world fhould fall,
And bow to me, the potent lord of all—
Curfe on his hopes, his councils, and his fchemes,
His plans of conqueft, and his golden dreams,
Thefe have allured me to the jaws of hell ;
By Satan tempted thus Ifcariot fell :
Divefted of majeftic pomp, I come,
My royal robes and airs I've left at home,
Speak freely, friend, whate'er you choofe to fay,
Suppofe me equal with yourfelf to day :
How fhall I fhun the mifchiefs that impend ?
How fhall I make Columbia, yet, my friend ?
I dread the power of each revolted State,

The trembling Eaſt hangs ballanc'd with their weight.
How ſhall I dare the rage of France and Spain,
And loſt dominion o'er the waves regain?
Adviſe me quick, for doubtful while we ſtand,
Deſtruction gathers o'er this wretched land:
Theſe hoſtile ſquadrons, to my ruin led,
Theſe gallic thunders fill my ſoul with dread:
If theſe ſhould triumph—Britain thou muſt fall,
And bend, a province to the conquering Gaul:
If this muſt be—thou earth, expanding wide,
Unlucky George in thy dark entrails hide——
Ye oceans, wrap me in your dark embrace—
Ye mountains, ſhroud me to your loweſt baſe——
Fall on my head, ye everlaſting rocks——
But why ſo penſive, my good Charly Fox?

Fox.

While in the arms of power and peace you lay,
Ambition led your reſtleſs ſoul aſtray.
Poſſeſt of lands, extending far and wide,
And more than Rome could boaſt in all her pride,
Yet, not contented with that mighty ſtore,
Like ſome baſe miſer, ſtill you ſought for more;
And, all in raptures for a tyrant's reign,
You ſtrove your ſubjects' deareſt rights to chain:
Thoſe ruffian hoſts, beyond the ocean ſent,
By your command, on blood and murder bent,
With cruel hand the form of man defac'd,
And laid the toils of art and nature waſte.

(For crimes like thefe imperial Britain bends,
For crimes like thefe her ancient glory ends.)
Thofe lands, once trueft to your name and race,
Which the wide ocean's utmoft waves embrace,
Your juft protection bafely you deny'd,
Their towns you plunder'd, and you burnt befide.
Virginia's flaves, without one blufh of fhame,
Againft their caufe you arm'd with fword and flame ;
At every port your fhips of war you laid,
And ftrove to ruin and diftrefs their trade,
Yet here, ev'n here, your mighty projects fail'd ;
For then from creeks their hardy feamen fail'd,
In flender barques they crofs'd a ftormy main,
And traffick'd for the wealth of France and Spain ;
O'er either tropic and the line they pafs'd,
And, deeply laden, fafe return'd at laft :
Nor think they yet had bow'd to Britain's fway,
Though diftant nations had not join'd the fray,
Alone they fought your armies and your fleet,
And made your Clintons and your Howes retreat,
And yet while France ftood doubting if to join,
Your fhips they captur'd, and they took Burgoyne !
　　How vain is Britain's ftrength, her armies now
Before Columbia's bolder veterans bow ;
Her gallant veterans all our force defpife,
Though late from ruin we beheld them rife ;
Before their arms our ftrongeft bulwarks fall ;
They ftorm the rampart and they fcale the wall ;
With equal dread, on either fervice fent,

They feize a fortrefs, or they ftrike a tent.

But fhould we bow beneath a foreign yoke,
And potent France atchieve the humbling ftroke,
Yet every power, and even ourfelves, muft fay,
"Juft is the vengeance of the fkies to-day :"
For crimes like ours dire vengeance muft atone ;
Forbear your fafts, and let the Gods alone—
By cruel kings, in fierce Britannia bred,
Such feas of blood have, firft and laft, been fhed,
That now, diftreft for each inhuman deed,
Our turn is come—our turn is come to bleed :
Forbear your groans ; for war and death array,
March to the foe, and give the fates their way.
Can we behold without one dying groan,
The fleets of France fuperior to our own ?
.Can we behold, without one poignant pang,
The foreign conquefts of the brave D'Eftaing ?
NORTH is your friend, and now deftruction knocks,
Still take his counfel, and regard not Fox.

George.

Ah ! fpeak not thus—your words will burft my heart,
Some fofter counfel to my ears impart.
How can I march to meet the infulting foe,
Who never yet to hoftile plains did go ?
When was I vers'd in battles or in blood ?
When have I fought upon the faithlefs flood ?
Much better could I at my palace door
Recline, and hear the diftant cannons roar.

Generals and admirals Britain yet can boaſt,
Some·fight on land, and ſome defend the coaſt;
The fame of theſe throughout the globe reſounds,
To theſe I leave the glory and the wounds;
But ſince this honour for no blood atones,
I muſt and will—be careful of my bones.

What pleaſure to your monarch would it be,
If Lords and Commons could at laſt agree;
Could *North* with *Fox* in firm alliance ſtand,
And *Burke* with *Sandwich* ſhake the ſocial hand,
Then ſhould we bring the rebels to our feet,
And France and Spain ingloriouſly retreat,
Her ancient glories to this iſle return,
And we no more for loſt Columbia mourn.

Fox.

Alliance!—what!—my maſter muſt be mad:
Say, what alliance can with theſe be had?
Can lambs and wolves in ſocial bands ally?——·
When theſe prove friendly, then will North and I.
Alliance! no—I curſe the abject thought;
Ally with thoſe their country's ruin ſought!
Who to perdition ſold their native land,
Leagu'd with the foe, a cloſe connected band—
Ally with theſe!—I ſpeak it to your face—
Alliance here, is ruin and diſgrace.
Angels·and devils in ſuch bonds unite,
So hell is allied to the realms of light—
Let *North* or *Sackville* ſtill my prayers deride,

Let turn-coat *Johnſtone* take the courtly ſide,
Even *Pitt*, if living, might with theſe agree ; ·
But no alliance ſhall they have with me.

   But ſince no ſhame forbids your tongue to own
A royal coward fills Britannia's throne ;
Since our beſt chiefs muſt fight your mad campaigns,
And be diſgrac'd, at laſt, by him who reigns,
No wonder, heaven ! ſuch ill ſucceſs attends !
No wonder North and Mansfield are your friends !
Take my advice, with them to battle go,
Theſe book-learn'd heroes may confront the foe—
Thoſe firſt who lead us tow'rds the brink of fate,
Should ſtill be foremoſt, when at Pluto's gate ;
Let them, grown deſperate by our weight of woes,
Collect new fury from this hoſt of foes,
And, ally'd with themſelves, to ruin ſteer,
The juſt concluſion of their mad career.

George.

No comfort in theſe cruel words I find—
Ungrateful words to my tormented mind !
With me alone, both France and Spain contend,
And not one nation can be call'd my friend :
Unpitying now the Dutchman ſees me fall,
The Ruſſian leaves me to the thundering Gaul,
The German, grown as careleſs as the Dane,
Conſigns my carcaſe to the jaws of Spain.
Where are the hoſts they promis'd me of yore,
When rich and great they heard my thunders roar

While yet confeſs'd the maſter of the ſea,
The Germans drain'd their wide domain for me,
And, aiding Britain with a friendly hand,
Help'd to ſubdue the rebels and their land?
Ah! rebels, rebels! inſolent and mad;
Our Scottiſh rebels were not half ſo bad——
They ſoon ſubmitted to ſuperior ſway;
But theſe grow ſtronger as my hoſts decay:
What crowds have periſh'd on their hoſtile ſhore!
They went for conqueſt, but return'd no more.
Columbia, thou a friend in better times!
Loſt are to me thy pleaſurable climes:
You wiſh me buried in eternal night,
You curſe the day when firſt I ſaw the light—
Your commerce vaniſh'd, hoſtile nations ſhare,
And thus you leave us naked, poor, and bare;
Deſpis'd by thoſe who ſhould our cauſe defend,
And helpleſs left, without one pitying friend.
Theſe dire afflictions ſhake my changeful throne,
And turn my brain—a very idiot grown:
Of all the iſles, the realms with which I part,
Columbia ſits the weightieſt at my heart,
She, ſhe provokes the deepeſt, heavieſt ſigh,
And makes me doubly wretched, ere I die.

Some dreary convent's unfrequented gloom
(Like Charles of Spain) had better be my doom:
There while in abſence from my crown I ſigh,
George, Prince of Wales, theſe ills may rectify;
A happier fortune may his crown await,

He yet, perhaps, may save this sinking state :
I'll to my prayers, my bishops, and my beads,
And beg God's pardon for my heinous deeds ;
Those streams of blood, that spilt by my command,
Call out for vengeance on this guilty land.

Fox.

In one short sentence take my whole advice,
(It is no time to flatter and be nice)
With all your soul for instant peace contend,
Thus shall you be your country's truest friend—
Peace, instant peace, may stay your tottering throne,
But wars and death and blood can profit none,
To *Catharine* send, in humble garb array'd,
And beg her intercession, not her aid :
Withdraw your armies from th' Americ' shore,
And vex her oceans with your fleets no more ;
Vain are their conquests, past experience shews,
For what this hour they gain, the next they lose.
Implore the friendship of those injur'd States ;
No longer strive against the stubborn fates.
Since heaven has doom'd *Columbia* to be free,
What is her commerce and her wealth to thee ?
Since heav'n that land of promise has denied,
Regain by cunning what you lost by pride :
Immediate ruin each delay attends,
Imperial Britain scarce her coasts defends ;
Hibernia sees the threat'ning foes advance,
And feels an ague at the thoughts of France ;

Jamaica mourns her half-protected ſtate,
Barbadoes ſoon may ſhare Grenada's fate,
And every iſle that owns your reign to-day,
May bow to-morrow to the Frenchman's ſway,
Yes—while I ſpeak, your empire, great before,
Contracts its limits, and is great no more.
Unhappy prince ! what madneſs has poſſeſt,
What worſe than madneſs ſeiz'd thy vengeful breaſt,
When white-rob'd peace before your portal ſtood,
To drive her hence, and ſtain the world with blood !
For this deſtruction threatens from the ſkies ;
See hoſtile navies to our ruin riſe ;
Our fleets inglorious ſhun the force of Spain,
And France, triumphant, ſtems the ſubject main.

    [*Anno,* 1779.]

THE BRITISH PRISON-SHIP.*

Amid thefe ills no tyrant dared refufe
My right to pen the dictates of the mufe,
To paint the terrors of the infernal place,
And fiends from Europe, infolent as bafe.

CANTO I.—*The Capture.*

ASSIST me, CLIO ! while in verfe I tell
    The dire misfortunes that a fhip befell,
Which outward bound, to St. Euftatia's fhore,
Death and difafter through the billows bore.
 ' From Philadelphia's happy port fhe came ;
(And there the builder plann'd her lofty frame,)
With wonderous fkill, and excellence of art
He form'd, difpos'd, and order'd every part,
With joy, beheld the ftately fabric rife
To a ftout bulwark, of ftupendous fize,
'Till launch'd at laft, capacious of the freight,
He left her to the pilots, and her fate.
    Firft, from her depths the tapering mafts afcend,
On whofe tall bulk the tranfverfe yards depend,
By fhrouds and ftays fecur'd from fide to fide

* Written towards the clofe of 1780, and firft publifhed by Mr. Francis Bailey, Philadelphia, early in the year 1781.

Trees grew on trees, fufpended o'er the tide :
Firm to the yards extended, broad and vaft,
They hung the fails, fufceptive of the blaft,
Far o'er the prow the lengthy bowfprit lay,
Supporting on the extreme the taut fore-ftay,
Twice ten fix pounders, at their port holes plac'd,
And rang'd in rows, ftood hoftile in the waift :
Thus all prepar'd, impatient for the feas,
She left her ftation with an adverfe breeze,
This her firft outfet from her native fhore,
To feas a ftranger, and untry'd before.
. From the fine radiance, that his glories fpread,
Ere from the eaft gay Phœbus lifts his head,
From the bright morn, a kindred name fhe won,
AURORA call'd, the daughter of the fun,
Whofe form, projecting, the broad prow difplays,
Far glittering o'er the wave, a mimic blaze.
   The gay fhip now, in all her pomp and pride,
With fails expanded, flew along the tide ;
'Twas thy deep ftream, O Delaware, that bore
This pile intended for a fouthern fhore,
Bound to thofe ifles where endlefs fummer reigns,
Fair fruits, gay bloffoms, and enamell'd plains ;
Where floping lawns the roving fwain invite ;
And the cool morn fucceeds the breezy night,
Where each glad day a heaven unclouded brings
And sky-topt mountains teem with golden fprings.
   From Cape HENLOPEN, urg'd by favouring gales,
When morn emerg'd, we fea-ward fpread our fails,

Then, eaſt-ſouth-eaſt, explor'd the briny way,
Cloſe to the wind, departing from the bay ;
No longer ſeen the hoarſe reſounding ſtrand,
With hearts elate we hurried from the land,
Eſcap'd the dangers of that ſhelving ground
To ſailors fatal, and for wrecks renown'd——

The gale increaſes as we plough the main,
Now ſcarce the hills their ſky-blue miſt retain :
At laſt they ſink beneath the rolling wave,
That ſeems their ſummits, as they ſink, to lave.
Abaft the beam the freſhening breezes play,
No miſts advancing, to deform the day,   .
No tempeſts riſing o'er the ſplendid ſcene,
A ſea unruffled, and a heaven ſerene.

Now *Sol's* bright lamp, the heaven-born ſource of light,
Had paſs'd the line of his meridian height,
And weſtward hung—retreating from the view
Shores diſappear'd, and every hill withdrew,
When, ſtill ſuſpicious of ſome neighbouring foe,
Aloft the Maſter bade a ſeaman go,
To mark if, from the maſt's aſpiring height,
Through all the round, a veſſel came in ſight.

Too ſoon the ſeaman's glance extending wide,
Far diſtant in the eaſt a ſhip eſpy'd,
Her lofty maſts ſtood bending to the gale,
Cloſe to the wind was brac'd each ſhivering ſail ;
Next from the deck we ſaw the approaching foe,
Her ſpangled bottom ſeem'd in flames to glow
When to the winds ſhe bow'd in dreadful haſte

And her lee-guns lay deluged in the waift ;
From her top-gallant wav'd an *Englifh Jack* ;——
With all her might fhe ftrove to gain our tack,
Nor ftrove in vain—with pride and power elate,
Wing'd on by winds, fhe drove us to our fate,
No ftop, no ftay her bloody crew intends,
(So flies a comet with its hoft of fiends)
Nor oaths, nor prayers arreft her fwift career,
Death in her front, and ruin in her rear.
 Struck at the fight, the mafter gave command
To change our courfe, and fteer toward the land—
Straight to the tafk the ready failors run,
And while the word was utter'd, half was done ;
As, from the fouth, the fiercer breezes rife
Swift from her foe alarm'd AURORA flies,
With every fail extended to the wind
She fled the unequal foe that chac'd behind.——
Along her decks, difpos'd in clofe array,
Each at its port, the grim artillery lay,
Soon on the foe with brazen throat to roar ;
But, fmall their fize, and narrow was their *bore ;*
Yet, faithful, they their deftin'd ftation keep
To guard the barque that wafts them o'er the deep,
Who now muft bend to fteer a homeward courfe
And truft her fwiftnefs rather than her force,
Unfit to combat with a powerful foe ;
Her decks too open, and her *waift* too low.
 While o'er the wave, with foaming prow, fhe flies,
Once more emerging, diftant landfcapes rife ;
 6

High in the air the *starry* ftreamer plays,
And every fail its various tribute pays ;
To gain the land, we bore the weighty blaft ;
And now the wifh'd for *cape* appear'd at laft ;
But the vext foe, impatient of delay,
Prepar'd for ruin, prefs'd upon his prey ;
Near, and more near, in aweful grandeur came
The frigate IRIS, not unknown to fame ;
IRIS her name, but HANCOCK once fhe bore,
Fram'd and completed on NEW ALBION's fhore,
By MANLY loft, the fwifteft of the train
That fly with wings of canvas o'er the main.*

Then, while for combat fome with zeal prepare,
Thus to the heavens the Boatfwain fent his prayer :
" Lift' all ye powers that rule the fkies and feas !
" Shower down perdition on fuch thieves as thefe,
" Winds, daunt their hearts with terror and difmay,
" And fprinkle on their powder falt fea fpray !
" May burfting cannon, while his aim he tries,
" Diftraft the gunner, and confound his eyes—
" The chief that awes the quarter-deck, may he
" Tripp'd from his ftand, be tumbled in the fea.
" May they who rule the *round-top's* giddy height

---

* "The Iris had been the United States' fhip Hancock, 32, Captain Manly,
and was captured by the Rainbow, 44, Sir George Collier. The Hancock, or
Iris, proved to be one of the fafteft fhips on the American ftation, and made the
fortunes of all who commanded her. Captain Manly is thought to have loft her
in confequence of having put her out of trim, by ftarting her water while chafed.
The fhip, in the end, fell into the hands of the French in the Weft Indies."—
COOPER's *Naval Hiftory*.

" Be canted headlong to perpetual night ;
" May fiends torment them on a leeward coaft,
" And help forfake them when they want it moft—
" From their wheel'd engines torn be every gun—
" And now, to fum up every curfe in one,
" May latent flames, to fave us, intervene,
" And hell-ward drive them from their magazine !"
 The Frigate, now, had every fail unfurl'd,
And rufh'd tremendous o'er the watery world ;
Thus fierce *Pelides*, eager to deftroy,
Chac'd the proud Trojan to the gates of Troy—
Swift o'er the waves while, hoftile, they purfue,
As fwiftly from their fangs AURORA flew,
At length HENLOPEN's cape we gain'd once more,
And vainly ftrove to force the fhip afhore ;
Stern fate forbade the barren fhore to gain ;
Denial fad, and fource of future pain !
For then the infpiring breezes ceas'd to blow,
Loft were they all, and fmooth'd the feas below ;
By the broad cape becalm'd, our lifelefs fails
No longer fwell'd their bofoms to the gales ;
The fhip, unable to purfue her way,
Tumbling about, at her own guidance lay,
No more the helm its wonted influence lends,
No oars affift us, and no breeze befriends ;
Mean time the foe, advancing from the fea,
Rang'd her black cannon, pointed on our *lee*,
Then up fhe *luff'd*, and blaz'd her entrails dire,
Bearing deftruction, terror, death, and fire.

Vext at our fate, we prim'd a piece, and then
Return'd the ſhot, to ſhew them we were men.
　　Dull night at length her duſky pinions ſpread,
And every hope to 'ſcape the foe was fled,
Cloſe to thy cape, Henlopen, though we preſs'd,
We could not gain thy defert, dreary breaſt ;
Though ruin'd trees beſhroud thy barren ſhore
With mounds of ſand half hid, or cover'd o'er,
Though ruffian winds diſturb thy ſummit bare,
Yet every hope and every wiſh was there :
In vain we fought to reach the joyleſs ſtrand,
Fate ſtood between, and barr'd us from the land.
　　All dead becalm'd, and helpleſs as we lay,
The ebbing current forc'd us back to ſea,
While vengeful IRIS, thirſting for our blood,
Flaſh'd her red lightnings o'er the trembling flood ;
At every flaſh a ſtorm of ruin came
'Till our ſhock'd veſſel ſhook through all her frame—
Mad for revenge, our breaſts with fury glow　　.
To wreak returns of vengeance on the foe ;
Full at his hull our pointed guns we rais'd,
His hull reſounded as the cannon blaz'd ;
Through his broad ſails while ſome a paſſage tore,
His ſides re-echo'd to the dreadful roar,
Alternate fires diſpell'd the ſhades of night—
But how unequal was this daring fight !
Our ſtouteſt guns threw but a ſix-pound ball,
Twelve pounders from the foe our ſides did maul ;
And, while no power to ſave him intervenes,

A bullet ſtruck our captain of marines ;
Fierce, though he bid defiance to the foe
He felt his death and ruin in the blow,
Headlong he fell, diſtracted with the wound,
The deck diſtain'd, and heart blood ſtreaming round.
    Another blaſt, as fatal in its aim
Wing'd by deſtruction, through our rigging came,
And aim'd aloft, to cripple in the fray,
Shrouds, ſtays, and braces tore at once away,
Sails, blocks, and oars in ſcatter'd fragments fly—
Their ſofteſt language was—SUBMIT, OR DIE.
    Repeated cries throughout the ſhip reſound ;
Now every bullet brought a different wound ;
Twixt *wind and water*, one aſſail'd the ſide :
Through this aperture ruſh'd the briny tide—
'Twas then the Maſter trembled for his crew,
And bade thy ſhores, O Delaware, adieu !—
And muſt we yield to yon' deſtructive ball,
And muſt our colours to theſe ruffians fall !——
They fall !—his thunders forc'd our ſtrength to bend,
The lofty topſails, with their yards, deſcend,
And the proud foe, ſuch leagues of ocean paſs'd,
His wiſh completed in our woe at laſt.
    Convey'd to YORK, we found, at length, too late,
That Death was better than the priſoner's fate,
There doom'd to famine, ſhackles, and deſpair,
Condemn'd to breathe a foul, infected air
In ſickly hulks, devoted while we lay,
Succeſſive funerals gloom'd each diſmal day——

But what on captives Britiſh rage can do,
Another Canto, friends, ſhall let you know.

CANTO II.—*The Priſon-Ships.**

THE various horrors of theſe hulks to tell,
Theſe Priſon Ships where pain and penance dwell,
Where death in tenfold vengeance holds his reign,
And injur'd ghoſts, yet unaveng'd, complain ;
This be my taſk—ungenerous Britons, you
Conſpire to murder whom you can't ſubdue.—

That Britain's rage ſhould dye our plains with gore,
And deſolation ſpread through every ſhore,
None e'er could doubt, that her ambition knew,——
This was to rage and diſappointment due ;
But that thoſe legions whom our ſoil maintain'd,
Who firſt drew breath in this devoted land,
Like famiſh'd wolves, ſhould on their country prey,

---

* Theſe priſon-ſhips were moſtly old tranſport veſſels, in which the Britiſh
troops had been brought to the city. They were moored, at firſt, off the Battery,
and afterwards in the Wallabout Bay, on the Long Iſland ſhore. One of theſe
ſhips, the Jerſey, was an old, condemned 64-gun ſhip, which had been employed
as a ſtore-ſhip. "In 1780," as we learn from Miſs Booth's 'Hiſtory of the City
of New York,' "when the priſoners on board the Good Hope [another of theſe
ſhips] burnt the veſſel, in the deſperate hope of regaining their liberty, the chief
incendiaries were removed to the Provoſt, and the remainder transferred to the
Jerſey, which was thenceforth uſed as a priſon-ſhip until the cloſe of the war,
when her inmates were liberated, and ſhe was henceforth ſhunned by all as a neſt
of peſtilence. The worms ſoon after deſtroyed her bottom, and ſhe ſank, bearing with her, on her planks, the names of thouſands of American priſoners. For
more than twenty years, her ribs lay expoſed at low water ; ſhe now lies buried
beneath the United States Navy Yard."

Affift its foes, and wreft our lives away,
This fhocks belief—and bids our foil difown
Such knaves, fubfervient to a bankrupt throne.
By them the widow mourns her partner dead,
Her mangled fons to darkfome prifons led,
By them—and hence my keeneft forrows rife,
My friend—companion—my *Oreftes* dies——
Still for that lofs muft wretched I complain,
And fad *Ophelia* mourn her lofs—in vain !

   Ah ! come the day when from this bleeding fhore
Fate fhall remove them, to return no more—
To fcorch'd Bahama fhall the traitors go
With grief, and rage, and unremitting woe,
On burning fands to walk their painful round,
And figh through all the folitary ground,
Where no gay flower their haggard eyes fhall fee,
And find no fhade—but from the cyprefs tree.

   So much we fuffer'd from the tribe I hate,
So near they fhov'd us to the brink of fate,
When two long months in thefe dark hulks we lay
Barr'd down by night, and fainting all the day
In the fierce fervours of the folar beam,
Cool'd by no breeze on Hudfon's mountain-ftream ;
That not unfung thefe threefcore days fhall fall
To black oblivion that would cover all !——

   No mafts or fails thefe crowded fhips adorn,
Difmal to view, neglected and forlorn ;
Here, mighty ills opprefs'd the imprifon'd throng,
Dull were our flumbers, and our nights were long——

From morn to eve along the decks we lay
Scorch'd into fevers by the folar ray;
No friendly *awning* caſt a welcome ſhade,
Once was it promis'd, and was never made;
No favours could theſe ſons of death beſtow,
'Twas endleſs vengeance, and unceaſing woe:
Immortal hatred does their breaſts engage,
And this loſt empire ſwells their ſouls with rage.

Two hulks on Hudſon's ſtormy boſom lie,
Two, on the eaſt, alarm the pitying eye——
There, the black SCORPION at her mooring rides,
There, STROMBOLO ſwings, yielding to the tides;
Here, bulky JERSEY fills a larger ſpace,
And HUNTER, to all hoſpitals diſgrace——

Thou, SCORPION, fatal to thy crowded throng,
Dire theme of horror and Plutonian ſong,
Requir'ſt my lay—thy ſultry decks I know,
And all the torments that exiſt below!
The briny wave that Hudſon's boſom fills
Drain'd through her bottom in a thouſand rills:
Rotten and old, replete with ſighs and groans,
Scarce on the waters ſhe ſuſtain'd her bones;
Here, doom'd to toil, or founder in the tide,
At the moiſt pumps inceſſantly we ply'd,
Here, doom'd to ſtarve, like famiſh'd dogs, we tore
The ſcant allowance, that our tyrants bore.

Remembrance ſhudders at this ſcene of fears—
Still in my view ſome tyrant chief appears,
Some baſe-born Heſſian ſlave walks threatening by,

Some fervile Scot, with murder in his eye,
Still haunts my fight, as vainly they bemoan
Rebellions manag'd fo unlike their *own !*
O may we never feel the poignant pain
To live fubjected to fuch fiends again,
Stewards and *Mates*, that hoftile Britain bore,
Cut from the gallows on their native fhore ;
Their ghaftly looks and vengeance-beaming eyes
Still to my view.in difmal vifions rife——
O may I ne'er review thefe dire abodes,
Thefe piles for flaughter, floating on the floods,——
And you, that o'er the troubled ocean go,
Strike not your ftandards to this venom'd foe,
Better the greedy wave fhould fwallow all,
Better to meet the death-conducting ball,
Better to fleep on ocean's oozy bed,
At once deftroy'd and number'd with the dead,
Than thus to perifh in the face of day
Where twice ten thoufand deaths one death delay.

When to the ocean finks the weftern fun,
And the fcorch'd Tories fire their evening gun,
" Down, rebels, down !" the angry Scotchmen cry,
" Bafe dogs, defcend, or by our broad fwords die !"

Hail dark abode ! what can with thee compare——
Heat, ficknefs, famine, death, and ftagnant air——
Pandora's box, from whence all mifchiefs flew,
Here real found, torments mankind anew !——
Swift from the guarded decks we rufh'd along,
And vainly fought repofe, fo vaft our throng ;

Four hundred wretches here, denied all light,
In crowded manfions pafs the infernal night,
Some for a bed their tatter'd veftments join,
And fome on chefts, and fome on floors recline ;
Shut from the bleffings of the evening air
Penfive we lay with mingled corpfes there,
Meagre and wan, and fcorch'd with heat, below,
We look'd like ghofts, ere death had made us fo—
How could we elfe, where heat and hunger join'd,
Thus to debafe the body and the mind,——
Where cruel thirft the parching throat invades,
Dries up the man, and fits him for the fhades.

No waters laded from the bubbling fpring
To thefe dire fhips thefe little tyrants bring——
By plank and ponderous beams completely wall'd
In vain for water and in vain we call'd——
No drop was granted to the midnight prayer,
To *rebels* in thefe regions of defpair !——
The loathfome cafk a deadly dofe contains,
Its poifon circling through the languid veins ;
" Here, *generous* Briton, generous, as you fay,
" To my parch'd tongue one cooling drop convey,
" Hell has no mifchief like a thirfty throat,
" Nor one tormentor like your *David Sproat.*" *

Dull pafs'd the hours, till, from the Eaft difplayed,
Sweet morn difpell'd the horrors of the fhade ;
On every fide dire objects met the fight,
And pallid forms, and murders of the night,——

* A Britifh fuperintendent of the prifon-fhips.

The dead were paſt their pain, the living groan,
Nor dare to hope another morn their own ;
But what to them is morn's delightful ray ?
Sad and diſtreſsful as the cloſe of day ;
O'er diſtant ſtreams appears the dewy green,
And leafy trees on mountain tops are ſeen,
But they no groves nor graſſy mountains tread,
Mark'd for a longer journey to the dead.

　Black as the clouds, that ſhade St. Kilda's ſhore, ˙
Wild as the winds, that round her mountains roar,
At every poſt ſome ſurly vagrant ſtands,
Cull'd from the Engliſh or the Heſſian* bands,—
Diſpenſing death triumphantly they ſtand,
Their muſquets ready to obey command ;
Wounds are their ſport, as ruin is their aim ;
On their dark ſouls compaſſion has no claim,
And diſcord only can their ſpirits pleaſe :
Such were our tyrants here, and ſuch were theſe.

　Ingratitude ! no curſe like thee is found
Throughout this jarring world's tumultuous round,
Their hearts with malice to our country ſwell
Becauſe, in former days, we us'd them well !—
This pierces deep, too deeply wounds the breaſt ;
We help'd them naked, friendleſs, and diſtreſt,
Receiv'd them, vagrants, with an open hand ;
Beſtow'd them buildings, privilege, and land—
Behold the change !—when angry Britain roſe,
Theſe thankleſs tribes became our fierceſt foes,

　　　* Scottiſh, in the edition of 1795.

By them devoted, plunder'd, and accurſt,
Stung by the ſerpents, whom ourſelves had nurs'd.
　But ſuch a train of endleſs woes abound,
So many miſchiefs in theſe hulks are found,
That on them all a poem to prolong
Would ſwell too far the horrors of our ſong—
Hunger and thirſt, to work our woe, combine,
And mouldy bread, and fleſh of rotten ſwine :
The mangled carcaſe, and the batter'd brain,
The doctor's poiſon, and the captain's cane,
The ſoldier's muſquet, and the ſteward's debt,
The evening ſhackle, and the noon-day threat.
　That balm, deſtructive to the pangs of care,
Which Rome of old, nor Athens could prepare,
Which gains the day for many a modern chief
When cool reflection yields a faint relief,
That *charm*, whoſe virtue warms the world beſide,
Was by theſe tyrants to our uſe denied ;
While yet they deign'd that healthſome balm to lade
The putrid water felt its powerful aid,
But when refus'd—to aggravate our pains—
Then fevers rag'd and revel'd through our veins ;
Throughout my frame I felt its deadly heat,
I felt my pulſe with quicker motions beat :
A pallid hue o'er every face was ſpread,
Unuſual pains attacked the fainting head ;
No phyſic here, no doctor to aſſiſt,
With oaths, they plac'd me on the ſick man's liſt ;
Twelve wretches more the ſame dark ſymptoms took,

And thefe were enter'd on the doctor's book ;
The loathfome HUNTER was our deftin'd place,
The HUNTER to all hofpitals difgrace ;
With foldiers, fent to guard us on our road,
Joyful we left the SCORPION's dire abode ;
Some tears we fhed for the remaining crew,
Then curs'd the hulk, and from her fides withdrew.

CANTO III.—*The Hofpital Prifon-Ship.*

Now tow'rds the HUNTER's gloomy decks we came,
A flaughter-houfe, yet *hofpital* in name ;
For none came there, 'till ruin'd with *their* fees,
And half confum'd, and dying of difeafe ;——
But when too near, with labouring oars we ply'd,
The *Mate*, with curfes, drove us from the fide ;
That wretch who, banifh'd from the navy crew,
Grown old in blood, did here his trade renew,
His rancorous tongue, when on his *charge* let loofe,
Utter'd reproaches, fcandal, and abufe,
Gave all to hell, who dar'd his *king* difown,
And fwore mankind were made for *George* alone.
A thoufand times, to irritate our woe,
He wifh'd us founder'd in the gulph below ;
A thoufand times, he brandifh'd high his ftick,
And fwore as often that we were not fick——
And yet fo pale !—that we were thought by fome
A freight of ghofts, from death's dominions come——
But calm'd at length—for who can always rage,

Or the fierce war of boundlefs paffion wage,
He pointed to the ftairs that led below
To damps, difeafe, and varied fhapes of woe—
Down to the gloom we took our penfive way,
Along the decks the dying captives lay ;
Some ftruck with madnefs, fome with fcurvy pain'd,
But ftill of putrid fevers moft complain'd !
On the hard floors thefe wafted objects laid,
There tofs'd and tumbled in the difmal fhade,
There no foft voice their bitter fate bemoan'd,
And death trode ftately, while the victims groan'd ;
Of leaky decks I heard them long complain,
Drown'd as they were in deluges of rain,
Deny'd the comforts of a dying bed,
And not a pillow to fupport the head——
How could they elfe but pine, and grieve, and figh,
Deteft a wretched life—and wifh to die.

   Scarce had I mingled with this difmal band
When a thin victim feiz'd me by the hand——
" And art thou come," (death heavy on his eyes)
" And art thou come to thefe abodes,"—(he cries ;)
" Why didft thou leave the *Scorpion's* dark retreat,
" And hither hafte, a furer death to meet ?
" Why didft thou leave thy damp infected cell ?—
" If *that* was purgatory, this is hell——
" We, too, grown weary of that horrid fhade
" Petition'd early for the doctor's aid ;
" His aid denied, more deadly fymptoms came,
" Weak, and yet weaker, glow'd the vital flame ;

" And when difeafe had worn us down fo low
" That few could tell if we were ghofts, or no,
" And all afferted death would be our fate——
" Then to the doctor we were fent—too late.
" Here waftes away *Eurymedon* the brave,
" Here young *Palemon* finds a watery grave,
" Here lov'd *Alcander*, now alas ! no more,
" Dies, far fequefter'd from his native fhore ;
" He late, perhaps, too eager for the fray,
" Chac'd the proud Briton o'er the watery way,
" 'Till fortune, jealous, bade her clouds appear,
" Turn'd hoftile to his fame, and brought him *here*.
 " Thus do our warriors, thus our heroes fall,
" Imprifon'd here, fure ruin meets them all,
" Or, fent afar to Britain's barbarous fhore,
" There pine neglected, and return no more :—
" Ah reft in peace, each injur'd, parted fhade,
" By cruel hands in death's dark weeds array'd.
" The days to come fhall to your memory raife
" Piles on thefe fhores, to fpread thro' earth your praife."
 From *Brooklyn* heights a Heffian doctor came,
Not great his fkill, nor greater much his fame ;
Fair Science never call'd the wretch her fon,
And Art difdain'd the ftupid man to own ;——
Can you admire that Science was fo coy,
Or Art refus'd his genius to employ ?——
Do men with brutes an equal dullnefs fhare,
Or cuts yon' grovelling mole the midway air——
In polar worlds can Eden's bloffoms blow,

Do trees of God in barren deferts grow.
Are loaded vines to Etna's fummit known,
Or fwells the peach beneath the frozen zone——
Yet ftill he put his genius to the rack
And, as you may fuppofe, was own'd a *quack*.
   He on his charge the healing work begun
• With antimonial mixtures, by the tun,
  Ten minutes was the time he deign'd to ftay,
The time of grace allotted once a day.——
He drench'd us well with bitter draughts, 'tis true,
Noftrums from hell, and *cortex* from Peru—
Some with his pills he fent to Pluto's reign,
And fome he blifter'd with his flies of Spain ;
His Tartar dofes walk'd their deadly round,
Till the lean patient at the potion frown'd
And fwore that hemlock, death, or what you will,
Were nonfenfe to the drugs that ftuff'd his bill.—
On thofe refufing, he beftow'd a kick,
Or menac'd vengeance with his walking ftick ;—
Here, uncontroul'd, he exercis'd his trade,
And grew experienc'd by the deaths he made.
By frequent blows we from his cane endur'd
He kill'd at leaft as many as he cur'd,
On our loft comrades built his future fame,
And fcatter'd fate where'er his footfteps came.
   Some did not bend, fubmiffive to his fkill,
And fwore he mingled poifon with his pill,
But I acquit him by a fair confeffion,
He was no *Myrmidon*—he was a Heffian—

Although a dunce, he had fome fenfe of fin
Or elfe the lord knows where we now had been ;
No doubt, in that far country fent to range
Where never prifoner meets with an exchange—
No centries ftand, to guard the midnight pofts,
Nor feal down hatch-ways on a crowd of ghofts.

Knave though he was, yet candour muft confefs
Not chief Phyfician was this man of Heffe—
One mafter o'er the murdering tribe was plac'd,
By him the reft were honour'd or difgrac'd ;
Once, and but once, by fome ftrange fortune led
He came to fee the dying and the dead—
He came—but anger fo deform'd his eye,
And fuch a faulchion glitter'd on his thigh,
And fuch a gloom his vifage darken'd o'er,
And two fuch piftols in his hands he bore !
That, by the gods !—with fuch a load of fteel,
He came, we thought, to murder, not to heal—
Rage in his heart and mifchief in his head,
He gloom'd deftruction, and had fmote us dead,
Had he fo dar'd—but fear with-held his hand—
He came—blafphem'd—and turn'd again to land.

From this poor veffel, and her fickly crew
A Britifh feaman all his titles drew,
Captain, efquire, commander, too, in chief,
And hence he gain'd his bread, and hence his beef,
But, fir, you might have fearch'd creation round
And fuch another ruffian not have found—
Though unprovok'd, an angry face he bore,

7

All were aftonifh'd at the oaths he fwore ;
He fwore, till every prifoner ftood aghaft,
And thought him Satan in a brimftone blaft ;
He wifh'd us banifh'd from the public light,
He wifh'd us fhrouded in perpetual night !
That were he king, no mercy would he fhow,
But drive all *rebels* to the world below ;
That if we *fcoundrels* did not fcrub the decks
His ftaff fhould break our bafe *rebellious* necks ;—
He fwore, befides, that fhould the fhip take fire
We too muft in the pitchy flames expire ;
And meant it fo—this tyrant, I engage,
Had loft his life, to gratify his rage.—

   If where he walk'd a murdered carcafe lay,
Still dreadful was the language of the day—
He call'd us dogs, and would have held us fo,
But terror check'd the meditated blow,
Of vengeance, from our injur'd nation due
To him, and all the bafe unmanly crew.

   Such food they fent, to make complete our woes,
It look'd like carrion torn from hungry crows :
Such vermin vile on every joint were feen,
So black, corrupted, mortified, and lean,
That once we try'd to move our flinty chief,
And thus addrefs'd him, holding up the beef :

   " See, captain, fee ! what rotten bones we pick,
" What kills the healthy cannot cure the fick :
" Not dogs on fuch by *Chriftian* men are fed,
" And fee, good mafter, fee, what loufy bread !"

" Your meat or bread" (this man of death replied)
" 'Tis not my care to manage or provide—
" But this, bafe rebel dogs, I'd have you know,
" That better than you merit we beftow :
" Out of my fight !"—nor more he deign'd to fay
But whifk'd about, and frowning, ftrode away.
     Each day, at leaft fix carcafes we bore
And fcratch'd them graves along the fandy fhore.
By feeble hands the fhallow graves were made,
No ftone, memorial, o'er the corpfes laid ;
In barren fands, and far from home, they lie,
No friend to fhed a tear, when paffing by ;
O'er the mean tombs the infulting Britons tread,
Spurn at the fand, and curfe the rebel dead.
     When to your arms thefe fatal iflands fall,
(For firft, or laft, they muft be conquer'd all)
Americans ! to rites fepulchral juft,
With gentleft footftep prefs this kindred duft,
And o'er the tombs, if tombs can then be found,
Place the green turf, and plant the myrtle round.
     Thefe all in Freedom's facred caufe allied,
For Freedom ventur'd and for Freedom died.
To bafe fubjection they were never broke,
They could not bend beneath a foreign yoke :
Had thefe furvived, perhaps in thraldom held,
To ferve the Britons they had been compelled—
Ungenerous deed !—can they the charge deny ?
This to avoid how many chofe to die.
     Americans ! a juft refentment fhew,

And glut revenge on this detefted foe ;
While the warm blood diftends the glowing vein
Still fhall refentment in your bofoms reign :
Can you forget the greedy Briton's ire,
Your fields in ruin, and your domes on fire,
No age, no fex, from luft and murder free,
And, black as night, the hell-born refugee !
Muft *York* forever your beft blood entomb,
And thefe gorg'd monfters triumph in our doom,
Who leave no art of cruelty untry'd ;——
Such heavy vengeance, and fuch hellifh pride !
Death has no charms—his realms dejefted lie
In the dull climate of a clouded fky,
Death has no charms, except in Britifh eyes,
See, arm'd for blood, the ambitious vultures rife,
See how they pant to ftain the world with gore,
And millions murder'd, ftill would murder more ;
That felfifh race, from all the world disjoin'd,
Perpetual difcord fpread among mankind,
Aim to extend their empire o'er the ball,
Subject, deftroy, abforb, and conquer all ;
As if the power, that form'd us, did condemn
All other nations to be flaves to them——
Roufe from your fleep, and crufh the invading band,
Defeat, deftroy, and fweep them from the land,
Ally'd like you, what madnefs to defpair,——
Attack the ruffians while they linger there ;
There *Tryon* fits, a tyrant all complete,
See *Vaughan*, there, with rude *Knyphaufen* meet,

And every wretch, whom honour fhould deteft
There finds a home—and *Arnold* with the reft.

Ah ! traitors, loft to every fenfe of fhame,
Unjuft fupporters of a tyrant's claim ;
Foes to the rights of freedom and of men,
Flufh'd with the blood of thoufands you have flain,
To the juft doom the righteous heavens decree
We leave you toiling ftill in cruelty,
Or on dark plans in future herds to meet,
Plans form'd in hell, and projects half complete :
The years approach that fhall to ruin bring
Your lords, your chiefs, your defolating* king,
Whofe murderous acts fhall ftamp his name accurs'd,
And his laft efforts more than damn the firft.

   [1780.]

* " Nero of a king."—EDITION OF 1795.

.CAPTAIN JONES'S INVITATION.*

THOU, who on some dark mountain's brow
   Hast toil'd thy life away till now,
And often from that rugged steep
Beheld the vast extended deep,
Come from thy forest, and with me
Learn what it is to go to sea.

There endless plains the eye surveys
As far from land the vessel strays;
No longer hill nor dale is seen,
The realms of death intrude between,
But fear no ill; resolve, with me
To share the dangers of the sea.

But look not there for verdant fields—
Far different prospects Neptune yields;
Green seas shall only greet the eye,
Those seas encircled by the sky,
Immense and deep—come then with me
And view the wonders of the sea.

* From the edition of 1786

Yet fometimes groves and meadows gay
Delight the feamen on their way;
From the deep feas that round us fwell
With rocks the furges to repel
Some verdant ifle, by waves embrac'd,
Swells, to adorn the wat'ry wafte.

Though now this vaft expanfe appear
With glaffy furface calm and clear;
Be not deceiv'd—'tis but a fhow,
For many a corpfe is laid below—
Even Britain's lads—it cannot be—
They were the *mafters* of the fea!

Now combating upon the brine,
Where fhips in flaming fquadrons join,
At every blaft the brave expire
'Midft clouds of fmoke, and ftreams of fire;
But fcorn all fear; advance with me—
'Tis but the cuftom of the fea.

Now we the peaceful wave divide,
On broken furges now we ride,
Now every eye diffolves with woe
As on fome lee-ward coaft we go—
Half loft, half buried in the main
Hope fcarcely beams on life again.

Above us ftorms diftract the fky,
Beneath us depths unfathom'd lie,

Too near we fee, a ghaftly fight,
The realms of everlafting night,
A wat'ry tomb of ocean green
And only one frail plank between!

But winds muft ceafe, and ftorms decay,
Not always lafts the gloomy day,
Again the fkies are warm and clear,
Again foft zephyrs fan the air,
Again we find the long-loft fhore,
The winds oppofe our wifh no more.

If thou haft courage to defpife
The various changes of the fkies,
To difregard the ocean's rage,
Unmov'd when hoftile fhips engage,
Come from thy foreft, and with me
Learn what it is to go to fea.

ON THE MEMORABLE VICTORY,

Obtained by the gallant Captain John Paul Jones, of the *Bon Homme Richard*, over the *Seraphis*, under the command of Captain Pearson.*

O'ER the rough main, with flowing sheet,
    The guardian of a numerous fleet,
      Seraphis from the Baltic came ;
A ship of less tremendous force
Sail'd by her side the self-same course,
    Countess of Scarb'ro' was her name.†

And now their native coasts appear,
Britannia's hills their summits rear
    Above the German main ;
Fond to suppose their dangers o'er,
They southward coast along the shore,
    Thy waters, gentle Thames, to gain.

* First published in Mr. Francis Bailey's *Freeman's Journal*, Philadelphia, August, 1781.

† This action was fought off Flamborough Head, on the 23d of September, 1779. It has been often described, and it is not required here to repeat the details of the admirable narratives of Cooper and Mackenzie. Few naval battles have made a greater popular impression. Jones, to this day, is a hero of the people, in England and America. His history has an air of romance and gallantry, of courage and adventure, the impression of which is by no means diminished by his personal vanity, occasional fopperies, and habit of self-assertion. His ability, as an officer and seaman, is not likely to be successfully disputed.

Full forty guns Seraphis bore,
And Scarb'ro's Countefs twenty-four,
  Mann'd with Old England's boldeft tars—
What flag that rides the Gallic feas
Shall dare attack fuch piles as thefe,
  Defign'd for tumults and for wars !

Now from the top-maft's giddy height
A feaman cry'd—" Four fail in fight
  " Approach with favouring gales,"
Pearfon, refolv'd to fave the fleet,
Stood off to fea, thefe fhips to meet,
  And clofely brac'd his fhivering fails.

With him advanc'd the Countefs bold,
Like a black tar in wars grown old :
  And now thefe floating piles drew nigh ;
But, mufe, unfold, what chief of fame
In the other warlike fquadron came,
  Whofe ftandards at his mast head fly.

'Twas JONES, brave JONES, to battle led
As bold a crew as ever bled
  Upon the fky-furrounded main ;
The ftandards of the weftern world
Were to the willing winds unfurl'd,
  Denying Britain's tyrant reign.

The *Good-Man-Richard* led the line ;
The *Alliance* next : with thefe combine

The Gallic fhip they *Pallas* call ;
The *Vengeance*, arm'd with fword and flame ;
Thefe to attack the Britons came—
   But *two* accomplifh'd all.

Now Phœbus fought his pearly bed :
But who can tell the fcenes of dread,
   The horrors of that fatal night !
Clofe up thefe floating caftles came :
The Good-Man-Richard burfts in flame ;
   Seraphis trembled at the fight.

She felt the fury of *her* ball :
Down, proftrate, down the Britons fall ;
   The decks were ftrew'd with flain :
Jones to the foe his veffel lafh'd ;
And, while the black artillery flafh'd,
   Loud thunders fhook the main.

Alas ! that mortals fhould employ
Such murdering engines, to deftroy
   That frame by heaven fo nicely join'd,;
Alas ! that e'er the god decreed
That brother fhould by brother bleed,
   And pour'd fuch madnefs in the mind.

But thou, brave Jones, no blame fhalt bear ;
The rights of men demand your care :
   For *thefe* you dare the greedy waves—

No tyrant, on deſtruction bent,
Has plann'd thy conqueſts—thou art ſent
　　To humble tyrants and their ſlaves.

See !—dread Seraphis flames again—
And art thou, JONES, among the ſlain,
　　And ſunk to Neptune's caves below——
He lives—though crowds around him fall,
Still he, unhurt, ſurvives them all ;
　　Almoſt alone he fights the foe.

And can your ſhip theſe ſtrokes ſuſtain ?
Behold your brave companions ſlain,
　　All claſp'd in ocean's cold embrace,
STRIKE, OR BE SUNK—the Briton cries—
SINK IF YOU CAN—the chief replies,
　· Fierce lightnings blazing in his face.

Then to the ſide three guns he drew,
(Almoſt deſerted by his crew)
　　And charg'd them deep with woe ;
By *Pearſon's* flaſh he aim'd hot balls ;
His main-maſt totters—down it falls——
　　O'erwhelming half below.

Pearſon had yet diſdain'd to yield,
But ſcarce his ſecret fears conceal'd,
　　And thus was heard to cry—
" With hell, not mortals, I contend ;

" What art thou—human, or a fiend,
    " That doſt my force defy ?

" Return, my lads, the fight renew !"——
So call'd bold Pearſon to his crew ;
    But call'd, alas ! in vain ;
Some on the decks lay maim'd and dead ;
Some to their deep receſſes fled,
    And hoſts were ſhrouded in the main.

Diſtreſs'd, forſaken, and alone,
He haul'd his tatter'd ſtandard down,
    And yielded to his gallant foe ;
Bold *Pallas* ſoon the *Counteſs* took,——
Thus both their haughty colours ſtruck,
    Confeſſing what the brave can do.

But, JONES, too dearly didſt thou buy
Theſe ſhips poſſeſt ſo gloriouſly,
    Too many deaths diſgrac'd the fray ;
Your barque that bore the conquering flame,
That the proud Britain overcame,
    Even ſhe forſook thee on thy way ;

For when the morn began to ſhine,
Fatal to her, the ocean brine
    Pour'd through each ſpacious wound ;
Quick in the deep ſhe diſappear'd :
But JONES to friendly Belgia ſteer'd,
    With conqueſt and with glory crown'd.

Go on, great man, to fcourge the foe,
And bid thefe haughty Britons know
    They to our *Thirteen Stars* fhall bend ;
The *Stars* that, veil'd in dark attire,
Long glimmer'd with a feeble fire,
     But radiant now afcend.

Bend to the Stars that flaming rife
On weftern worlds, more brilliant fkies,
    Fair Freedom's reign reftor'd——
So when the Magi, come from far,
Beheld the God-attending Star,
    They trembled and ador'd.

AN ANCIENT PROPHECY.

WHEN a certain great King, whofe initial is G,
   Forces STAMPS upon papér, and folks to drink TEA ;
When thefe folks burn his tea and ftampt paper, like ftubble,—
You may guefs that this king is then coming to trouble.

But when a PETITION he treads under feet,
And fends over the ocean an army and fleet,
When that army, half famifh'd, and frantic with rage
Is coop'd up with a leader, whofe name rhymes to *cage* ;
When that leader goes home, dejeded and fad ;
You may then be affur'd the king's profpeds are bad.

But when B. and C. with their armies are taken
This king will do well, if he·faves his own bacon :
In the year Seventeen hundred and eighty and two
A ftroke he fhall get, that will make him look blue :
And foon, very foon, fhall the feafon arrive,
When *Nebuchadnezzar* to pafture fhall drive.

In the year eighty-three, the affair will be over
And he fhall eat turnips that grow in *Hanover :*

The face of the Lion will then become pale,
He fhall yield fifteen teeth, and be fheer'd of his tail——
O king, my dear king, you fhall be very fore,
From the *Stars* and the *Stripes* you will mercy implore,
And your Lion fhall growl, but hardly bite more.——

AN ADDRESS

TO THE COMMANDER IN CHIEF, OFFICERS, AND SOLDIERS OF THE AMERICAN ARMY.

ACCEPT, great men, that fhare of honeft praife
    A grateful nation to your merit pays :
Verfe is too mean that merit to difplay,
And words too weak our praifes to convey.

    When firft proud Britain rais'd her hoftile* hand
With claims unjuft to bind our native land,
Tranfported armies, and her millions fpent
To enforce the mandates that a tyrant fent ;
" Refift ! refift !" was heard through every ftate,
You heard the call, and fear'd your country's fate :
Then rifing fierce in arms, for war array'd,
You taught to vanquifh thofe who dar'd invade.

    Those *Britifh chiefs* whom former wars had crown'd
With conqueft—and in every clime renown'd ;
Who forc'd new realms to own their monarch's law,
And *whom* even George beheld with fecret awe—
Thofe mighty chiefs, compell'd to fly or yield,
Scarce dar'd to meet you on the embattled field ;

* "Heavy."—ED. 1795.

8

To Bofton's port you chas'd the trembling crew,
Quick, even from thence the Britifh veterans flew—
Through wintry waves they fled, and thought each wave
Their laft, beft fafety from a foe fo brave.

    What men, like you, our warfare could command,
And bring us fafely to the promis'd land?
Not fwoln with pride, with victory elate—
'Tis in misfortune you are doubly great:
When *Howe* victorious our weak armies chas'd,
And, fure of conqueft, laid *Cefarea* wafte,
When proftrate, bleeding, at his feet fhe lay,
And the proud victor tore her wreathes away,
Each gallant chief put forth his warlike hand,
And rais'd the drooping genius of the land,
Repell'd the foe, their choiceft warriors flain,
And drove them howling to their fhips again.

    While *others* kindle into martial rage
Whom fierce ambition urges to engage,
An iron race, by angry heav'n defign'd
To conquer firft, and then enflave mankind;
Here, chiefs and heroes more humane we fee,
They venture life, that others may be free.

    O! MAY you live to hail that glorious day
When Britain homeward fhall purfue her way—
That race fubdu'd, who fill'd the world with flain
And rode tyrannic o'er the fubject main!—
What few prefum'd, you boldly have atchiev'd,
A tyrant humbled, and a world reliev'd.

    O WASHINGTON, who leadft this glorious train,

Still may the fates thy valued life maintain—
Rome's boafted chiefs, who, to their own difgrace,
Prov'd the worft fcourges of the human race,
Pierc'd by whofe darts a thoufand nations bled,
Who captive princes at their chariots led ;
Born to enflave, to ravage, and fubdue—
Return to *nothing*, when compar'd to you ;
Throughout the world your growing fame has fpread,
In every country are your virtues read ;
Remoteft *India* hears your deeds of fame,
The hardy Scythian ftammers at your name ;
The haughty Turk, now longing to be free,
Neglects his *Sultan* to enquire of thee ;
The barbarous Briton hails you to his fhores,
And calls him *Rebel*—whom his heart adores.

Still may the heavens prolong your vital date,
And ftill may conqueft on your banners wait :
Whether afar to ravag'd lands you go,
Where wild *Potowmac's* rapid waters flow,
Or where *Saluda* laves the fertile plain
And, fwoln by torrents, rufhes to the main ;
Or if again to *Hudfon* you repair
To fmite the cruel foe that lingers there—
Revenge *their* caufe, whofe virtue was their crime,
The exil'd hofts from Carolina's clime.

Late from the world, in quiet may'ft thou rife
And, mourn'd by millions, reach your native fkies—
With patriot kings and generous chiefs to fhine,
Whofe virtues rais'd them to be deem'd divine :

May VASA* only equal honours claim,
Alike in merits, and alike in fame !
    [*Anno*, 1781.]

* GUSTAVUS VASA, of Sweden, the deliverer of his country.

A NEW YORK TORY,

TO HIS FRIEND IN PHILADELPHIA.

DEAR Sir, I'm ſo anxious to hear of your health,
 I beg you would ſend me a letter by ſtealth :
I hope a few months will quite alter the caſe,
When the wars are concluded, we'll meet and embrace.

For I'm led to believe from our brilliant ſucceſs,
And, what is as clear, your amazing diſtreſs,
That the cauſe of rebellion has met with a check
That will bring all its patrons to hang by the neck.

Cornwallis has manag'd ſo well in the South,
Thoſe rebels want victuals to put in their mouth ;
And Arnold has ſtript them, we hear, to the buff—
Has burnt their tobacco, and left them—the ſnuff.

Dear Thomas, I wiſh you would move from that town
Where meet all the rebels of fame and renown ;
When our armies, victorious, ſhall clear that vile neſt
You may chance, though a Tory, to ſwing with the reſt.

But again—on reflection—I beg you would stay—
You may serve us yet better than if mov'd away—
Give advice to Sir HARRY of all that is passing,
What vessels are building, what cargoes amassing ;

Inform, to a day, when those vessels will sail,
That our cruisers may capture them all, without fail—
By proceedings, like these, your peace shall be made,
The rebellious shall swing, but be you ne'er afraid.

I cannot conceive how you do to subsist—
The rebels are starving, except those who 'list ;
And as you reside in the land of Gomorrah,
You must fare as the rest do, I think, to your sorrow.

Poor souls ! if ye knew what a doom is decreed,
(I mean not for you, but for rebels indeed)
You would tremble to think of the vengeance in store,
The halters and gibbets—I mention no more.

The rebels must surely conclude they're undone,
Their navy is ruin'd, their armies have run ;
It is time they should now from delusion awaken—
The rebellion is done—for the TRUMBULL* is taken !

---

* The American frigate Trumbull, 20, Captain James Nicholson, was chased
off the capes of the Delaware, August 8th, 1781, by three British cruisers. As it
was blowing heavily towards night, the fore-topmast of the Trumbull was carried
away by a squall, bringing down with it, on deck, the main-topgallant mast.
About ten o'clock at night, one of the British vessels, the Iris, 32, came up and
closed with her while still encumbered with the wreck. "In the midst of rain

and fqualls, in a tempeftuous night, with moft of the forward hamper of the fhip
over her bows, or lying on the forecaftle, with one of the arms of the fore-topfail
yard run through her fore-fail, and the other jammed on deck, and with a difor-
ganized crew, Captain Nicholfon found himfelf compelled to go to quarters, or to
ftrike without refiftance. He preferred the firft; but the Englifh volunteers, inftead of obeying orders, went below, extinguifhed the lights, and fecreted themfelves. Near half of the remainder of the people imitated this example, and
Captain Nicholfon could not mufter fifty of even the diminifhed crew he had,
at the guns. The battle that followed might almoft be faid to have been fought
by the officers. Thefe brave men, fuftained by a party of the petty officers and
feamen, managed a few of the guns for more than an hour, when the General
Monk, 18, coming up and joining in the fire of the Iris, the Trumbull fubmitted."—Cooper's *Naval Hiftory.*

TO LORD CORNWALLIS,

AT YORK, VIRGINIA.*

HAIL, great deftroyer (equall'd yet by none)
  Of countries not your mafter's, nor your own ;
Hatch'd by fome demon on a ftormy day,
Satan's beft fubftitute to burn and flay ;
Confin'd at laft ; hem'd in by land and fea,
Burgoyne himfelf was but a type of thee !
  Like his, to freedom was your deadly hate,
Like his your bafenefs, and be his your fate :
To you, like him, no profpect Nature yields
But ruin'd waftes and defolated fields—
In vain you raife the interpofing wall,
And hoift thofe ftandards that, like you, muft fall,

---

* Charles, Marquis of Cornwallis, came to New York with his regiment in
1776. After ferving for a while as Major-General in the campaigns in the
Jerfeys, he was engaged in the expedition to the Chefapeake, and fubfequently,
in 1780, in the fiege of Charlefton, S. C., which ended in its furrender. Left in
command in the State, he fought the battles of Camden and Guilford, making
his way northerly, with his army, through the Carolinas to Virginia, where he
maintained himfelf in a fortified pofition, at Yorktown, till he was compelled to
furrender to Wafhington, in October, 1781. Cornwallis was at this time at the
age of forty-three. His fubfequent career, in India, was diftinguifhed. He was
in 1798 Lord Lieutenant of Ireland. In 1805 he was fent to India, as Gov-
ernor-General, and died fhortly after his arrival at Calcutta.

In you conclude the glories of your race,
Complete your monarch's, and your own difgrace.

    What has your lordfhip's pilfering arms attain'd ?—
Vaft ftores of *plunder*, but no STATE regain'd—
That may return, though you perhaps may groan.
Reftore it, CHARLEY, for 'tis not your own—
Then, lord and foldier, headlong to the brine
Rufh down at once—the devil and the fwine.

    Would'ft thou at laft with *Wafhington* engage,
Sad object of his pity, not his rage ?
See, round thy pofts how terribly advance
The chiefs, the armies, and the fleets of France ;
Fight while you can, for warlike *Rochambeau*
Aims at your head his laft decifive blow ;
Unnumber'd ghofts from earth untimely fped,
Can take no reft till you, like them, are dead—
Then die, my Lord ; that only chance remains
To wipe away difhonourable ftains,
For fmall advantage would your capture bring,
The *plundering fervant of a bankrupt king.*

    [*October* 8. 1781.]

A LONDON DIALOGUE,

BETWEEN MY LORDS, DUNMORE AND GERMAINE.

Dunmore.

EVER fince I return'd to my dear native fhore,
   No poet in *Grubftreet* was ever dunn'd more—
I'm dunn'd by my barber, my taylor, my groom ;
How can I do elfe than to fret and to fume ?
They join to attack me with one good accord,
From morning 'till night 'tis " my lord, and my lord."
And there comes the cobler, fo often deny'd—
If I had him in private, I'd threfh his tough hide.

Germaine.

Would you worry the man that has found you in fhoes ?
Come, courage, my lord, I can tell you good news—
Virginia is conquered, the rebels are bang'd,
You are now to go over and fee them fafe hang'd :
I hope it is not to your nature abhorrent
To fign for thefe wretches a handfome death warrant—
Were I but in your place, I'm fure it would fuit
To fign their death warrants, and hang them to boot.

Dunmore.

My lord !—I'm amaz'd—have we routed the foe ?—
I fhall govern again then, if matters be fo—
And as to the hanging, in fhort, to be plain,
I'll hang them fo well, they'll ne'er want it again.
With regard to the wretches who thump at my gates,
I'll difcharge all their dues with the rebel eftates ;
In lefs than three months I fhall fend a polacca
As deep as fhe'll fwim, fir, with corn and tobacco.

Germaine.

And fend us fome rebels—a dozen or fo—
They'll ferve here in *London* by way of a fhow ;
And as to the Tories, believe me dear coufin,
We can fpare you fome hundreds to pay for the dozen.

LORD CORNWALLIS TO SIR HENRY CLINTON.

FROM YORK, VIRGINIA.

FROM clouds of fmoke, and flames that round me glow,
    To you, dear Clinton, I difclofe my woe.
Here cannons flafh, bombs glance, and bullets fly ;
Not ARNOLD's felf endures fuch mifery.
Was I foredoom'd in tortures to expire,
Hurl'd to perdition in a blaze of fire ?
With thefe blue flames can mortal man contend—
What arms can aid me, or what walls defend ?
Even to thefe gates laft night a phantom ftrode,
And hail'd me trembling to his dark abode :
Aghaft I ftood, ftruck motionlefs and dumb,
Seiz'd with the horrors of the world to come.

    Were but my power as mighty as my rage,
Far different battles would Cornwallis wage,
Beneath his fword yon' threat'ning hofts fhould groan,
The earth fhould quake with thunders all his own.
O crocodile ! had I thy flinty hide,
Swords to defy, and glance the balls afide,
By my own prowefs would I rout the foe,
With my own javelin would I work their woe—

But fates averſe, by heaven's ſupreme decree,
Nile's ſerpent form'd more excellent than me.

   Has heaven, in ſecret, for ſome crime decreed
That I ſhould ſuffer, and my ſoldiers bleed ?
Or is it by the jealous ſkies conceal'd,
That I muſt bend, and they ignobly yield ?
Ah ! no—the thought o'erwhelms my ſoul with grief,
Come, bold ſir Harry, come to my relief ;
Come, thou brave man, whom rebels *Tombſtone* call,
But Britons, *Graves*—come Digby, devil, and all ;
Come, princely WILLIAM, with thy potent aid,
Can George's blood by Frenchmen be diſmay'd ?
From a king's *uncle* once Scotch rebels run,
And ſhall not theſe be routed by a *ſon ?*
Come with your ſhips to this diſaſt'rous ſhore,
Come—or I ſink—and ſink to riſe no more.
By every motive that can ſway the brave
Haſte, and my feeble, fainting army ſave ;
Come, and loſt empire o'er the deep regain,
Chaſtiſe theſe upſtarts that uſurp the main :
I ſee their firſt rates to the charge advance,
I ſee loſt *Iris* wear the flags of France ;*
There a ſtrict rule the wakeful Frenchman keeps,
There, on no bed of down, lord *Rawdon* ſleeps !

   Tir'd with long acting on this bloody ſtage,
Sick of the follies of a wrangling age,
Come with your fleet, and help me to retire

* Note ante, page 82.

To Britain's coaſt, the land of my deſire—
For, me the foe their certain captive deem,
And every trifler takes me for his theme—
Long, much too long, in this hard ſervice try'd,
Beſpatter'd ſtill, bedevil'd, and bely'd ;
With the firſt chance that favouring fortune ſends
I'll fly, converted, from this land of fiends,
Convinc'd, for me, ſhe has no gems in ſtore,
Nor leaves one triumph, even to hope for, more.

    [1781.]

ON THE FALL OF GENERAL EARL CORNWALLIS,

Who, with about feven thoufand Men, furrendered themfelves prifoners of war, to the Allied Armies of AMERICA and FRANCE, on the memorable 19th of October, 1781.

> " One brilliant game our arms have won to-day,
> Another, *Princes*, yet remains to play ;
> Another mark our arrows muft attain—
> *Gallia** affift !—nor be our efforts vain."
>
> Hom. *Odyffey*, Book xxii.

A CHIEFTAIN, form'd on *Howe*, *Burgoyne*, and *Gage*,
Once more, nor this the laft, provokes my rage--
Who saw thefe *Nimrods* firft for conqueft burn !
Who has not feen them to the duft return ?
This *conqueror* next, who ravag'd all our fields,
Foe to the Rights of Man, Cornwallis yields !—
None e'er before effay'd fuch defperate crimes,
Alone he ftood, arch-butcher of the times,
Rov'd, uncontroul'd, this wafted country o'er,
Strew'd plains with dead, and bath'd his jaws with gore.

'Twas thus the wolf, who fought by night his prey,
And plunder'd all he met with on his way,
Stole what he could, and murder'd as he pafs'd,
Chanc'd on a trap, and loft his head at laft.

---

* In the original,—" Phœbus affift !—nor be the labour vain."—*Author's Note*.

What pen can write, what human tongue declare
The endleſs murders of this LORD OF WAR !
Nature in him diſgrac'd the form divine ;
Nature miſtook, ſhe meant him for a—ſwine :
That eye his forehead, to her ſhame, adorns ;
Bluſh ! Nature, bluſh—beſtow him tail and horns !—
By him the orphan mourns—the widow'd dame
Saw ruin ſpreading in the waſteful flame ;
Gaſh'd o'er with wounds, beheld with ſtreaming eye
A ſon, a brother, or a conſort, die !——
Through ruin'd realms bones lie without a tomb,
And ſouls he ſped to their eternal doom,
Who elſe had liv'd, and ſeen their toils again
Bleſs'd by the genius of the rural reign.

Convinc'd we are, no foreign ſpot of earth
But Britain only, gave this warrior birth :
That white-cliff'd iſle, the vengeful tyrants' den,
Has ſent us monſters, where we look'd for men.
When memory paints their horrid deeds anew,
And brings theſe murdering miſcreants to our view,
We aſk the leaders of theſe bloody bands,
Can they expect compaſſion at our hands ?—

But may this year, the glorious EIGHTY-ONE,
Conclude ſuccefsful, and all wars be done ;
This brilliant year their total downfall ſee,
And what Cornwallis *is*, Sir HENRY* *be*.

O come the time, nor diſtant be the day,

* Sir Henry Clinton.

When our fwift navy fhall its wings difplay ;
Mann'd by brave fouls, to feek the Britifh fhore,
The wrongs revenging that their fathers bore :
As earthquakes fhook the huge COLOSSUS down,
So fhake the wearer of the Britifh crown ;
Unpitying next his hated offspring flay,
Or into foreign lands by force convey :
Give them their turn to pine and die in chains,
'Till. not one tyrant of the race remains.

Thou, who refideft on thofe thrice happy fhores,
Where white-rob'd peace her envied blefllings pours,
Stay, and enjoy the pleafures that fhe yields ;
But come not, ftranger, to our wafted fields,
For warlike hofts on every plain appear,
War damps the beauties of the rifing year :
In vain the groves their bloomy fweets difplay ;
War's clouded winter chills the charms of May :
Here human blood the trampled harveft ftains ;
Here bones of men yet whiten all the plains ;
Seas teem with dead ; and our unhappy fhore
Forever blufhes with its children's gore.

But turn your eyes—behold the tyrant fall,
Nor fay—Cornwallis has achiev'd it all.—

All mean revenge AMERICANS difdain,
Oft have they prov'd it, and now prove again ;
With nobler fires their generous bofoms glow ;
Still in the captive they forget the foe :—
But when a *nation* takes a wrongful caufe,
And hoftile turns to heaven's and nature's laws ;

9

When, facrificing at ambition's fhrine,
Kings flight the mandates of the power divine,
And devaftation fpread on every fide,
To gratify their malice or their pride,
And fend their flaves their projects to fulfil,
To wreft our freedom, or our blood to fpill :—
Such to forgive, is virtue too fublime ;
For, even compaffion has been found a crime.

A prophet once, for miracles renown'd,
Bade *Joafh* fmite the arrows on the ground—
Taking the myftic fhafts, the prince obey'd,
Thrice fmote them on the earth—and then he ftay'd—
Griev'd when he faw full victory deny'd,
" Six times you fhould have fmote," the prophet cry'd,
" Then had proud *Syria* funk beneath your power ;—
" Now thrice you fmite her—but fhall fmite no more."

Cornwallis ! thou art rank'd among the great ;
Such was the will of all-controuling fate.
As mighty men, who liv'd in days of yore,
Were figur'd out fome centuries before ;
So you with them in equal honour join,
Your great precurfor's name was *Jack Burgoyne !*
Like you was he, a man in arms renown'd,
Who, hot for conqueft, fail'd the ocean round ;
This, this was he, who fcour'd the woods for praife,
And burnt down cities to defcribe the blaze !

So, while on fire, his harp Rome's tyrant ftrung,
And as the buildings flam'd, old Nero fung.

Who could have guefs'd the purpofe of the fates,

When that *vain boaſter* bow'd to conquering GATES!
Then ſung the ſiſters as the wheel went round,
(Could we have heard the invigorating ſound)
Thus ſurely did the fatal ſiſters ſing—
" When juſt four years do this ſame ſeaſon bring,
" And in his annual journey, when the ſun
" Four times completely ſhall his circuit run,
" An *Angel* then ſhall rid you of your fears,
" By binding Satan* for a thouſand years,
" Shall laſh his godſhip to the infernal ſhore,
" To waſte the nations, and deceive no more ;
" Make wars, and blood, and tyranny to ceaſe,
" And huſh the rage of Europe into peace."
    Joy to your lordſhip, and your high deſcent,   ·
You are the Satan that the *ſiſters* meant.
Too ſoon you found your race of ruin run,
Your conqueſts ended, and your battles done !
But that to live is better than to die,
And life you choſe, though life with infamy,
You ſhould have climb'd your loftieſt veſſel's maſt,
Took one ſad ſurvey of your wanton waſte,
Then plung'd forever to the wat'ry bed,
Loſt all your honours—even your memory dead.
    Aſham'd to live, and yet afraid to die,
Your courage ſlacken'd as your foe drew nigh—
Ungrateful chief, to yield your *favorite band*
To chains and priſons, in a hoſtile land :

* " Pluto."—ED. 1795.

To the wide world your *Negro friends* to caſt,
And leave your *Tories* to be hang'd at laſt !—
You ſhould have fought with horror and amaze,
'Till ſcorch'd to cinders in the cannon blaze,
'Till all your hoſt of Gog-magogs was ſlain,
Doom'd to diſgrace no human ſhape again—
From depths of woods this hornet hoſt he drew—
Swift from the ſouth the envenom'd ruffians flew ;—
Deſtruction follow'd at their *cloven* feet,
'Till you, *Fayette*, conſtrain'd them to retreat,
And held them cloſe, 'till thy fam'd ſquadron came,
De Grasse, completing their eternal ſhame.

When the loud cannon's unremitting glare,
And red hot balls compell'd *you* to deſpair,
How could you ſtand to meet your generous foe ?
Did not the fight confound with rage and woe ?—
In thy great ſoul what god-like virtues ſhine,
What inborn greatneſs, Washington, is thine !—
Elſe had no priſoner trod theſe lands to-day,
All, with his lordſhip, had been ſwept away,
All doom'd alike death's vermin to regale,
Nor one been left to tell the dreadful tale !
But his own terms the mean invader nam'd—
He nobly gave the *priſoner* all he claim'd,
And bade Cornwallis, conquer'd and diſtreſs'd,
Bear all his torments in one tortur'd breaſt.

Now curſt with life, a *foe* to man and God,
Like *Cain*, we drive you to the land of *Nod :*
He with a brother's blood his hands did ſtain,

One brother he—you have a thoufand flain.
On eagles' wings explore your homeward flight,
Plan future conquefts, and new battles fight :
Such horrid deeds your murdering hoft defame
We grieve to think their form, and ours, the fame:
Remorfe be theirs !—even you, though much too late,
Shall curse the day you languifh'd to be great:
And, may deftruction rufh, with fpeedy wing,
Low as yourfelf, to drag each tyrant king ;
Swept from this ftage, the race that vex our ball,
Deep in the duft may every monarch fall,
To wafted nations bid a long adieu,
Shrink from an injur'd world—and fare like YOU.

TO THE MEMORY OF THE BRAVE AMERICANS,

Under General Greene, in South Carolina, who fell in the action of September 8, 1781.*

A T Eutaw Springs the valiant died :
    Their limbs with duſt are cover'd o'er—
Weep on, ye ſprings, your tearful tide ;
    How many heroes are no more !

If in this wreck of ruin, they
    Can yet be thought to claim a tear,
O ſmite thy gentle breaſt, and ſay
    The friends of freedom ſlumber here !

* The battle of Eutaw Springs was one of the beſt conteſted fields of the Revolution. Both ſides fought with extraordinary heroiſm. General Greene was in command of the Americans, and Lieutenant-Colonel Stuart of the Britiſh, in this engagement. Greene had about two thouſand men in the field, and the ſtrength of the enemy was about the ſame. The battle laſted nearly four hours; the bayonet was freely uſed. The loſs on both ſides was extraordinary for the numbers engaged. "Never," wrote General Greene of his army, in a letter to Congreſs, "did men and officers offer their blood more willingly in the ſervice of their country." The advantage was, at firſt, with the Americans, and afterwards with the Britiſh. Both ſides claimed the victory. "The truth ſeems to be," ſays Chief-Juſtice Marſhall, in his "Life of Waſhington," "that, unconnected with its conſequences, the fortune of the day was nearly balanced. But, if the conſequences be taken into the account, the victory unqueſtionably belonged to Greene. The reſult was the expulſion of the hoſtile army from the territory, which was the immediate object of conteſt."

Thou, who fhalt trace this bloody plain,
    If goodnefs rules thy generous breaft,
Sigh for the wafted rural reign ;
    Sigh for the fhepherds, funk to reft !

Stranger, their humble graves adorn ;
    You too may fall, and afk a tear ;
'Tis not the beauty of the morn
    That proves the evening fhall be clear—

They faw their injur'd country's woe ;
    The flaming town, the wafted field ;
Then rufh'd to meet the infulting foe ;
    They took the fpear—but left the fhield.

Led by thy conquering genius, GREENE,
    The Britons they compell'd to fly :
None diftant view'd the fatal plain,
    None griev'd, in fuch a caufe, to die—

But, like the Parthian, fam'd of old,
    Who, flying, ftill their arrows threw ;
Thefe routed Britons, full as bold
    Retreated, and retreating flew.

Now reft in peace, our patriot band ;
    Though far from Nature's limits thrown,
We truft, they find a happier land,
    A brighter fun-fhine of their own.

THE ROYAL ADVENTURER.*

PRINCE William, of the Brunſwick race,
  To witneſs George's ſad diſgrace
  The royal lad came over,
Rebels to kill, by Right Divine—
Deriv'd from that illuſtrious line,
  The beggars of Hanover.

* Prince William Henry, the third ſon of George III., afterwards William
IV., entered the navy as midſhipman at the age of fourteen, in 1779. He failed
in the Prince George, of 98 guns, to Gibraltar, in the courſe of which cruiſe he
ſaw ſome ſervice, under Rodney, in conflict with the Spaniſh fleet; and it was
in this ſhip, accompanied by Admiral Digby, that he arrived at New York, in
September, 1781. He had juſt completed his ſixteenth year. He was ceremo-
niouſly welcomed by the Commander-in-chief, Sir Henry Clinton, by Governor
Robertſon, and "other great officers of the crown, conducted to Commodore
Affleck's, where his royal Highneſs dined, and, in the evening, retired to apart-
ments provided for his accommodation in Wall ſtreet." Soon after his arrival,
the Governor, in the name of himſelf, his Majeſty's council, and the inhabitants,
preſented him with an addreſs overflowing with fulſome expreſſions of loyalty.
"On the report of your coming," was its language, "we felt our obligation to
our gracious king for this new and ſignal proof of his regard. Your royal Highneſs' appearance augments our gratitude, by improving our idea of the extent of
his goodneſs. Your preſence animates every loyal breaſt. The glow in our own
perſuades us you are formed to win every heart. A rebellion that grew upon
prejudice, ſhould ſink at the approach of ſo fair a repreſentation of the royal virtues. But if a miſled faction, not to be vanquiſhed by goodneſs, perſiſts in the
war, every man of ſpirit will be proud to fight in a cauſe for which you expoſe
your life." The Prince remained in the city during the winter and the enſuing
ſummer, partaking of the hoſpitalities of the officers and others, and, during the

So many chiefs got broken pates
In vanquiſhing the rebel States,
    So many nobles fell,
That George the third in paſſion cry'd,
" Our royal blood muſt now be try'd ;
    " 'Tis that muſt break the ſpell :

" To you (the fat pot-valiant SWINE
" To DIGBY ſaid) dear friend of mine,
    " To you I truſt my boy ;
" The rebel tribes ſhall quake with fears,
" Rebellion die when he appears,
    " My Tories leap with joy."

So ſaid, ſo done—the lad was ſent,
But never reach'd the continent,
    An iſland held him faſt—
Yet there his friends danc'd rigadoons,
The Heſſians ſung, in High Dutch tunes,
    " Prince William's come at laſt."

ſkating ſeaſon, enjoying that paſtime on the ponds in the vicinity. In March,
1782, there was a plan on foot, originated by Colonel Matthias Ogden, of New
Jerſey, to " ſurpriſe in their quarters and bring off" the Prince and Admiral
Digby; but though the ſcheme had the approval of Waſhington, who coun-
ſelled that, if captured, the priſoners ſhould be treated " with all poſſible re-
ſpect," nothing appears to have been attempted in the matter. On the 4th of
June, the Prince received, as is duly recorded in the *Royal Gazette*, the congratu-
lations of the Commander-in-chief, with a proceſſion of officers, on occaſion of
his father's birth-day; and on the 21ſt of Auguſt, his own was celebrated with
" the uſual felicitations." The Prince was afterwards transferred to the Bar-
fleur, commanded by Sir Samuel Hood, and left the ſtation for the Weſt Indies
prior to his return to England, in the ſummer of 1783.

" Prince William comes !"—The Briton cry'd—
" Our labours now will be repaid—*
　　" Dominion be reſtored—
" Our monarch is in William ſeen,
" He is the image of our queen,
　　" Let William be ador'd !"

The Tories came with long addreſs,
With poems groan'd the *Royal Preſs,*
　　And all in William's praiſe—
The youth aſtoniſh'd look'd about
To find their *vaſt dominions* out,
　　Then anſwer'd, in amaze :

" Where all your *vaſt domain* can be,
" Friends, for my ſoul I cannot ſee :
　　" 'Tis but an empty name :
" Three waſted iſlands, and a town
" In rubbiſh buried—half burnt down,
　　" Is all that we can claim :

" I am of royal birth, 'tis true,
" But what, my ſons, can princes do,
　　" No armies to command ?
" Cornwallis conquer'd and diſtreſt—
" Sir Henry Clinton grown a jeſt—
　　" I curſe—and quit the land."　　　[1782.]

　　　* " The glory of our empire wide
　　　" Shall now be ſoon reſtor'd."—Ed. 1795.

LORD DUNMORE'S PETITION

TO THE LEGISLATURE OF VIRGINIA:

Humbly Sheweth,

THAT a filly old fellow, much noted of yore,
 And known by the name of John, earl of Dunmore,
Has again ventur'd over to vifit your fhore.

The reafon of this he begs leave to explain—
In England they faid you were conquer'd and flain,
(But the devil take him that believes them again)—

So, hearing that moft of you Rebels were dead,
That fome had fubmitted, and others had fled,
I mufter'd my Tories, myfelf at their head,

And over we fcudded, our hearts full of glee,
As merry as ever poor devils could be,
Our *ancient dominion*, Virginia, to fee ;

Our fhoe-boys, and tars, and the very cook's mate
Already conceiv'd he poffefs'd an eftate,
And the Tories no longer were curfing their fate.

Myfelf, (the don Quixote) and each of the crew,
Like Sancho, had iflands and empires in view—
They were captains, and kings, and the devil knows who :

But now, to our forrow, difgrace, and furprife,
No longer deceiv'd by the *Father of Lies*,*
We hear with our ears, and we fee with our eyes :—

I have therefore to make you a modeft requeft,
(And I'm fure, in my mind, it will be for the beft)
Admit me again to your manfions of reft.

There are Eden, and Martin, and Franklin, and Tryon,†
All waiting to fee you fubmit to the Lion,
And may wait 'till the devil is king of Mount Sion :—

Though a brute and a dunce, like the reft of the clan,
I can govern as well as moft Englifhmen can ;
And if I'm a drunkard, I ftill am a man :

I mifs'd it fome how in comparing my notes,
Or fix years ago I had join'd with your votes ;
Not aided the negroes in cutting your throats.

Altho' with fo many hard names I was branded,
I hope you'll believe, (as you will, if you're candid)
That I only perform'd what my mafter commanded.

---

* Rivington, the printer of the *Royal Gazette* at New York.

† The laft royal governors : Robert Eden, of Maryland ; Jofeph Martin, of North Carolina ; William Franklin, of New Jerfey ; William Tryon, of New York.

Give me lands, whores and dice, and you ſtill may be free ;
Let who will be maſter, we ſha'nt diſagree ;
If king or if Congreſs—no matter to me ;—

I hope you will ſend me an anſwer ſtraightway,
For 'tis plain that at Charleſton we cannot long ſtay—
And your humble petitioner ever ſhall pray.

    [Charleſton, Jan. 6, 1782.]

EPIGRAM

Occasioned by the *Title* of Mr. Rivington's New York Royal Gazette being scarcely legible.*

SAYS Satan to Jemmy, " I hold you a bet
" That you mean to abandon our Royal Gazette,
" Or, between you and me, you wou'd manage things better
" Than the Title to print on so sneaking a letter.

* " James Rivington, the king's printer in New York, in this era of the Revolution, an Englishman by birth, having failed as a bookseller in London, came to America in 1760. He conducted a bookstore in Philadelphia previous to his establishment in New York; at first in that business, and afterwards as a printer. In 1773, he began the publication of the *New York Gazetteer*, and, as the crisis of the Revolution approached, excited the hostility of the popular party by his devotion to the royal cause. In November, 1775, his press was broken up by an incursion of the whig leader, Captain Isaac Sears, from Connecticut. Rivington then left for England, and returning, with a new press, was appointed king's printer. The *Royal Gazette*, which he now published, soon attained a reputation for its unscrupulous partisanship.—It was popularly called, by the patriots who suffered from its misrepresentations, 'The Lying Gazette.' Freneau, who knew the man, took a humorous delight in replying to the squibs and attacks with which the *Gazette* abounded; and as the war closed, and Rivington, who, it was found, had assisted Washington as a spy, made overtures for reconciliation, the wits, including, with Freneau, Francis Hopkinson, Dr. Witherspoon, and Trumbull, mingling severity with ridicule, opened all their batteries upon him. Rivington, a supple courtier, stood the fire as best he might, took down the royal arms of which Freneau had made sport, and continued his paper with the title, *Rivington's New York Gazette and Universal Advertiser*. But the people were

" Now being connected fo long in the art,
" It would not be prudent at prefent to part ;
" And people, perhaps, would be frighten'd, and fret
" If the devil alone carry'd on the Gazette."

Says Jemmy to Satan (by way of a wipe)
" Who gives me the matter fhould furnifh the type ;
" And why you find fault, I can fcarcely divine,
" For the types, like the printer, are certainly thine.

" 'Tis yours to deceive with the femblance of truth,
" Thou friend of my age, and thou guide of my youth !
" But, to profper, pray fend me fome further fupplies,
" A fett of new types, and a fett of new lies."

    [*Feb.* 13, 1782.]

not difpofed to forget his mifdeeds, and the *Gazette* languifhed and came to an
early termination. Rivington continued to refide in New York till his death, in
1802, at the age of feventy-eight."—*Cyclopædia of American Literature*, I., ·
278–83.

LINES

Occasioned by Mr. Rivington's new Titular types to his Royal Gazette, of
February 17, 1782.

WELL—now (said the devil) it looks something better!
    Your title is struck on a *charming* new *Letter* :
Last night in the dark, as I gave it a squint,
I saw my dear partner had taken the hint.
    I ever surmis'd (though 'twas doubted by some)
That the old types were shadows of substance to come :
But if the NEW LETTER is pregnant with charms
It grieves me to think of those cursed King's Arms.
The *Dieu et mon droit* (his God and his right)
Is so dim, that I hardly know what is meant by't
The paws of the Lion can scarcely be seen,
And the Unicorn's guts are most shamefully lean !
The *Crown* is so worn of your master the despot,
That I hardly know which 'tis (a crown or a pisspot)—
When I rub up my day-lights, and look very sharp
I just can distinguish the Irishman's harp ;
Another device appears rather silly,
Alas ! it is only the shade of the LILLY !
For the honour of George, and the fame of our nation
Pray, give his escutcheons a rectification—

Or I know what I know (and I'm a queer fhaver)
Of HIM and his Arms I'll be the engraver.*
   [1782.]

---

* The pun in the laft word is diftinctly marked in the earlier edition of 1726,
—" the *In*-grave-r."

10

ON MR. RIVINGTON'S NEW ENGRAVED KING'S ARMS TO HIS ROYAL GAZETTE.

FROM the regions of night, with his head in a fack,
    Afcended a perfon accoutred in black,
And upward directing his circular eye whites ;
(Like the Jure-divino political Levites)
And leaning his elbow on Rivington's fhelf,
While the printer was bufy, thus mus'd with himfelf :
" My mandates are fully complied with at laft,
" New ARMS are engrav'd, and new letters are caft ;
" I therefore determine and freely accord,
" This fervant of mine fhall receive his reward."
Then turning about, to the printer he faid,
" Who late was my *fervant* fhall now be my *Aid;*
" Since under my banners fo bravely you fight,
" Kneel down !—for your merits I dubb you a KNIGHT,
" From a paffive *fubaltern* I bid you to rife
" The INVENTOR, as well as the PRINTER OF LIES."

    [1782.]

A SPEECH

That should have been spoken by the KING of the island of BRITAIN to his PARLIAMENT.

MY lords, I can hardly from weeping refrain,
　　When I think of this year, and its cursed campaign;
But still it is folly to whine and to grieve,
For things will yet alter, I hope and believe.

Of the four southern States we again are bereav'd,
They were just in our grasp (or I'm sadly deceiv'd):
There are wizzards and witches that dwell in those lands
For the moment we gain them, they slip from our hands.

Our prospects, at present, most gloomy appear;
Cornwallis returns, with a flea in his ear,
Sir Henry is sick of his station, we know—
And Amherst, though press'd, is unwilling to go.

The HERO* that steer'd for the cape of Good Hope
With Monsieur Suffrein was unable to cope—
Many months are elaps'd, yet his task is to do—
To conquer the Cape, and to conquer Peru:

---

* Commodore George Johnstone, commanding the British East India fleet, was attacked by the French fleet under M. de Suffrein at St. Jago, one of the Cape de Verd Islands, in 1781. Johnstone's flag-ship was the Rodney, 50.

When his squadron at Portsmouth he went to equip,
He promis'd great things from his FIFTY-GUN SHIP;
But, let him alone—while he knows which is which,
He'll not be so ready to " *die in a ditch.*"

This session, I thought to have told you thus much,
" A treaty concluded, and peace with the Dutch"—
But, as stubborn as ever, they vapour and brag,
And sail by my nose with the Prussian flag.

The empress refuses to join on our side,
As yet with the Indians we're only ally'd:
(Though such an alliance is rather improper,
We English are white, but their colour is copper.)

The Irish, I fear, have some mischief in view;
They ever have been a most troublesome crew—
If a truce or a treaty hereafter be made,
They shall pay very dear for their present free trade.

Dame Fortune, I think, has our standard forsaken,
For Tobago, they say, by Frenchmen is taken:
Minorca's besieg'd—and as for Gibraltar,
By Jove, if it's taken I'll take to the halter.

It makes me so wroth, I could scold like Xantippe
When I think of our losses along Missisippi—
And see in the Indies that horrible Hyder
His conquests extending still wider, and wider.

'Twixt Wafhington, Hyder, Don Galvez, De Graffe,
By my foul, we are brought to a very fine pafs—
When we've reafon to hope new battles are won,
A packet arrives—and an army's undone !—

In the midft of this fcene of difmay and diftrefs,
What is beft to be done, is not eafy to guefs,
For things may go wrong though we plan them aright,
And blows they muft look for, whofe trade is to fight.

In regard to the Rebels, it is my decree
That dependent on Britain they ever fhall be ;
Or I've captains and hofts, that will fly at my nod
And flaughter them all—by the bleffing of God.

But if they fucceed, as they're likely to do,
Our neighbours muft part with their colonies too ;
Let them laugh and be merry, and make us their jeft,
When La Plata revolts, we will laugh with the reft—

'Tis true that the journey to caftle St. Juan
Was a project that brought the projectors to ruin ;
But ftill, my dear lords, I would have you reflect,
Who nothing do venture can nothing expect.

If the Commons agree to afford me new treafures,
My fentence once more is for vigorous meafures :
Accuftom'd fo long to head winds and bad weather,
Let us conquer—or go to the devil together.
    [1782.]

RIVINGTON'S LAST WILL AND TESTAMENT.

SINCE life is uncertain, and no one can ſay,
    How ſoon we may go, or how long we ſhall ſtay,
Methinks he is wiſeſt who ſooneſt prepares,
And ſettles, in ſeaſon, his worldly affairs :

Some folks are ſo weak they can ſcarce avoid crying,
And think when they're making their wills they are dying ;
'Tis ſurely a ſerious employment—but ſtill,
Who e'er died the ſooner for making his will ?

Let others be ſad, when their lives they review,
But I know *whom* I've ſerv'd—and *him* faithfully too ;
And though it may ſeem a fanatical ſtory
He often has ſhow'd me a glimpſe of his glory.

IMPRIMIS, my carcaſe I give and deviſe
To be made into cakes of a moderate ſize,
To nouriſh thoſe Tories whoſe ſpirits may droop,
And ſerve the king's army with portable ſoup.

Unleſs I miſtake, in the ſcriptures we read
That "worms on the dead ſhall deliciouſly feed,"
The ſcripture ſtands true—and that I am firm in,
For what are our Tories and ſoldiers but vermin ?—

This foup of all foups can't be call'd that of beef,
(And this may to fome be a matter of grief:)
But I am certain the BULL would occafion a laugh,
That beef-portable-foup fhould be made of a CALF.

To the king, my dear mafter, I give a full fett
(In volumes bound up) of the ROYAL GAZETTE,
In which he will find the vaft records contain'd
Of provinces conquer'd, and victories gain'd.

As to ARNOLD, the traitor, and Satan, his brother,
I beg they will alfo accept of another;
And this fhall be bound in Morocco red leather,
Provided they'll read it, like brothers, together.

But if Arnold fhould die, 'tis another affair,
Then Satan, furviving, fhall be the fole heir;
He often has told me he thought it quite clever,
So to him and his heirs I bequeath it forever.

I know there are fome (that would fain be thought wife)
Who fay my Gazette is a record of lies;
In anfwer to this, I fhall only reply—
All the choice that I had was, to ftarve or to lie.

My fiddles, my flutes, French horns and guittars*
I leave to our HEROES, now weary of wars—

* Rivington's advertifements of liqueurs, mufical inftruments, fifhing-tackle,
and various articles of ufe and luxury, which he kept in his ftore for the wants
of the officers, are mingled with recommendations of the popular literature of the

To the wars of the stage they more boldly advance,
The captains fhall play, and the foldiers fhall dance.*

To Sir *Henry Clinton*, his ufe and behoof,
I leave my French brandy, of very good proof;
It will give him frefh fpirits for battle and flaughter
And make him *feel bolder* by land and by water:

Yet I caution the knight, for fear he do wrong
'Tis *avant la viande, et après le poiffon*†—
It will ftrengthen his ftomach, prevent it from turning,
And digeft the affront of his effigy—burning.

To Baron KNYPHAUSEN, his heirs and affigns,‡
I bequeath my *old Hock*, and my Burgundy wines,
To a true Heffian drunkard, no liquors are fweeter,
And I know the old man is no foe to the *creature*.

To a GENERAL, my namefake,§ I give and difpofe
Of a purfe full of clipp'd, *light, fweated* half joes;

---

day, in a farcical ftyle. He feems to have prided himfelf in particular on his
fupply of "good fiddles." The advertifements, in fact, of the *Royal Gazette*,—
a quaint prefentment of the times,—afford no fmall part of the amufement of the
journal to readers of the prefent day.

* It became fafhionable at this period with the Britifh officers, to affume the
bufinefs of the Drama, to the no fmall mortification of thofe who had been holding them up as the undoubted conquerors of North America.—*Author's note*, ED.
1809.

† Before flefh and after fifh.—*See Royal Gazette*.

‡ Baron William Von Knyphaufen, Lieutenant-General in the Britifh fervice,
in command of the Heffian mercenaries, celebrated during the war about New
York and the Jerfeys, where he was much engaged.

§ General James Robertfon, a Scotchman, a native of Fifefhire, an old officer

I hereby defire him to take back his trafh,
And return me my HANNAY's infallible WASH.

My cheffmen and tables, and other fuch chattels
I give to CORNWALLIS, renowned in battles :
By moving of thefe (not tracing the map)
He'll explain to the king how he got in a TRAP.

To good DAVID MATTHEWS* (among other flops)
I give my whole cargo of Maredants drops,
If they cannot do all, they may cure him in part,
And fcatter the poifon that cankers his heart :

Provided, however, and neverthelefs,
That what other eftate I enjoy and poffefs
At the time of my death (if it be not then fold)
Shall remain to the Tories, TO HAVE AND TO HOLD.

As I thus have bequeath'd them both carcafe and fleece,
The leaft they can do is to wait my deceafe ;
But to give them what fubftance I have, ere I die,
And be eat up with vermin, while living—not I—

of the army in America who had refided in New York previous to the Revolution, and was governor of the city during its occupation by the Britifh.   In
1780, Lieutenant-General James Robertfon was a member of the commiffion
fent by Sir Henry Clinton from New York up the Hudfon, to intercede with
Wafhington for the life of André.   Robertfon was met at Dobb's Ferry by
Greene, when the conference proceeded between the two, the former urging a
reconfideration of the cafe with great earneftnefs.

   * David Matthews was mayor of New York during the time the city was
held by the Britifh, in the Revolution.

In WITNESS whereof (though no ailment I feel)
Hereunto I fet both my hand and my feal;
(As the law fays) in prefence of witneffes twain,
'Squire *John Coghill Knap*,* and brother *Hugh Gaine.*
 [1782.]

---

* "Knapp," fays Dawfon, in a note to "New York City during the Revolution," was "a notorious pettifogger, a convict who had fled from England for his
own benefit."

THE POLITICAL BALANCE; OR, THE FATES OF BRITAIN AND AMERICA COMPARED.

A TALE.

Deciding Fates, in Homer's ſtíle, I ſhew,
And bring contending Gods once more to view.

AS Jove the Olympian (who both I and you know,
Was brother to Neptune, and huſband to Juno)
Was lately reviewing his papers of ſtate,
He happen'd to light on the records of Fate

In Alphabet order this volume was written—
So he open'd at B, for the article Britain—
She ſtruggles ſo well, ſaid the god, I will ſee
What the ſiſters in Pluto's dominions decree.

And, firſt, on the top of a column, he read
" Of a king, with a mighty ſoft place in his head,
" Who ſhould join in his temper the aſs and the mule,
" The third of his name, and by far the worſt fool :

" His reign ſhall be famous for multiplication,
" The ſire and the king of a *whelp* generation :

" But fuch is the will and the purpofe of fate,
" For each child he begets, he fhall forfeit a *State:*

" In the courfe of events, he fhall find to his coft
" That he cannot regain what he foolifhly loft;
" Of the nations around he fhall be the derifion,
" And know, by experience, the Rule of Divifion."

So Jupiter read—a god of firft rank—
And ftill had read on—but he came to a blank :
For the Fates had neglected the reft to reveal—
They either forgot it, or chofe to conceal :

When a leaf is torn out, or a blot on a page
That pleafes our fancy, we fly in a rage—
So, curious to know what the Fates would fay next,
No wonder if Jove, difappointed, was vext.

But ftill, as true genius not frequently fails,
He glanc'd at the *Virgin*, and thought of the *Scales ;*
And faid, " To determine the will of the Fates,
" One fcale fhall weigh *Britain*, the other the *States.*"

Then turning to Vulcan, his maker of thunder,
Said he, " My dear Vulcan, I pray you look yonder,
" Thofe *creatures* are tearing each other to pieces,
" And inftead of abating, the carnage increafes.

" Now, as you are a blackfmith, and lufty ftout ham-eater,
" You muft make me a globe of a fhorter diameter ;

" The world in abridgment, and juſt as it ſtands
" With all its proportions of waters and lands ;

" But its various diviſions muſt ſo be deſign'd,
" That I can unhinge it whene'er I've a mind—
" How elſe ſhould I know what the portions will weigh,
" Or which of the combatants carry the day ?"

Old Vulcan comply'd, (we've no reaſon to doubt it)
So he put on his apron and ſtraight went about it—
Made center, and circles as round as a pancake,
And here the Pacific, and there the Atlantic.

An axis he hammer'd, whoſe ends were the poles,
(On which the whole body perpetually rolls)
A brazen meridian he added to theſe,
Where four times repeated were ninety degrees.

I am ſure you had laugh'd to have ſeen his droll attitude,
When he bent round the ſurface the circles of latitude,
The zones, and the tropics, meridians, equator,
And other fine things that are drawn on ſalt water.

Away to the ſouthward (inſtructed by Pallas)
He plac'd in the ocean the Terra Auſtralis,
New Holland, New Guinea, and ſo of the reſt—
AMERICA lay by herſelf in the weſt :

From the regions where winter eternally reigns,
To the climes of Peru he extended her plains ;

Dark groves, and the zones did her bofom adorn,
And the *Crofiers*,* new burnifh'd, he hung at Cape Horn.

The weight of two oceans fhe bore on her fides,
With all their convulfions of tempefts and tides ;
Vaft lakes on her furface did fearfully roll,
And the ice from her rivers furrounded the pole.

Then Europe and Afia he northward extended,
Where under the Arctic with Zembla they ended ;
(The length of thefe regions he took with his garters,
Including Siberia, the land of the Tartars).

In the African clime (where the cocoa-nut tree grows)
He laid down the defarts, and even the Negroes,
The fhores by the waves of four oceans embrac'd,
And elephants ftrolling about in the wafte.

In forming Eaft India, he had a wide fcope,
Beginning his work at the cape of Good Hope ;
Then eaftward of that he continued his plan,
'Till he came to the empire and ifles of Japan.

Adjacent to Europe he ftruck up an ifland,
(One part of it low, but the other was high land)
With many a comical creature upon it,
And one wore a hat, and another a bonnet.

---

* Stars, in the form of a crofs, which mark the South Pole in fouthern lati-
tudes.

Like emmits or ants in a fine fummer's day,
They ever were marching in battle array,
Or fkipping about on the face of the brine,
Like witches in egg-fhells (their fhips of the line).

Thefe poor little creatures were all in a flame,
To the lands of America urging their claim,
Still biting, or ftinging, or fpreading their fails :
(For Vulcan had form'd them with ftings in their tails).

So poor and fo lean, you might count all their ribs,*
Yet were fo enraptur'd with crackers and fquibs,
That Vulcan with laughter almoft fplit afunder,
" Becaufe they imagin'd their crackers were thunder."

Due weftward from thefe, with a channel between,
A fervant to flaves, HIBERNIA was feen,
Once crowded with monarchs, and high in renown,
But all fhe retain'd was the Harp and the Crown !

Infulted forever by nobles and priefts,
And manag'd by bullies, and govern'd by beafts,
She look'd !—to defcribe her I hardly know how,
Such an image of death in the fcowl on her brow :

For fcaffolds and halters were full in her view,
And the fiends of perdition their cutlaffes drew :

* Their national debt being now above £200,000,000 fterling.—*Author's note.*

And axes and gibbets around her were plac'd,
And the demons of murder her honours defac'd—
With the blood of the WORTHY her mantle was ftain'd :
And hardly a trace of her beauty remain'd.*

Her genius, a female, reclin'd in the fhade,
And, merely for mufic, fo mournfully play'd,
That Jove was uneafy to hear her complain,
And order'd his blackfmith to loofen her chain.:

Then tipt her a wink, faying, " Now is your time,
" (To *rebel* is the fin, to *revolt.* is no crime)
" When your fetters are off, if you dare not be free
" Be a flave if you will, but complain not to me."

But finding her timid, he cry'd in a rage—
" Tho' the doors are flung open, fhe ftays in the cage !
" Subfervient to Britain then let her remain,
" And her freedom fhall be, *but the choice†* *of her chain.*"

At length, to difcourage all ftupid pretenfions,
Jove look'd at the globe, and approv'd its dimenfions,
And cry'd in a tranfport—" Why ! what have we here !
" Friend Vulcan, it is a moft beautiful fphere !

" Now while I am bufy in taking apart
" This globe that is form'd with fuch exquifite art,

* This ftanza and the preceding are additions, from the edition of 1809.
† "Length."—ED. 1795.

" Go, Hermes, to Libra, (you're one of her gallants)
" And afk, in my name, for the loan of her balance."

Away pofted Hermes, as fwift as the gales,
And as fwiftly return'd with the ponderous Scales,
And hung them aloft to a beam in the air,
So equally pois'd, they had turn'd with a hair.

Now Jove to COLUMBIA his fhoulders apply'd,
But aiming to lift her, his ftrength fhe defy'd—
Then, turning about to their godfhips, he fays—
" A BODY SO VAST is not eafy to raife ;

" But if you affift me, I ftill have a *notion*
" Our *forces*, *united*, can put her in motion,
" And fwing her aloft, (tho' alone I might fail)
" And place her, in fpite of her bulk, in our fcale ;

" If fix years together the Congrefs have ftrove,
" And more than *divided the empire with Jove ;*
" With a JOVE like myfelf, who am *nine* times as great,
" You can join, like their foldiers, to heave up this weight."

So to it they went, with handfpikes and levers,
And upward fhe fprung, with her mountains and rivers !
Rocks, cities, and iflands, deep waters and fhallows,
Ships, armies, and forefts, high heads, and fine fellows :

" Stick to it !" cries Jove—" Now heave one and all !
" At leaft we are lifting '*one eighth of the ball !*'

11

" If backward fhe tumbles—then trouble begins,
" And then have a care, my dear boys, of your fhins !"

When gods are determin'd, what project can fail ?
So they gave a hard fhove, and fhe mounted the fcale ;
Sufpended aloft, Jove view'd her with awe—
And the *gods** for their *pay*, had a hearty—huzza !

But Neptune bawl'd out—" Why Jove you're a noddy,
" Is Britain fufficient to poife that vaft body ?
" 'Tis nonfenfe fuch caftles to build in the air—
" As well might an oyfter with Britain compare."

" Away to your waters, you bluftering bully,"
Said Jove, " or I'll make you repent of your folly,
" Is Jupiter, fir, to be tutor'd by you ?—
" Get out of my fight, for I know what to do !"

Then fearching about with his fingers for Britain,
Thought he, " this fame ifland I cannot well hit on :
" The devil take him that firft call'd her the GREAT :
" If fhe was—fhe is *vaftly* diminifh'd of late !"

Like a man that is fearching his thigh for a flea,
He peep'd and he fumbled, but nothing could fee ;
At laft he exclaim'd—" I am furely upon it—
" I think I have hold of a highlander's bonnet."

* American Soldiers.

But finding his error, he faid with a figh,
" This bonnet is only the ifland of Skie !"*
So away to his *namefake* the PLANET he goes,
And borrow'd *two moons* to hang on his nofe.

Thro' thefe, as through glaffes, he faw her quite clear,
And in raptures cry'd out—" I have found her—fhe's here !
" If this be not Britain, then call me an afs,
" She looks *like a gem in an ocean of glafs.*

' But, faith, fhe's fo fmall I muft mind how I fhake her :
" In a box I'll inclofe her, for fear I fhould break her :
" Though a god, I might fuffer for being aggreffor,
" Since fcorpions, and vipers, and hornets poffefs her ;

" The white cliffs of Albion I think I defcry,
" And the hills of Plinlimmon appear rather nigh—
" But, Vulcan, inform me what creatures are thefe,
" That fmell fo of onions, and garlick, and cheefe ?"

Old Vulcan reply'd—" Odds fplutter a nails !
" Why, thefe are the Welch, and the country is Wales !
" When Taffy is vext, no devil is ruder—
" Take care how you trouble the offspring of TUDOR !

" On the crags of the mountains *hur* living *hur* feeks,
" *Hur* country is planted with garlick and leeks ;

* An ifland on the north-weft of Scotland.

" So great is *hur* choler, beware how you teize *hur*,
" For thefe are the Britons—unconquer'd by Cæfar."

" But now, my dear Juno, pray give me my mittens,
" (Thefe infects I am going to handle are Britons)
" I'll draw up their ifle with a finger and thumb,
" As the doctor extracts an old tooth from the gum."

Then he rais'd her aloft—but to fhorten our tale,
She look'd like a CLOD in the oppofite fcale—
Britannia fo fmall, and COLUMBIA fo large—
A fhip of firft rate, and a ferryman's barge !

Cry'd Pallas to Vulcan, " Why, Jove's in a dream—
" Obferve how he watches the turn of the beam !
" Was ever a mountain outweigh'd by a grain ?
" Or what is a drop when compar'd to the main ?"

But Momus alledg'd—" In my humble opinion,
" You fhould add to Great Britain her foreign dominion,
" When this is appended, perhaps fhe will rife,
" And equal her rival in weight and in fize."

" Alas ! (faid the monarch) your project is vain,
" But little is left of her foreign domain ;
" And, fcatter'd about in the liquid expanfe,
" That little is left to the mercy of France ;

" However, we'll lift them, and give her fair play—"
And foon in the fcale with their miftrefs they lay ;

But the gods were confounded and ſtruck with ſurpriſe,
And Vulcan could hardly believe his own eyes !

For (ſuch was the purpoſe and guidance of fate)
Her foreign dominions diminiſh'd her weight—
By which it appear'd, to Britain's diſaſter,
Her foreign poſſeſſions were changing their maſter.

Then, as he replac'd them, ſaid Jove with a ſmile—
" Columbia ſhall never be rul'd by an iſle—
" But vapours and darkneſs around her ſhall riſe,
" And tempeſts conceal her a-while from our eyes ;

" So locuſts in Egypt their ſquadrons diſplay,
" And riſing, disfigure the face of the day :
" So the moon, at her full, has a frequent eclipſe,
" And the ſun in the ocean diurnally dips.

" Then céaſe your endeavours, ye vermin of Britain—
(And here, in deriſion, their iſland he ſpit on)
" 'Tis madneſs to ſeek what you never can find,
" Or to think of uniting what Nature disjoin'd :

" But ſtill you may flutter awhile with your wings,
" And ſpit out your venom and brandiſh your ſtings ·
" Your hearts are as black, and as bitter as gall,
" A curſe to mankind—and a blot on the Ball."
        [*April*, 1782.]

SIR HARRY'S INVITATION.*

COME, gentlemen Tories, firm, loyal, and true,
　　Here are axes and fhovels, and fomething to do !
　　　　For the fake of our king,
　　　　Come, labour and fing ;
You left all you had for his honour and glory,
And he will remember the fuffering Tory :
　　　　We have, it is true,
　　　　Some fmall work to do ;
　　　　But here's for your pay
　　　　Twelve coppers a day,
And never regard what the rebels may fay,
But throw off your jerkins and labour away.

To raife up the rampart, and pile up the wall,
To pull down old houfes and dig the canal,
　　　　To build and deftroy—
　　　　Be this your employ,
In the day time to work at our fortifications,
And fteal in the night from the rebels your rations ;
　　　　The king wants your aid
　　　　Not empty parade ;

* Sir Henry Clinton, at New York, to the Refugees.

Advance to your places
Ye men of *long faces,*
Nor ponder too much on your former difgraces,
This year, I prefume, will quite alter your cafes.

Attend at the call of the fifer and drummer,
The French and the Rebels are coming next fummer,
And forts we muft build
Though Tories are kill'd—
Then courage, my jockies, and work for your king,
For if you are taken no doubt you will fwing—
If *York* we can hold
I'll have you enroll'd;
And after you're dead
Your names fhall be read
As who for their monarch both labour'd and bled,
And ventur'd their necks for their *beef* and their *bread.*

'Tis an honour to ferve the braveft of nations,
And be left to be hang'd in their capitulations—
Then fcour up your mortars
And ftand to your quarters,
'Tis nonfenfe for Tories in battle to run,
They never need fear fword, halberd, or gun;
Their hearts fhould not fail 'em,
No balls will affail 'em,
Forget your difgraces
And *fhorten* your *faces,*
For 'tis true as the gofpel, believe it or not,
Who are born to be hang'd, will never be fhot.

DIALOGUE,

Burgoyne.

LET thofe, who will, be proud and fneer,
    And call you an unwelcome peer,
But I am glad to fee you here :
The prince that fills the Britifh throne,
Unlefs fuccefsful, honours none ;
Poor Jack Burgoyne !—you're not alone.

Cornwallis.

Thy fhips, De Graffe, have caus'd my grief—
To rebel fhores and their relief
There never came a luckier chief :
In fame's *black* page it fhall be read,
By Gallic arms my foldiers bled—
The rebels *thine* in triumph led.

Burgoyne.

Our fortunes different forms affume :—
I call'd and call'd for *elbow-room*,
'Till GATES *difcharg'd* me to my doom ;

But you, that conquer'd far and wide,
In little York thought fit to hide,
The *fubject ocean* at your fide.

Cornwallis.

And yet no force had gain'd that poft—
Not Wafhington, his country's boaft,
Nor Rochambeau, with all his hoft,
Nor all the Gallic fleet's parade—
Had Clinton hurried to my aid,
And Sammy Graves been not afraid.

Burgoyne.

For head knock'd off, or broken bones,
Or mangled corpfe, no price atones;
Nor all that prattling rumour fays,
Nor all the piles that art can raife,
The poet's or the parfon's praife.

Cornwallis.

Though I am brave, as well as you,
Yet ftill I think your notion true;
Dear brother Jack, our toils are o'er—
With foreign conquefts plagu'd no more,
We'll ftay and guard our native fhore.

ON THE LATE

ROYAL SLOOP OF WAR, GENERAL MONK,

[FORMERLY THE WASHINGTON]

Mounting Six quarter deck Wooden Guns.

WHEN the Washington ship by the English was beat,
    They sent her to England to shew their great feat,
And Sandwich straightway, as a proof of his spunk,
Dash'd out her old name, and call'd her the Monk.*

" This MONK hated Rebels (said *Sandy*)—'od rot 'em,
" So heave her down quickly, and copper her bottom ;
" With the sloops of our navy we'll have her enroll'd,
" And mann'd with pick'd sailors, to make her *feel bold.*

" To shew that our king is both *valiant* and *good,*
" Some guns shall be *iron,* and others be *wood ;*
" And, in truth, (tho' I wish not the secret to spread)
" All her guns should be wooden—to suit with his head."

  * General Monk, who was the most active agent in restoring Charles II.—
Author's note.

BARNEY'S INVITATION.

COME, all ye lads that know no fear,
    To wealth and honour we will fteer
In the Hyder Ali privateer,
        Commanded by brave Barney.*

She's new and true, and tight and found,
Well rigg'd aloft, and all well found—
Come and be with laurel crown'd,
        Away—and leave your laffes.

Accept our terms without delay,
And make your fortunes while you may,
Such offers are not every day
        In the power of the jolly failor.

---

* The "Hyder Ali," or Ally, as fhe was popularly called, was a fmall mer-
chantman, purchafed in the fpring of 1782 by the State of Pennfylvania, and fitted out, with the affiftance of funds furnifhed by the merchants of Philadelphia,
to free the Delaware of the marauding cruifers of the enemy. Lieutenant Jofhua
Barney was feledted as her commander. He entered upon the fervice with fpirit.
His action in the Delaware Bay with the Britifh floop-of-war General Monk, the
brilliant firft-fruits of his appointment, on the 8th of April, is the fubjedt of the
following poem. The General Monk had formerly been the American privateer
General Wafhington; fhe had been captured and her name changed by the
Britifh. Her old name was now reftored. She was fubfequently employed by
the General Government as a packet.

Succe∫s and fame attend the brave,
But death the coward and the ∫lave,
Who fears to plough the Atlantic wave,
      To ∫eek the bold invaders.

Come, then, and take a crui∫ing bout,
Our ∫hip ∫ails well, there is no doubt,
She has been try'd both in and out,
      And an∫wers expectation.

Let no proud foes whom Europe* bore
Di∫tre∫s our trade, in∫ult our ∫hore—
Teach them to know their reign is o'er,
      Bold Philadelphia ∫ailors !

We'll teach them how to ∫ail ∫o near,
Or to venture on the Delaware,
When we in warlike trim appear,
      And crui∫e without Henlopen.

Who cannot wounds and battles dare
Shall never cla∫p the blooming fair ;
The brave alone their charms ∫hall ∫hare,
      The brave are their protectors.

With hand and heart united all,
Prepar'd to conquer or to fall,
Attend, my lads, to honour's call,
      Embark in our Hyder Ali.

* "That Britain."—ED. 1786.

From an eaſtern prince ſhe takes her name,
Who, ſmit with freedom's ſacred flame,
Uſurping Britons brought to ſhame,
          His country's wrongs avenging ;

See, on her ſtern the waving ſtars—
Inur'd to blood, inur'd to wars,
Come, enter quick, my jolly tars,
          To ſcourge theſe haughty Britons.

Here's grog enough—then drink about,
I know your hearts are firm and ſtout ;
American blood will ne'er give out,
          And often we have prov'd it.

Though ſtormy oceans round us roll,
We'll keep a firm undaunted ſoul,
Befriended by the cheering bowl,
          Sworn foes to melancholy :

While timorous landſmen lurk on ſhore,
'Tis ours to go where cannons roar—
On a coaſting cruiſe we'll go once more,
          Deſpiſers of all danger ;

And Fortune ſtill that crowns the brave
Shall guard us o'er the gloomy wave—
A fearful heart betrays a knave ,
          Succeſs to the Hyder Ali.

SONG, ON CAPTAIN BARNEY'S VICTORY OVER THE SHIP GENERAL MONK.

O'ER the waſte of waters cruiſing,
    Long the General Monk had reign'd ;
All ſubduing, all reducing,
    None her lawleſs rage reſtrain'd :
Many a brave and hearty fellow
    Yielding to this warlike foe,
When her guns began to bellow
    Struck his humbled colours low.

But grown bold with long ſucceſſes,
    Leaving the wide wat'ry way,
She, a ſtranger to diſtreſſes,
    Came to cruiſe within Cape May :
" Now we ſoon (ſaid Captain Rogers)
    " Shall their men of commerce meet ;
" In our hold we'll have them lodgers,
    " We ſhall capture half their fleet.

" Lo ! I ſee their van appearing—
    " Back our topſails to the maſt—
" They toward us full are ſteering
    " With a gentle weſtern blaſt :

" Ive a lift of all their cargoes,
  " All their guns, and all their men :
" I am fure thefe modern Argo's
  " Can't efcape us one in ten :

" Yonder comes the Charming Sally
  " Sailing with the General Greene—
" Firft we'll fight the HYDER ALI,
  " Taking her is taking them :
" She intends to give us battle,
  " Bearing down with all her fail—
" Now, boys, let our cannon rattle !
  " To take her we cannot fail.

" Our eighteen guns, each a nine pounder,
  " Soon fhall terrify this foe ;
" We fhall maul her, we fhall wound her,
  " Bringing rebel colours low."—
While he thus anticipated
  Conquefts that he could not gain,
He in the Cape May channel waited
  For the fhip that caus'd his pain.

Captain Barney then preparing,
  Thus addrefs'd his gallant crew—
" Now, brave lads, be bold and daring,
  " Let your hearts be firm and true ;
" This is a proud Englifh cruifer,
  " Roving up and down the main,

" We muſt fight her—muſt reduce her,
    " Tho' our decks be ſtrew'd with ſlain.

" Let who will be the ſurviver,
        " We muſt conquer or muſt die,
" We muſt take her up the river,
        " Whate'er comes of you or I :
" Tho' ſhe ſhows moſt formidable
        " With her eighteen pointed nines,
" And her quarters clad in ſable,
        " Let us baulk her proud deſigns.

" With four nine pounders, and twelve ſixes
        " We will face that daring band ;
" Let no dangers damp your courage,
        " Nothing can the brave withſtand.
" Fighting for your country's honour,
        " Now to gallant deeds aſpire ;
" Helmſman, bear us down upon her,
        " Gunner, give the word to fire !"

Then yard-arm and yard-arm meeting,
    Strait began the diſmal fray,
Cannon mouths, each other greeting,
    Belch'd their ſmoky flames away :
Soon the langrage, grape, and chain-ſhot,
    That from Barney's cannons flew,
Swept the Monk, and clear'd each round to
    Kill'd and wounded half her crew.

Captain Rogers ftrove to rally :
    But they from their quarters fled,
While the roaring Hyder Ali
    Cover'd o'er his decks with dead.
When from their tops their dead men tumbled,
    And the ftreams of blood did flow,
Then their proudeft hopes were humbled
    By their brave inferior foe.

All aghaft, and all confounded,
    They beheld their champions fall,
And their captain, forely wounded,
    Bade them quick for quarters call.
Then the Monk's proud flag defcended,
    And her cannon ceas'd to roar ;
By her crew no more defended,
    She confefs'd the conteft o'er.

Come, brave boys, and fill your glaffes,
    You have humbled one proud foe,
No brave action this furpaffes,
    Fame fhall tell the nations fo—
Thus be Britain's woes completed,
    Thus abridg'd her cruel reign,
'Till fhe ever, thus defeated,
    Yields the fceptre of the main.
    12

THE HESSIAN DEBARKATION.

REJOICE, O Death ! Britannia's tyrant fends
    From German plains his myriads to our fhore ;
The fierce Hibernian with the Heffian join'd—
    Bring them, ye winds, but waft them back no more !

To thefe far climes with ftately ftep they come,
    Refolv'd all prayers, all prowefs to defy :
Smit with the love of countries not their own
    They come—alas ! to conquer, not to die.

In the flow breeze I hear their funeral fong
    The dance of ghofts the infernal tribes prepare ;
To hell's dark manfions hafte the abandon'd throng,
    Tafting from German fculls great ODIN's beer.

From dire Cefarea—forc'd thefe flaves of kings—
Quick let them take their way on eagles' wings ;
To thy ftrong pofts, MANHATTAN's ifle, repair,
To meet the vengeance that awaits them there.

THE NORTHERN SOLDIER.

IN vain you talk of fruits and flowers,
　　When rude December chills the plain,
And nights are cold, and long the hours,
　　To damp the ardour of the ſwain;
　　Who, parting from his ſocial fire,
　　　　All comfort muſt forego,
　　　　　And here, and there,
　　　　　And every where
　　　　Purſue the invading foe.

But we muſt ſleep in froſts and ſnows;
　　No ſeaſon breaks up our campaign:
Hard as the oaks, we dare oppoſe
　　The autumnal, or the wintry reign.
　　Alike to us, the winds that blow
　　　　In Summer's ſeaſon gay,
　　　　　Or thoſe that rave
　　　　　On Hudſon's wave,
　　　　And drift his ice away.

Traitors and death may cloud our ſcene,
　　The ball may pierce, the cold may kill,

And dire misfortunes intervene :
⠀But Freedom fhall be potent, ftill,
⠀⠀To drive thefe Britons from our fhore,
⠀⠀⠀Who, cruel and unkind,
⠀⠀⠀⠀With flavifh chain
⠀⠀⠀⠀Attempt, in vain,
⠀⠀⠀Our free-born limbs to bind.

TRUTH ANTICIPATED.

WHAT brilliant events have of late come to pafs,
 No lefs than the capture of Monfieur DE GRASSE !*
His Majefty's Printer has told it for true,
As we had it from him, fo we give it to you.

Many folks of difcernment the ftory believ'd,
And the devil himfelf it at firft had deceiv'd,

---

* Admiral Rodney's decifive engagement with the French fleet, under the
Count de Graffe, was fought off the ifland of Martinique, April 12, 1782. The
battle lafted from feven in the morning till evening, when the action ended in
the utter defeat of the French. Rodney, in the Formidable, engaged the Ville
de Paris, the flag-fhip of De Graffe, and forced her furrender. De Graffe was
taken to England a prifoner of war. For this diftinguifhed fervice, Rodney was
raifed to the peerage.

Sir George Rodney's "Letter on his late glorious victory over the French fleet
in the Weft Indies," appeared in Rivington's *Gazette* of May 15, 1782. It was
addreffed to Mr. Charles Kerr, at Antigua, on the 18th of April, and read:
"The French fleet, after an action that lafted from feven in the morning till
funfet, on the 12th of April, 1782, met with a total defeat. The Ville de Paris,
with four other fhips taken and the Diadem funk, graced the victory, and their
whole fleet fo extremely fhattered, that had there been but two hours more day-
light, more than half would have been taken. Two hundred and thirty Britifh
killed, feven hundred and fifty-nine wounded. I would have compounded for
three thoufand at leaft; the French muft have loft many more than five thoufand. Their whole army was on board." The following French fhips were
taken: La Ville de Paris, 110; Le Glorieux, 74; Le Cæfar, 74; Le Hector,
74; L'Ardent, 64; Le Diadem, 74, funk.

Had it not been that Satan imported the ſtuff,
And ſign'd it *George Rodney*, by way of high proof.

Said *Satan* to *Jemmy*, " Let's give them the *whappers*—
" Some news I have got that will bring in the coppers,
" And *truth* it ſhall be, though I paſs it for *lies*,
" And making a page of your Newſpaper ſize.

" A wide field is open to favour my plan,
" And the rebels may prove that I lie—if they can ;
" Since they jeſted and laugh'd at our lying before,
" Let it paſs for a lie, to torment them the more.—

" My wings are yet wet with the *Weſt-India* dew,
" And *Rodney* I left, to come hither to you,
" I left *him* bedevil'd with brimſtone and ſmoke,
" The *French* in diſtreſs, and their armament broke.

" For news ſo delightful, with heart and with voice
" The Tories of every degree ſhall rejoice ;
" With charcoal and ſulphur ſhall utter their joy
" 'Till they all get as black as they paint the *old Boy*."

Thus, pleas'd with the motion, each cutting a caper,
Down they ſat at the table, with pen, ink, and paper ;
In leſs than five minutes the matter was ſtated,
And Jemmy turn'd ſcribe, while Satan dictated.

" Begin (ſaid the devil) in the form of a *Letter*,
" (If you call it *true copy*, 'tis ſo much the better)

" Make Rodney affert that he met the French fleet,
" Engag'd it, and gave 'em a *total defeat*.

" But the better to vamp up a fhow of reality,
" The tale muft be told with circumftantiality,
" What veffels were conquer'd by Britain's bold fons,
" Their quotas of men, and their numbers of guns.

" There's the *Ville de Paris*—one hundred and ten—
" Write down, that George Rodney has kill'd half her men;
" That her hull and her rigging are fhatter'd and fhaken,
" Her flag humbled down, and her admiral taken:

" *Le Cefar*, 'tis true, is a feventy-four,
" But the *Ville de Paris* was thirty-fix more;
" With a grey goofe's quill if that fhip we did feize on,
" Le Cefar muft fall, or I'll know what's the reafon.

" The next that I fix on to take, is the *Hector*,
" (Her name may be Trojan, but fhall not protect her)
" Don't faulter, dear comrade, and look like a goofe,
" If we've taken thefe three, we can take *Glorieufe*.

" The laft mention'd fhip runs their lofs up to four,
" *Le Diadem* funk, fhall make it one more;
" And now, for the fake of round numbers, dear coufin,
" Write *Ardent*, and then we have juft half-a-dozen!"

Jemmy fmil'd at the notion, and whifper'd, " O fy!
" Indeed 'tis a fhame to perfuade one to lie"—

But Satan replied—" Confider, my fon,
" I am prince of the winds, and have feen what is done :

" With a conqueft like this, how bright we fhall fhine !
" That Rodney has taken *fix fhips of the Line*,
" Will be in your paper a brilliant affair ;
" How the *tories* will laugh, and the *rebels* will fwear !

" But farther, dear Jemmy, make Rodney to fay,
" *If the fun two hours longer had held out the day*,
" *The reft were fo beaten, fo baifted, fo tore*,
" *He had taken them* ALL, *and he knew not but* MORE."

So the *partners* broke up as good friends as they met,
And foon it was all in the *Royal Gazette ;*
The Tories rejoic'd at the very good news,
And faid, *There's no fear we fhall die in our fhoes.*

Now let us give credit to Jemmy, forfooth,
Since once in a way he has hit on the truth :
If again he returns to his practice of lies,
He hardly reflects where he'll go when he dies.

But ftill, when he dies, let it never be faid
That he refts in his grave with no verfe at his head ;
But furnifh, ye poets, fome fhort epitaph,
And fomething like this, that readers may laugh :

Here *lies* a King's Printer, we needn't fay who :
There is reafon to think that he tells what is true :

But if he *lies* here, 'tis not over-ſtrange,
His preſent poſition is but a ſmall change,
So, reader, paſs on—'tis a folly to ſigh,
For all his life long he did little but LIE.

    [1782.]

ON SIR HENRY CLINTON'S RECALL.

THE *dog that is beat has a right to complain—*
   Sir Harry returns a difconfolate *man*,
To the face of his mafter, the Lord's oil-anointed,
To the country provided for thieves difappointed.

Our FREEDOM, he thought, to a tyrant muft fall,
He concluded the weakeft muft go to the wall;
The more he was flatter'd, the bolder he grew—
He quitted the old world to conquer the new.

But in fpite of the deeds he has done in his garrifon,
(And they have been curious beyond all comparifon)
He now muft go home, at the call of his king,
To anfwer the charges that Arnold may bring.

But what are the acts that this chief has atchiev'd ?—
If good, it is hard he fhould now be aggriev'd,
And the more, as he fought for his national glory,
Nor valued, a farthing, the RIGHT of the ftory.

This famous great man, and two birds* of his feather,
In the Cerberus frigate came over together;

      * Generals Howe and Burgoyne.

But of all the bold chiefs that re-meafure the trip,
Nor two have been known to return in one fhip.

Like children that wreftle and fcuffle in fport,
They are very well pleas'd as long as unhurt,
But a thump on the nofe, or a blow in the eye,
Ends the fray—and they go to their *daddy* and cry.

Sir Clinton, thy deeds have been mighty and many,
You faid all our *paper* was not worth a penny,
('Tis nothing but rags,* quoth honeft Will Tryon,
Are *rags* to difcourage the *Sons of the Lion?*)

But Clinton thought thus—" It is folly to fight,
" When things may by eafier methods come right,
" There is fuch an art as counterfeit-ation—
" And I'll do my utmoft to honour our nation ;

" I'll fhew this damn'd country that I can enflave her,
" And that by the help of a fkilful engraver,
" And then let the rebels take care of their bacon,——
" We'll play them a trick, or I'm vaftly miftaken."

But the project fucceeded not quite to your liking,
So you paid off your *artift*, and gave up BILL STRIKING;
But 'tis an affair I am glad you are quit on,
Yet had furely been hang'd had you try'd it in Britain.

* See his Letter to General Parfons.

At the taking of Charleſton you cut a great figure,
The terms you propounded were terms full of rigour,
Yet could not foreſee poor CHARLEY's* diſgrace,
Nor how ſoon your own COLOURS would go to the CASE.

When the town had ſurrender'd, the more to diſgrace ye,
(Like another *true Briton* that did it at 'Statia)
You broke all the terms yourſelf had extended,
Becauſe you ſuppos'd the rebellion was ended ;

Whoever the tories mark'd out as a whig,
If gentle, or ſimple, or little, or big,
No matter to you—to kill 'em and ſpite 'em,
You ſoon had 'em up where the dogs couldn't bite 'em.

Then thinking theſe rebels were ſnug and ſecure,
You left them to Rawdon and Neſbit Balfour ;
(The face of the latter no maſk need be draw'd on,
And to fiſh for the Devil my bait ſhould be *Rawdon*.)

Returning to York with your ſhips and your plunder,
And boaſting that rebels muſt ſhortly knock under,
The firſt thing that ſtruck you as ſoon as you landed
Was the fortreſs at Weſt-Point, where Arnold commanded.

Thought you, " If friend Arnold this fort will deliver,
" We then ſhall be maſters of all Hudſon's river,

* Cornwallis.

" The *eaft* and the *fouth* lofing communication,
" The Yankies will die by the Act of *Starvation*."

So off you fent Andrè (not guided by Pallas)
Who foon purchas'd Arnold, and with him the gallows;
Your *lofs* I conceive than your *gain* was far greater,
You loft a good fellow, and got a vile traitor.

Now Carleton comes over to give you relief,
A knight like yourfelf, and commander in *chief*.
But the *chief* he will get, you may tell the *dear honey*,
Will be a black eye, hard knocks, and *no* money.

Now with—" Britons, ftrike home!" your forrows difpel,
Away to your mafter, and honeftly tell
That his *arms* and his *artifts* can nothing avail,
His men are too few, and his tricks are too ftale.

Advife him at length to be juft and fincere;
Of which not a fymptom as yet doth appear,
As we plainly perceive from his fending Sir Guy
The TREATY to break with our gallic ally.

SIR GUY CARLETON'S ADDRESS TO THE AMERICANS.*

FROM Britain's fam'd iſland once more I come over,
(No iſland on earth is in proweſs above her)
With powers and commiſſions your hearts to recover !

Our king, I muſt tell you, is plagu'd with a phantom
(Independence they call it) that hourly doth haunt him,
And relief, my dear rebels, you only can grant him.

Tom Gage and Sir Harry, Sir William, (our boaſt)
Lord Howe, and the reſt that have ſcouted the coaſt,
All fail'd in their projects of laying this ghoſt :

So unleſs the damn'd ſpectre myſelf can expel
It will yet kill our monarch, I know very well,
And gallop him off on his lion to hell.

* Sir Guy Carleton, " Commander-in-chief of his Majeſty's forces, and Com-
miſſioner for making peace or war in North America," to follow the announce-
ment of *Rivington's Gazette*, arrived at New York, as the ſucceſſor of Sir Henry
Clinton, in the Ceres man-of-war, Captain Hawkins, on Sunday, May 5, 1782.
He remained in the city till the concluſion of peace, leaving, with his troops, on
the 25th of November of the following year. He was born in Ireland, in 1724.
Previouſly to the American Revolution he had ſeen much ſervice, having diſtin-
guiſhed himſelf at the ſieges of Louiſburg and Quebec. He was wounded in
1762, at the ſiege of Havannah. In 1772 he was Governor of Quebec. He
died in 1808.

But I heartily wiſh, that, inſtead of Sir Guy,
They had ſent out a ſeer from the iſland of Skie,
Who rebels, and devils, and ghoſts could defy :

So great is our proſpect of failing at laſt,
When I look at the preſent, and think of the paſt,
I wiſh with our heroes I had not been claſſed ;

For though, to a man, we are bullies and bruiſers,
And cover'd with laurels, we ſtill are the loſers,
'Till each is recall'd with his tory accuſers :

But the war now is alter'd, and on a new plan ;
By negociation we'll do what we can—
And I am an honeſt, well-meaning old man ;

Too proud to retreat, and too weak to advance,
We muſt ſtay where we are, at the mercy of chance,
'Till Fortune ſhall help us to lead you a dance.

Then lay down your arms, dear rebels—O hone !
Our king is the beſt man that ever was known,
And the greateſt that ever was ſtuck on a throne ;

His love and affection by all ranks are ſought ;
Here take him, my honies, and each pay a groat—
Was ever a monarch more eaſily bought ?

In pretty good caſe, and very well found,
By night and by day we carry him round ;
He muſt go for a groat, if we can't get a pound.

Break the treaties you made with Louis Bourbon !
Abandon the Congrefs, no matter how foon,
And then, all together, we'll play a new tune.

'Tis ftrange that they always would manage the roaft,
And force you their healths and the Dauphin's to toaft;
Repent, my dear fellows, and each get a *poft* :

Or, if you objeçt that *one poft* is too few,
We generous Britons will help you to *two*
With a beam laid acrofs—that will certainly do.

The folks that rebell'd in the year forty-five,
We us'd them fo well, that we left few alive,
But fent them to heaven in fwarms from their hive.

Your noble refiftance we cannot forget,
'Tis nothing but right we fhould honour you yet;
If you are not rewarded, we die in your debt.

So, quickly fubmit, and our mercy implore,
Be as loyal to George as you once were before,
Or I'll flaughter you all—and probably more.

What puzzled Sir Harry, Sir Will, and his brother,
Perhaps may be done by the fon of my mother,
With the *Sword* in one hand and a *Branch* in the other.

My bold predeceffors (as fitting their ftation)
At their firft coming out, all fpoke PROCLAMATION ;
'Tis the cuftom with us, and the way of our nation.

Then Kil-al-la-loo !—Shelaly, I fay ;—
If we cannot all fight, we can all run away—
And further at prefent I choofe not to fay.

[1782.]

13

MODERN IDOLATRY, OR ENGLISH QUIXOTISM.

MY native fhades delight no more,
    I hafte to meet the ocean's roar,
I feek a wild rebellious fhore
      Beyond the Atlantic main :

'Tis honour calls !—I muft away !—
Nor eafe nor pleafure tempts my ftay,
Nor all that Love himfelf can fay,
      A moment fhall detain.

To meet thofe hofts that dare difown
Allegiance to Britannia's throne
I draw the fword that pities none,
      I draw their rebel blood ;

Amazement fhall their troops confound
When gafping, proftrate on the ground,
My fword fhall drink from every wound
      A life deftroying flood !

The fwarthy Indian, yet unbroke,
Shall bend his neck to Britain's yoke,

Or flee from her avenging ftroke
 To defarts yet unknown ;

The Atlantic ifles fhall own her fway,
Peru and Mexico obey,
And thofe who yet to Satan pray
 Beyond the fouthern zone.

For George the third I dare to go
Through Etna's fire and Greenland's fnow,
Where'er our kindred waters flow,
 The vaft unbounded main.

In him true glory fhines complete,
In him a thoufand virtues meet—
'Twere heaven to die at George's feet.
 Could I that blefling gain !

For George the third I dare to fall,
Since he to me is all in all—
May he fubdue this earthly ball,
 And nations tribute bring ;—

Yon' rebel States fhall wear his chain
Where traitors now with tyrants reign—
And fubjeƈt fhall be all the main
 To George our potent king.

When honour calls to guard his throne,
My life I dare not call my own—

My life I yield, without a groan,
    For him whom I adore :

In endlefs glory he fhall reign—
'Tis he fhall conquer France and Spain—
Though I perphaps may ne'er again
    Behold my native fhore !

EPILOGUE.

'TIS fo well known 'tis hardly worth relating
That men have worfhipp'd gods, though of their own crea-
        ting ;
Art's handy work they thought they might adore,
And bow'd to gods that were but logs before.

Idols, of old, were made of clay or wood,
And, in themfelves, did neither harm nor good,
Acted as though they knew the good old rule,
" Friend, hold thy peace, and you'll be thought no fool."

Britons ! their cafe is yours—and link'd in fate
You, like your Indian allies—good and great—
Bow to fome frowning block yourfelves did rear,
And worfhip *wooden monarchs*—out of fear—

ON GENERAL ROBERTSON'S PROCLAMATION.*

OLD Judas the traitor (nor need we much wonder)
   Falling down from the gallows, his paunch split asunder,
Affording, 'tis likely, a horrible scent
Rather worse than the sulphur of hell, where he went.

* The following proclamation, dated New York, June 22, 1782, appeared in Rivington's *Royal Gazette* of the 26th of that month, surmounted by the Royal Arms :—" By His Excellency Lieutenant-General JAMES ROBERTSON, *Governor of New York, &c., &c.* The Commander-in-Chief having shown the great confidence he reposes in the Citizens of New York by trusting his Majesty's interest there, to their Zeal, Loyalty, and Gallantry, I persuade myself that every citizen will with alacrity claim his title to a share of the Militia duty ; that none may be deprived of this, and that those whose zeal would lead them to appear whenever called for, may not be called for too often, I think proper to declare :

"That all persons are to perform the Militia duty, excepting the Ministers of God's Word, his Majesty's Counsellors and principal servants whose avocations to religious and civil, necessarily prevents their attendance on Military duties.

"All persons who from age or infirmity are unable to act, may do duty by substitutes, providing those they offer are judged sufficient by the Colonel of the regiment, or commanding officer of the corps to which they belong.

"If any of the Gentlemen of the learned professions find themselves so usefully employed as to be induced to avoid the honour of appearing in person, they are supposed to be judges of the importance of their own time, and may act by proper substitutes.

"As no person deserves protection in a place of which he refuses to contribute to the defence ; every person who refuses to appear when summoned to his Militia duty is to be confined in the Main-Guard by the Colonel or commanding Officer of the corps to which he belongs, where he is to be kept till further orders."

So now this bra' chieftain, who long has fufpended
And kept out of view, what his mafter intended,
Burfts out all at once, and an infide difclofes,
Difgufting the tories, who ftop up their nofes.

The fhort of the matter is this, as I take it—
New York of true Britons is plainly left naked,
And their conduct amounts to an honeft confeffion,
They cannot depend on the run-a-way Heffian.

In fuch a dilemma, pray what fhould they do ?
Hearts loyal, to whom fhould they look but to You ?—
You know pretty well how to handle the fpade,
To dig their canals, and to make a parade ;

The city is left to your valiant defence,
And, of courfe, it will be but of little expence,
Since there is an old fellow that looks fomewhat sooty
Who, *gratis*, will help you in doing your duty—

" In doing our duty !—'tis duty indeed
" (Says a Tory) if this be the way that we fpeed ;
" We never lov'd fighting, the matter is clear—
" If we had, I am fure, we had never come here.

" George we own'd for our king, as his true loyal fons,
" But why will he force us to manage his guns ?—
" Who 'lift in the army or cruife on the wave,
" Let them do as they will—'tis their trade to be brave.

" Guns, mortars, and bullets, we eafily face,
" But when they're in motion—it alters the cafe ;
" To fkirmifh with Huddies* is all our defire—
" *For though we can murder, we cannot ſtand fire.*

" To the ſtandards of Britain we fled for proteétion,
" And here we are gather'd, a goodly colleétion ;
" And moſt of us think it is rather too hard
" For refuſing to arm, to be put under guard ;

" Who knows *under guard* what ills we may feel !—
" It is an expreſſion that means a great deal—
" 'Mongſt the rebels they *fine* 'em who will not turn out,
" But here we are left in a ſorrowful doubt—

" Theſe Britons were always ſo ſharp and ſo ſnifty——
" The rebels excuſe you from ſerving, when fifty,
" But here we are counted ſuch wonderful men
" We are kept in the ranks, 'till we're four ſcore and ten.

" Kick'd, cuff'd, and ill-treated from morning 'till night—
" We have room to conjeéture, *that all is not right :*
" For Freedom, we fled from our country's defence,
" And freedom we'll get—when death ſends us hence.

" If matters go thus, it is eaſy to ſee
" That as idiots we've been, ſo ſlaves we ſhall be ;

* Captain Huddy, an American captain, who, after capitulating in a block-houfe, was hanged by refugees, called new levies.—*Author's note.*

" And what will become of that peaceable train
" Whofe tenets enjoin them from war to abstain ?

" Our city commandant muft be an odd fhaver,
" Not a fingle exception to make in their favour !—
" Come, let us turn round and *rebellioufly* fing,
" Huzza for the CONGRESS !—the de'il take the king."
    [1782.]

ARNOLD'S DEPARTURE.*

Mala foluta navis exit alite
Ferens olentem Mævium, &c.
Imitated from Horace.

WITH evil omens from the harbour fails
    The ill-fated fhip that worthlefs ARNOLD bears,
God of the fouthern winds, call up thy gales,
    And whiftle in rude fury round his ears.

With horrid waves infult his veffel's fides,
    And may the eaft wind on a leeward fhore
Her cables fnap, while fhe in tumult rides,
    And fhatter into fhivers every oar.

And let the north wind to her ruin hafte,
    With fuch a rage, as when from mountains high
He rends the tall oak with his weighty blaft,
    And ruin fpreads, where'er his forces fly.

May not one friendly ftar that night be feen;
    No Moon, attendant, dart one glimmering ray,

* General Arnold failed from New York, with his family, in December, 1781.
He furvived in England for nearly twenty years, dying in London in 1801, at the
age of fixty-one.

Nor may fhe ride on oceans more ferene
　　Than Greece, triumphant, found that ftormy day,

When angry Pallas fpent her rage no more
　　On vanquifh'd Ilium, then in afhes laid,
But turn'd it on the barque that Ajax bore,*
　　Avenging thus her temple, and the maid.

When tofs'd upon the vaft Atlantic main
　　Your groaning fhip the fouthern gales fhall tear,
How will your failors fweat, and you complain
　　And meanly howl to Jove, that will not hear!

But if, at laft, upon fome winding fhore
　　A prey to hungry cormorants you lie,
A wanton goat to every ftormy power,†
　　And a fat lamb, in facrifice, fhall die.‡
　　　　　[Dec., 1782.]

---

* Ajax the younger, fon of Oileus, king of the Locrians.　He debauched
Caffandra in the temple of Pallas, which was the caufe of his misfortune, on his
return from the fiege of Troy.—Author's note.

† The Tempeſts were Goddeſſes amongft the Romans.—Author's note

‡ This is a clever imitation of Horace's Tenth Epode, "In Mævium poetam,"
the foul fatirift whom Virgil has commemorated with Bavius.　Freneau's rendering is quite fkilful, and fhows his fcholar's appreciation of the original.　The
reader may be pleafed to compare it with Theodore Martin's recent direct verfion
of the ode :—

　　　　　Fool fall the day, when from the bay
　　　　　　The veffel puts to fea,
　　　　　That carries Mævlus away,
　　　　　　That wretch unfavoury !

　　　　　Mind, Aufter, with appalling roar
　　　　　　That you her timbers fcourge ;
　　　　　Black Eurus, fnap each rope and oar
　　　　　　With the o'ertoppling furge !

Rife, Aquilo, as when the far
　High mountain-oaks ye rend ;
When ftern Orion fets, no ftar
　Its friendly luftre lend !

Seethe, ocean, as when Pallas turn'd
　Her wrath from blazing Troy
On impious Ajax' bark, and fpurn'd
　The victors in their joy !

I fee them now, your wretched crew,
　All toiling might and main,
And you, with blue and death-like hue,
　Imploring Jove in vain !

" Mercy, O Mercy ! fpare me, pray !"
　With craven moan ye call,
When founders in the Ionian bay
　Your bark before the fquall :

But if your corpfe a banquet forms
　For fea-birds, I 'll devote
Unto the powers that rule the ftorms
　A lamb and liquorifh goat.

A PICTURE OF THE TIMES; WITH OCCASIONAL REFLECTIONS.

STILL round the world triumphant Difcord flies,
  Still angry kings to bloody conteft rife;
Hofts bright with fteel, in dreadful order plac'd,
And fhips contending on the watery wafte;
Diftracting demons every breaft engage,
Unwearied nations glow with mutual rage;
Still to the charge the routed Briton turns,
The war ftill rages and the battle burns;
See, man with man in deadly combat join,
See, the black navy form the flaming line;
Death fmiles alike at battles loft or won—
Art does for him what Nature would have done.

  Can fcenes like thefe delight the human breaft?—
Who fees with joy humanity diftreft;
Such tragic fcenes fierce paffion might prolong,
But flighted Reafon fays, they muft be wrong.

  Curs'd be the day, how bright foe'er it fhin'd,
That firft made kings the mafters of mankind;
And curs'd the wretch who firft with regal pride
Their equal rights to equal men deny'd;
But curs'd, o'er all, who firft to flavery broke,

Submiſſive bow'd, and own'd a monarch's yoke :
Their ſervile ſouls his arrogance ador'd
And baſely own'd a brother for a lord ;
Hence wrath, and blood, and feuds, and wars began,
And man turn'd monſter to his fellow-man.

   Not ſo that age of innocence and eaſe
When men, yet ſocial, knew no ills like theſe ;
Then dormant yet, Ambition (half unknown)
No rival murder'd to poſſeſs a throne ;
No ſeas to guard, no empires to defend—
Of ſome ſmall tribe the father and the friend,
The hoary ſage beneath his ſylvan ſhade
Impos'd no laws but thoſe which reaſon made ;
On peace, not war ; on good, not ill, intent,
He judg'd his brethren by their own conſent ;
Untaught to ſpurn thoſe brethren to the duſt ;
In virtue firm, and obſtinately juſt,
For him no navies rov'd from ſhore to ſhore,
No ſlaves were doom'd to dig the glitt'ring ore ;
Remote from all the vain parade of ſtate,
No ſlaves in ſcarlet ſaunter'd at his gate,
Nor did his breaſt the angry paſſions tear,
He knew no murder, and he felt no fear.

   Was this the patriarch ſage ?—Then turn thine eyes
And view the contraſt that our age ſupplies ;
Touch'd from the life, we trace no ages fled,
We draw no curtain that conceals the dead ;
To diſtant Britain let thy view be caſt,
And ſay, the preſent far exceeds the paſt ;

Of all the plagues that e'er the world have curs'd,
Name George, the tyrant, and you name the worſt !
   What demon, hoſtile to the human kind,
Planted theſe fierce diſorders in the mind ?
All, urg'd alike, one phantom we purſue,
But what has war with human kind to do ?
In death's black ſhroud our bliſs can ne'er be found ;
'Tis madneſs aims the life-deſtroying wound,
Sends fleets and armies to theſe ravag'd ſhores,
Plots conſtant ruin, and no peace reſtores.
   O dire Ambition !—thee theſe horrors ſuit :
Loſt to the human, ſhe aſſumes the brute ;
She, proudly vain, or inſolently bold,
Her heart revenge, her eye intent on gold,
Sway'd by the madneſs of the preſent hour
Lays worlds in ruin for *extent of power ;*
That ſhining bait, which dropt in folly's way
Tempts the weak mind, and leads the heart aſtray,
   Thou Happineſs ! ſtill ſought but never found,
We, in a circle, chace thy ſhadow round ;
Meant all mankind in different forms to bleſs,
Which, yet poſſeſſing, we no more poſſeſs :
Thus far remov'd and painted on the eye
Smooth verdant fields ſeem blended with the ſky,
But where they both in fancied contact join
In vain we trace the viſionary line ;
Still, as we chace, the empty circle flies,
Emerge new mountains, or new oceans riſe.

   [1782.]

PRINCE WILLIAM HENRY'S SOLILOQUY.

[Occaſioned by the Public Rejoicings in Philadelphia for the birth of the Dauphin of France, ſon to Louis XVI.]

PEOPLE are mad, thus to adore the Dauphin—
   Heaven grant the brat may ſoon be in his coffin—
The honours here to this young Frenchman ſhown,
Of right, ſhould be Prince George's or my own;
And all thoſe wreathes, that bloom on Louis now,
Should hang, unfading, on my father's brow.

   To theſe far ſhores with longing hopes I came,
(By birth a Briton, not unknown to fame)
Pleaſures to ſhare that loyalty imparts,
Subdue the *rebels*, and regain their hearts.

   Weak, ſtupid expeɛtation—all is done !
Few are the prayers that riſe for George's ſon !
Nought through the waſte of theſe wide realms I trace,
But rage, contempt, and curſes on our race,
Hoſts, with their chiefs, by bold uſurpers won,
And not a bleſſing left for George's ſon !

   Here on theſe iſles* (my terrors not a few)
I walk attended by an exil'd crew :

---

* New York and the neighbouring iſlands.

Thefe from the firft have done their beft to pleafe,
But who would herd with fycophants like thefe?
This vagrant race, who their loft fhores bemoan,
Would bow to Satan, if he held our throne—
Rul'd by their fears—and what is meaner far,
Have worfhipp'd William only for his STAR!
To touch my hand their thronging thoufands ftrove,
And tir'd my patience with unceafing love—
In fame's fair annals told me I fhould live,
And, a FOURTH WILLIAM, to late times arrive;
Muft Digby's royal pupil walk the ftreets,
And fmile on every ruffian that he meets;
Or teach them, as he has done—he knows when—
That kings and princes are no more than men!

  Muft I, alas! difclofe, to our difgrace,
That Britain is too fmall for George's race?
Here in the weft, where all did once obey,
Three iflands only, now, confefs our fway;
And in the *eaft* we have not much to boaft,
For HYDER ALI drives us from that coaft :—
Yield, rebels, yield—or I muft go once more
Back to the white cliffs of my native fhore;
(Where, in procefs of time, fhall go Sir GUY,*
And where Sir HARRY has return'd to figh,
Whofe hands grew weak when things began to crofs,
Nor made one effort to retrieve our lofs)
Oatmeal and Scottifh kale-pots round me rife,

---

* Sir Guy Carleton, who had fucceeded Sir Henry Clinton at New York.

And Hanoverian turnips greet mine eyes ;—
Welch goats and naked rocks my bofom fwell,
And Teague ! dear Teague !—to thee I bid farewell—
    Curfe on the Dauphin and his friends, I fay,
He fteals our honours and our rights away.
DIGBY !—our anchors !—weigh them to the bow,
And eaftward through the wild waves let us plough :
Such dire refentments in my bofom burn,
That to thefe fhores I never will return,
'Till fruits and flowers on Zembla's coafts are known,
And feas congeal beneath the torrid zone !

    [1782.]
    14

BEELZEBUB'S REMONSTRANCE.

(On a late Rivingtonian *Apology* for LYING)

YOUR golden dreams, your flattering fchemes,
　　Alas! where are they fled, Sir?
Your plans derang'd, your profpects chang'd,
You now may go to bed, Sir.—

How could you thus, impell'd by fear,
Give up the hopes of many a year?—
Your fame retriev'd, and foaring high
In TRUTH's refemblance feem'd to fly:
But now you grow fo wondrous wife,
You turn, and own that all is—lies.

A fabric that from hell was rais'd,
On which aftonifh'd rebels gaz'd,
And which the world fhall ne'er forget,
No lefs than RIVINGTON's GAZETTE,
Demolifh'd at a fingle ftroke—
The angel Gabriel might provoke.

" That all was lies," might well be true,
But why muft this be told by you?

Great mafter of the fcheming head,
Where is thy wonted cunning fled?
It was a folly to engage
That truth henceforth fhould fill your page;
When you muft know, as well as I,
Your firft great object is—to LIE.

Your fortune was as good as made,
Great artift in the fibbing trade!
But now I fee, with grief and pain,
Your credit cannot rife again:
No more the favorite of my heart,
No more will I my gifts impart.

Yet fomething fhall you gain at laft
For lies contriv'd in feafons paft—
When prefling to the *narrow gate*
I'll fhow the portal mark'd by fate,
Where all mankind, as preachers fay,
Are apt to take the wider way,
And though the ROYAL Printer fwear,
Will bolt him in, and keep him there!

BEELZEBUB.

[1782.]

THE REFUGEES' PETITION TO SIR GUY CARLETON.

Humbly Sheweth,

THAT your Honour's petitioners, Tories by trade,
 From the firſt of the war have lent Britain their aid,
And done all they could, both in country and town,
In ſupport of the king and the rights of his crown ;
But, now to their grief and confuſion, they find
" The de'il may take them who are fartheſt behind."

In the rear of all raſcals they ſtill have been plac'd
And Rebels and Frenchmen full often have fac'd,
Have been in the midſt of diſtreſſes and doubt
Whene'er they came in or whene'er they went out ;
Have ſupported the king and defended *his church*,
And now, in the end, muſt be left in the lurch.

Though often, too often, his arms were diſgrac'd,
We ſtill were in hopes he would conquer at laſt,
And reſtore us again to our ſweethearts and wives,
The pride of our hearts and the joy of our lives—
But he promis'd *too far*, and we truſted *too much*,
And who could have look'd for a war with the Dutch ?

Our *board* broken up, and difcharg'd from our ftations,
Sir Guy ! it is cruel to cut off our *rations ;*
Of a project, like that, whoe'er was the mover,
It is, we muft tell you, a fneaking manœuvre ;
A plan to deftroy us—the bafeft of tricks
By means of ftarvation, a ftigma to fix.

If a peace be intended, as people furmife,
(Though we hope from our fouls thefe are nothing but lies)
Inform us at once what we have to expect,
Nor treat us, as ufual, with furly neglect ;
Or, elfe, while you Britons are fhipping your freights,
We'll go to the Rebels, and get our eftates.—

SIR GUY'S ANSWER.

WE have reafon to think there will foon be a peace,
      And that war with the Rebels will certainly ceafe ;
But, be that as it will, I would have you to know
That as matters are changing, we foon may change too ;
In fhort, I would fay, (fince I have it at heart)
Though the war fhould continue, yet *we* may depart.

Four offers in feafon I therefore propofe,
(As much as I can do in reafon, God knows)
In which, though there be not too plentiful carving,
There ftill is fufficient to keep you from ftarving.

And, firft, of the firft, it would mightily charm me
To fee you, my children, *enlift in the army,*

Or *enter the navy*, and get for your pay
A *farthing* an hour, which is *sixpence* per day—
There's Hector Clackmannan, and Arthur O'Gregor
And Donald M'Donald shall rule you with vigour :

If these do not suit you, then take your new plan,
Make your peace with the rebels (march off, to a man :)
There rank and distinction perhaps you may find
And rise into offices fit to your mind——
But if still you object—I advise you to take a
Farewell of New-York—and away to *Jamaica*.

RIVINGTON'S REFLECTIONS.*

I.

THE more I reflect, the more plain it appears,
 If I ſtay, I muſt ſtay at the riſque of my ears,
I have ſo be-pepper'd the foes of *our* throne,
Be-rebel'd, be-devil'd, and told them their own,
That if we give up to theſe rebels at laſt,
'Tis a chance if my ears will atone for the paſt.
 'Tis always the beſt to provide for the worſt—
So evacuation I'll mention the firſt:
If Carleton ſhould ſail for our dear native ſhore
(As Clinton, Cornwallis, and Howe did before)
And take off the ſoldiers that ſerve for our guard,
(A ſtep that the Tories would think rather hard)
Yet ſtill I ſurmiſe, for aught I can ſee,
No Congreſs or *Senates* would meddle with me.

* The firſt part of this poem was republiſhed in the *Royal Gazette*, at New
York, of December 14, 1782, with the following introduction:—"Mr. Rivington, having been applied to by many Gentlemen for a pleaſant publication reſpect-
ing himſelf, exhibited in the Philadelphia *Freeman's Journal*, of December 4th,
takes leave to copy it into this Day's Gazette, and aſſures the Author that a
Column ſhall at any time be moſt cheerfully reſerved to convey that Gentleman's
lively Lucubrations to the Public." The original publication of the "Reflections" had the motto from Virgil: *Incluſus pœnam expectat.*

For, what have I done, when we come to confider,
But fold my commodities to the beft bidder?
If I offer'd to lie for the fake of a poft,
Was I to be blam'd if the king offer'd moft?
The King's Royal Printer!—Five hundred a year!——
Between you and me, 'twas a handfome affair:
Who would not for that give matters a ftretch
And lie back and forward, and carry and fetch.
May have fome pretenfions to *honour* and *fame*:—
But what are they both but the found of a name,
Mere words to deceive us, as I have found long fince,
Live on them a week, and you'll find them but nonfenfe.

The late news from Charlefton my mind has perplext,
If that is abandon'd,—I know what goes next:
This city of YORK is a place of great note,
And that we fhould hold it I now give my vote;
But what are our votes againft Shelburne's decrees?
Thefe people at helm fteer us juft where they pleafe,
So often they've had us all hands on the brink,
They'll fteer us at laft to the devil, I think.
And though in the danger themfelves have a fhare,
It will do us fmall good that they alfo go there.

It is true that the Tories, their children, and wives
Have offer'd to ftay, at the rifque of their lives,
And gain to themfelves an immortal renown
By ALL turning foldiers, and keeping the town:
Whoe'er was the Tory that ftruck out the plan,
In my humble conceit, was a very good man:
But our words on this fubject need be very few—

Already I fee that it never will do :
For, fuppofe a few fhips fhould be left us by Britain
With Tories to man them, and other things fitting,
In truth we fhould be in a very fine box,
As well they might guard us with fhips on the ftocks,
And when I beheld them aboard and afloat,
I am fure I fhould think of *the bear in the boat.*

   On the faith of a Printer, things look very black—
And what fhall we do, alas ! and alack !
Shall we quit our young princes and full blooded peers,
And bow down to vifcounts and French chevaliers ?
Perhaps you may fay, " As the very laft fhift
" We'll go to New Scotland, and take the king's gift :"

   Good folks, do your will—but I vow and I fwear,
I'll be boil'd into foup before I'll live there :
Is it thus that our monarch his fubjects degrades ?—
Let him go and be damn'd with his axes and fpades :—
Of all the vile countries that ever were known
In the frigid, or torrid, or temperate zone,
(From accounts that I've had) there is not fuch another ;
It neither belongs to this world or the other :
A favour they think it to fend us there *gratis*,
To fing like the Jews at the river Euphrates,
And, after furmounting the rage of the billows,
Hang ourfelves up at laft with our harps on the willows :
Ere I fail for that fhore, may I take my laft nap—
Why, it gives me the palfy to look on its map !
And he that goes there (though I mean to be civil)
May fairly be faid to have gone to the Devil.

Shall I puſh for Old England, and whine at the throne ?
Alas ! they have JEMMIES enough of their own !
Beſides, ſuch a name I have got from my trade,
They would think I was lying, whatever I ſaid ;
Thus ſcheme as I will, or contrive as I may,
Continual difficulties riſe in the way :
In ſhort, if they let me remain in this realm,
What is it to Jemmy who ſtands at the helm ?
I'll petition the rebels (if York is forſaken)
For a place in their Zion which ne'er ſhall be ſhaken ;
I am ſure they'll be clever : it ſeems their whole ſtudy :
They hung not young ASGILL for old captain HUDDY,*

---

* Irving thus tells the ſtory of "Old Huddy :"—"A marauding New York
refugee, in 1782, had been captured by the Jerſey people, and killed in attempting to eſcape from thoſe who were conduċting him to Monmouth jail. His
partiſans in New York determined on a ſignal revenge. Captain Joſeph Huddy,
an ardent whig, who had been captured when bravely defending a block-houſe
in Monmouth County, and carried captive to New York, was now drawn forth
from priſon, conduċted into the Jerſeys by a party of refugees, headed by a Captain Lippencott, and hanged on the heights of Middletown, with a label affixed
to his breaſt, bearing the inſcription, ' Up goes Huddy for Philip White.' A
popular outcry for retaliation enſued. Waſhington felt the neceſſity for aċtion,
ſubmitted the matter to a board of officers, and, in accordance with their deter-
mination, demanded of Sir Henry Clinton, that Captain Lippencott or the officer
who had ordered the execution ſhould be given up. If this were not complied
with, wrote Waſhington, ' I ſhall hold myſelf juſtifiable in the eyes of God and
man for the meaſure to which I will reſort.' Clinton declined to ſurrender
Lippencott, but ſtated that he had ordered an inveſtigation into the circumſtances,
and would bring the perpetrator of the deed to trial. Waſhington, ſtrengthened
in his purpoſe by a reſolution of Congreſs, then ordered one of the Britiſh officers,
priſoners at Lancaſter, Pa., to be choſen by lot for retaliation. The lot fell upon
Captain Charles Aſgill of the Guards, an amiable youth of nineteen, and the ſon
of a wealthy baronet. His ſituation excited the ſympathy of his brother Britiſh
officers, and their indignation at Clinton in ſubjeċting him to the penalty by not
giving up the offender. One of their number, Captain Ludlow, was allowed to

And it muſt be a truth that admits no denying,
If they ſpare us for MURDER they'll ſpare us for LYING.

II.

FOLKS may think as they pleaſe, but to me it would ſeem,
That our great men at home have done nothing but dream:
Such trimming and twiſting and ſhifting about,
And ſome getting in, and others turn'd out;
And yet, with their bragging and looking ſo big,
All they did was to dance a theatrical jig.

Seven years now, and more, we have try'd every plan,
And are juſt as near conquering as when we began,
Great things were expected from Clinton and Howe,
But what have they done, or where are they now?
Sir Guy was ſent over to kick up a duſt,
Who already prepares to return in *diſguſt*—
The object deluſive we wiſh to attain

go to New York to repreſent the matter to Sir Guy Carleton, the new Commander-in-chief. Aſgill, meanwhile, was courteouſly treated, but firmly detained
to await the reſult. Lippencott was finally tried by a court-martial, and acquit-
ted, on the ground of having received verbal orders from Governor Franklin,
preſident of the board of aſſociated loyaliſts. The Britiſh commander reprobated
the death of Captain Huddy, and broke up the board. Under theſe circumſtances, Waſhington, reluctant to preſs the penalty involved, admitted Captain
Aſgill on parole, and requeſted the action of Congreſs to ſet him at liberty. Lady
Aſgill, the mother of the youth, anxious for her ſon's ſafety, had, in the mean
time, gained the ear of the French miniſter, the Count de Vergennes, with a ſup-
plication for his interceſſion, which, under the direction of the king and queen,
was made. Waſhington laid the Count's application before Congreſs, which
now took a favourable view of the matter, and Captain Aſgill, greatly to the
relief of Waſhington, was releaſed."—IRVING's *Life of Waſhington*, iv. 394-7.
SPARKS's *Life and Writings of Waſhington*, viii. 301, and sequel.

Has been in our reach, and may be fo again—
But fo oddly does heaven its bounties difpenfe,
And has granted our king fuch a fmall fhare of fenfe
That, let Fortune favour or fmile as fhe will,
We are doom'd to drive on, like a horfe in a mill,
And though we may feem to advance on our rout,
'Tis but to return to where we fat out.

From hence I infer (by way of improvement)
That nothing is got by this circular movement;
And I plainly perceive, from this fatal delay,
We are going to ruin the round-about way!
Some nations, like fhips, give up to the gale,
And are hurry'd afhore with a full flowing fail;
So Sweden fubmitted to abfolute power,
And freemen were chang'd to be flaves in an hour;
Thus THEODORE foon from his grandeur came down,
Forfaking his fubjects and Corfican crown;*

* Theodore Baron Newhoff, an enthufiaftic German military adventurer, who
was proclaimed king of Corfica in 1736. After paffing eight months on the
ifland, affuming various marks of royalty, he left his "kingdom" to folicit aid on
the Continent; but failed to carry his further fchemes of fovereignty into effect.
He ended his days in great poverty in London, where he was confined, not long
before his death, which happened in 1756, as a prifoner for debt. Horace Walpole took an imaginative intereft in his fortunes, and wrote a very pleafant paper
in the *World* (No. viii., Feb. 22, 1753) in his behalf, fuggefting a fubfcription
for his relief. A confiderable fum was, in confequence, collected for the fallen
monarch. "How muft I blufh for my countrymen," writes Walpole, "when I
mention a monarch! an unhappy monarch, now actually fuffered to languifh for
debt in one of the common prifons of this city! A monarch whofe courage
raifed him to a throne, not by a fucceffion of ambitious, bloody acts, but by the
voluntary election of an injured people, who had the common right of mankind
to freedom, and the uncommon refolution of determining to be free! This
prince is Theodore, king of Corfica! a man whofe claim to royalty is as indifpu-

But we—'tis our fate, without ally or friend,
To go to perdition, *cloſe haul'd* to the wind.
    The caſe is too plain, that if I ſtay here
I have ſomething to hope and ſomewhat to fear :
In regard to my carcaſe, I ſhould n't mind that—
I can ſay " I have liv'd," and have grown very fat ;
Have been in my day remarkably ſhifty,
And ſoon, very ſoon, will be verging on fifty.
'Tis time for the ſtate of the dead to prepare,
'Tis time to conſider how things will go there ;
Some few are admitted to Jupiter's hall,
But the dungeons* of Pluto are open to all—
The day is approaching as faſt as it can
When Jemmy ſhall be a mere moderate man,
Shall ſleep under ground both ſummer and winter,
The huſk of a man, and the ſhell of a printer,
And care not a farthing for George or his line,
What empires ſtart up, or what kingdoms decline.
    Our parſon laſt Sunday brought tears from my eyes,
When he told us of heaven, I thought of my lies—
To his flock he deſcrib'd it, and laid it before 'em,
(As if he had been in its *Sanctum Sanctorum*)
Recounted its beauties that never ſhall fade,
And quoted John Bunyan to prove what he ſaid ;

---

table as the moſt ancient titles to any monarchy can pretend to be; that is, the
choice of his ſubjects; the only kind of title allowed in the excellent Gothic
conſtitutions, from whence we derive our own; the ſame kind of title which
endears the preſent royal family to Engliſhmen; and the only kind of title againſt
which, perhaps, no objection can lie."
    * " But the kitchen of Pluto is open to all."—ED. 1795.

Debarr'd from the gate who the Truth fhould deny,
Or " whofoe'er loveth or maketh a lie."
   Thro' the courfe of my life it has ftill been my lot
In fpite of myfelf, to fay " things that are not,"
And therefore fufpect that upon my deceafe
Not a poet will leave me to flumber in peace,
But at leaft once a week be-fcribble the ftone
Where Jemmy, poor Jemmy, lies fleeping alone!
   Howe'er in the long run thefe matters may be,
If the fcripture is true, it has bad news for me—
And yet, when I come to examine the text,
And the learn'd annotations that POOLE has annex'd,
Throughout the black lift of the people that fin
I cannot once find that I'm mention'd therein;
Whoremongers, idolaters, all are left out,
And wizzards, and dogs (which is proper, no doubt)
But he who fays I'm there, miftakes or forgets—
It mentions no PRINTERS of ROYAL GAZETTES!
   In truth, I have need of a manfion of reft,
And *here* to remain might fuit me the beft—
PHILADELPHIA in fome things would anfwer as well,
(Some Tories are there, and my papers might fell)
But then I fhould live amongft wrangling and ftrife,
And be forc'd to fay *credo* the reft of my life:
For their fudden converfion I'm much at a lofs—
I am told that they bow to the wood of the crofs,
And worfhip the reliques tranfported from Rome,
St. Peter's toe-nails and St. Anthony's comb.—
If thus the true faith they no longer defend

I fcarcely can think where the madnefs will end—
If the greateft among them fubmit to the Pope,
What reafon have I for indulgence to hope?
If the Congrefs themfelves to the CHAPEL did pafs,*
Ye may fwear that poor JEMMY would have to fing mafs.

[*Dec.* 1782.]

* "On the 4th of November laft, the clergy and felectmen of Bofton paraded
"through the ftreets after a crucifix, and joined in a proceffion in praying for a
"departed foul out of Purgatory; and for this they gave the example of Con-
"grefs, and other American leaders, on a former occafion at Philadelphia, fome
"of whom, in the height of their zeal, even went fo far as to fprinkle themfelves
"with what they call *Holy water*."—*Royal Gazette*, of December 11. inft.

POLITICAL BIOGRAPHY.

GAINE'S LIFE.

City of New-York, *Jan.* 1, 1783.*

TO the *Senate*† of York, with all due fubmiffion,
Of honeſt HUGH GAINE‡ the humble *Petition ;*
An *Account of his Life* he will alſo prefix,
And ſome trifles that happened in *ſeventy-ſix ;*
He hopes that your honours will take no offence,
If he ſends you ſome groans of contrition from hence,
And, further, to prove that he's truly ſincere,
He wiſhes you all a *happy New Year.*

I.

AND, firſt, he informs, in his repreſentation,
 That he once was a printer of good reputation,
And dwelt in the ſtreet call'd Hanover Square,
(You'll know where it is, if you ever was there)

* The Britiſh army evacuated New York the November following.
† The Legiſlature of the State were at this time in ſeffion at Fishkill.
‡ Hugh Gaine, a native of Ireland, commenced the printing bufineſs in New
York in 1750. In 1752, he began the publication of the *New York Mercury,*
a weekly newfpaper, which appeared every Monday. It was fubfequently entitled *The New York Gazette and the Weekly Mercury.* In 1777, Gaine ſet up the
King's Arms in the title, in place of a figure of Mercury. "During the political
conteſt with Great Britain," ſays Thomas, in his "Hiſtory of Printing," "the
Mercury appeared rather as a neutral paper. Gaine ſeemed deſirous to ſide with
the ſucceſsful party ; but, not knowing which would eventually prevail, he ſeems
to have been unſtable in his politics. After the war commenced, he leaned to-

Next door to the dwelling of doctor Brownjohn,
(Who now to the drug-fhop of Pluto is gone)
But what do I fay—who e'er came to town,
And knew not Hugh Gaine at the *Bible* and *Crown*.
  Now, if I was ever fo given to lie,
My dear native country I wouldn't deny;
(I know you love Teagues) and I fhall not conceal
That I came from the kingdom where Phelim O'Neale
And other brave worthies ate butter and cheefe,
And walk'd in the clover-fields up to their knees:
Full early in youth, without bafket or burden,
With a ftaff in my hand, I pafs'd over Jordan,
(I remember my comrade was doctor Magraw,*
And many ftrange things on the waters we faw,
Sharks, dolphins, and fea-dogs, bonettas, and whales,
And birds at the tropic, with quills in their tails)
And came to your city and government feat,
And found it was true you had fomething to eat;
When thus I wrote home—" The country is good,

ward the country. When the Britifh army approached New York, in 1776,
Gaine removed to Newark in New Jerfey, and there, during a few weeks, publifhed the *Mercury*. Soon after the Britifh gained poffeffion of the city of New
York, he returned and printed, under the protection of the King's army; and,
like Rivington, devoted his paper to the royal caufe. Gaine publifhed the *Mercury* until peace was eftablifhed, and it was then difcontinued, after an exiftence of
about thirty-one years."

  In compliance with a petition to the State Legiflature, which is the fubject
of Freneau's humorous poem, Hugh Gaine was permitted, at the clofe of the
war, to remain in the city in peace. There he continued engaged in his bufinefs
as a bookfeller, in which he enjoyed the reputation of great probity, till his
death, in 1807, at the age of eighty-one.

  * A cynical and very eccentric phyfician.—*Author's note.*

  15

" They have plenty of victuals and plenty of wood :
" The people are kind, and, whate'er they may think,
" I fhall make it appear I can fwim where they'll fink ;
" And yet they're fo brifk, and fo full of good cheer,
" By my foul, I fufpect they have always new year,
" And therefore conceive *it is good to be here.*"

So faid, and fo acted—I put up a prefs,
And printed away with amazing fuccefs ;
Neglected my perfon, and look'd like a fright,
Was bother'd all day, and was bufy all night,
Saw money come in, as the papers went out,
While Parker and Weyman* were driving about,
And curfing, and fwearing, and chewing their cuds,
And wifhing Hugh Gaine and his prefs in the fuds :
Ned Weyman was printer, you know, to the king,
And thought he had got all the world in a ftring,
(Though riches not always attend on a throne)
So he fwore I had found the philofopher's ftone,
And call'd me a rogue, and a fon of a bitch,
Becaufe I knew better than him to get rich.

To malice like that 'twas in vain to reply—
You had known by his looks he was telling a lie.

Thus life ran away, fo fmooth and ferene—
Ah ! thefe were the happieft days I had feen !
But the faying of Jacob I've found to be true,
" The days of thy fervant are evil and few !"
The days that to me were joyous and glad,
Are nothing to thofe which are dreary and fad !

---

* New-York Printers, before the Revolution.

The feuds of the *Stamp-Act* foreboded foul weather,
And war and vexation all coming together:
Thofe days were the days of riots and mobs,
Tar, feathers, and tories, and troublefome jobs—
Priefts preaching up war for the *good of our fouls*,
And libels, and lying, and Liberty-Poles,
From which, when fome whimfical *colours* you wav'd,
We had nothing to do, but look up and be fav'd—
(You thought, by *refolving*, to terrify Britain—
Indeed, if you did, you were damnably *bitten*)
I knew it would bring an eternal reproach,
When I faw you a-burning Cadwallader's* coach;
I knew you would fuffer for what you had done,
When I faw you lampooning poor *Sawney* his fon,
And bringing him down to fo wretched a level,
As to ride him about in a cart with the devil.—

II.

WELL, as I predicted that matters would be—
To the ftamp-act fucceeded a tax upon *Tea:*
What cheft-fulls were fcatter'd, and trampled, and drown'd,
And yet the whole tax was but three pence *per* pound!
May the hammer of Death on my noddle defcend,
And Satan torment me to time without end,
If this was a reafon to fly into quarrels,
And feuds that have ruin'd *our* manners and morals;
A parfon himfelf might have fworn round the compafs,

---

* Lieutenant-Governor Cadwallader Colden.

That folks for a trifle fhould make fuch a *rumpus*,
Such a rout as to fet half the world in a rage,
Make France, Spain, and Holland with Britain engage,
While the Emperor, the Swede, the Rufs, and the Dane
All pity JOHN BULL—and run off with his gain.
    But this was the feafon that I muft lament—
I firft was a whig with an honeft intent ;
Not a Rebel among them talk'd louder or bolder,
With his fword by his fide, or his gun on his fhoulder ;
Yes, I was a whig, and a whig from my heart,
But ftill was unwilling with Britain to part—
I thought to oppofe her was foolifh and vain,
I thought fhe would turn and embrace us again,
And make us happy as happy could be,
By renewing the æra of mild SIXTY-THREE :
And yet, like a cruel undutiful fon,
Who evil returns for the good *to be done*,
Unmerited odium on Britain to throw,
I printed fome treafon for PHILIP FRENEAU,
Some damnable poems reflecting on GAGE,
The KING and his COUNCIL, and writ with fuch rage,
So full of invective, and loaded with fpleen,
So fneeringly fmart, and fo hellifhly keen,
That, at leaft in the judgment of half our wife men,
ALECTO herfelf put the nib to his pen.

III.

AT this time arofe a certain king SEARS,*
Who made it his ftudy to banifh our fears:
He was, without doubt, a perfon of merit,
Great knowledge, fome wit, and abundance of fpirit;
Could talk like a lawyer, and that without fee,
And threaten'd perdition to all that drank TEA.
Long fermons did he againft Scotchmen prepare,
And drank like a German, and drove away care.
Ah! don't you remember what a vigorous hand he put
To drag off the great guns, and plague captain *Vandeput?*
That *night* when the HERO (his patience worn out)
Put fire to his cannons and folks to the rout,
And drew up his fhip with *a fpring on her cable,*

---

* Isaac Sears, a popular leader of the "Sons of Liberty," in New York, at
the outbreak of the Revolution, and hence called "King Sears," from his authority and influence, was born in Connecticut, in 1729. He was a failor in early
life, and, when he appeared as an actor in public affairs in New York, in 1765,
as Chairman of the Committee of Correfpondence of the patriots of that period,
was a merchant and fea-captain of that city. In Auguft, 1775, he was engaged
with a number of citizens, among whom was Alexander Hamilton, then a ftudent of Columbia College, in removing the cannon from the Battery at the foot
of Broadway, while Captain Vandeput, in command of the *Afia* in the harbour,
fired upon the party and the city. The tavern of Samuel Fraunces, in Broad
ftreet, the building in which Wafhington took leave of his officers at the end of
the war, was, according to Freneau, ftruck by a fhot. In the edition of 1786,
the lines referring to this incident read :—

> " At firft we fuppos'd it was only a fham,
> Till he drove a round ball through the roof of black Sam ;"—

Fraunces being of a dark complexion. Sears, making a voyage to China as
fupercargo, after the war was ended, was, on his arrival at Canton, ftruck with a
fever, which there terminated his life in October, 1785.

And gave us a fecond confufion of *Babel*,
And (what was more *folid* than *fcurrilous language*)
Pour'd on us a tempeft of *round fhot* and *langrage ;*
Scarce a broadfide was ended 'till another began again--
By Jove! it was nothing but *Fire away Flannagan !**
Some thought him SALUTING his *Sally's* and *Nancy's*
'Till he drove a *round fhot* thro' the roof of *Sam Francis.*
The town by his flafhes was fairly enlighten'd,
The women mifcarry'd, the beaus were all frighten'd ;
For my part, I hid in a cellar (as fages
And Chriftians were wont in the *primitive ages :*
Thus the *Prophet of old that was rapt to the fky,*
Lay fnug in a cave 'till the tempeft went by,
But, as foon as the comforting fpirit had fpoke,
He rofe and came out with his myftical cloak) :
Yet I hardly could boaft of a moment of *reft,*
The dogs were a-howling, the town was diftreft !—
But our terrors foon vanifh'd, for fuddenly SEARS
Renew'd our loft courage and dry'd up our tears.

Our memories, indeed, muft have ftrangely decay'd
If we cannot remember what SPEECHES he made,
What handfome *harangues* upon every occafion,
How he laugh'd at the whim of a *Britifh Invafion !*

"P—x take 'em, (faid he) do ye think they will come ?
"If they fhou'd—we have only to beat on *our drum,*
"And *run up the flag of American freedom,*
"And people will *mufter* by millions to *bleed 'em !*
"What *freeman* need value fuch blackguards as thefe !

* A cant phrafe among privateerfmen.—*Author's note.*

" Let us fink in our channel fome *Chevaux de frife*—
" And then let 'em come—and we'll fhow 'em fair play—
" But they are not madmen—I tell you—not they !"

IV.

FROM this very day 'till the *Britifh* came in,
We liv'd, I may fay, in the *Defert of Sin*;—
Such beating, and bruifing, and *fcratching, and tearing;*
Such kicking, and cuffing, and *curfing, and.fwearing !*——
But when *they* advanc'd with *their numerous* fleet,
And WASHINGTON made his *noƐturnal retreat,**
(And which *they permitted,* I fay, to *their* fhame,
Or else *your* NEW EMPIRE had been but a name)
We townfmen, like women, of *Britons* in *dread,*
Miftrufted *their* meaning, and foolifhly fled ;
Like the *reft* of the dunces I mounted my fteed,
And.gallop'd away with *incredible* fpeed,
To NEWARK I haftened—but *trouble* and *care*
Got up on the crupper and follow'd me there!
There I fcarcely got fuel to keep myfelf warm,
And fcarcely found fpirits to *weather the ftorm ;*
And was quickly convinc'd I had little to do,
(The *Whigs* were in arms, and my *readers* were few)
So, after remaining one cold winter feafon,
And ftuffing my *papers* with *fomething like treafon,*
And meeting misfortunes and endlefs difafters,
And forc'd to fubmit to a hundred *new mafters,*
I thought it more prudent to hold to the *one*—

* From Long Ifland.

And (after repenting of what I had done,
And curfing my folly and idle purfuits)
Return'd to the city, and hung up my boots.

V.

AS matters have gone, it was plainly a blunder,
But *then* I expected the Whigs muft knock under,
And I always adhere to the fword that is longeft,
And ftick to the party that's like to be ftrongeft :
That you have fucceeded is merely a chance,
I never once dreamt of the conduct of France !—
If alliance with her you were promis'd—at leaft
You ought to have fhow'd me your STAR *in the eaft*,
Not let me go off uninform'd as a beaft.
When your army I faw without ftockings or fhoes,
Or victuals—or *money*, to pay them their dues,
(Excepting your wretched Congreffional *paper*,   .
That ftunk in my nofe like the fnuff of a taper,
A cart load of which for a dram might be fpent all,
That damnable bubble, the *old Continental*
That *took* people *in* at this wonderful crifis,
With its *mottoes* and *emblems*, and cunning *devices ;*
Which, bad as it was, you were forc'd to admire,
And which was, in fact, the *pillar of fire*,
To which you directed your wandering nofes,
Like the Jews in the defert conducted by MOSES)
When I faw them attended with *famine* and *fear*,
Diftrefs in their front, and *Howe* in their rear ;
When I faw them for debt inceffantly dunn'd,

Nor a fhilling to pay them laid up in your fund ;
Your ploughs at a ftand, and your fhips run afhore—
When this was apparent (and need I fay more ?)
I *handled* my cane, and I *look'd* at my hat,
And cry'd—" God have mercy on armies like that !"
I took up my bottle, difdaining to ftay,
And faid—" Here's a health to the *Vicar* of *Bray*,"
And cock'd up my beaver, and—ftrutted away.

VI.

ASHAM'D of my conduct, I fneak'd into town,
(Six hours and a quarter the fun had been down)
It was, I remember, a cold frofty night,
And the ftars in the firmament glitter'd as bright
As if (to affume a poetical ftile)
Old Vulcan had give them a rub with his file.
'Till this curfed night, I can honeftly fay,
I ne'er before dreaded the dawn of the day ;
Not a wolf or a fox that is caught in a trap
E'er was fo afham'd of his nightly mifhap—
I couldn't help thinking what ills might befal me,
What rebels and rafcals the Britifh would call me,
And how I might fuffer in credit and purfe,
If not in my perfon, which ftill had been worfe :
At length I refolv'd (as was surely my duty)
To go for advice to parfon AUCHMUTY :*

* The Rev. Samuel Auchmuty, a graduate of Harvard College of the clafs of
1742, fucceeded the Rev. Dr. Barclay as Rector of Trinity Church, New York,
in 1764. His fympathies with the old monarchy were decided. Sabine, in his

(The parfon, who now I hope is in glory,
Was then upon earth, and a terrible tory,
Not COOPER himfelf, of ideas perplext,
So nicely could handle and torture a text,
When bloated with lies, thro' his trumpet he founded
The damnable fin of oppofing a crown'd head)
Like a penitent finner, and dreading my fate,
In the grey of the morning I knock'd at his gate ;
(No doubt he was vex'd that I rous'd him fo foon,
For his worfhip was moftly in blankets till noon.)
    At length he approach'd in his *veftments of black*—
(Alas, my poor heart ! it was then on the rack,
Like a man in an ague or one to be *try'd*;
I fhook—and recanted, and flobber'd, and figh'd)
His gown, of it felf, was amazingly big,
Befides, he had on his canonical wig,

"Loyalifts of the Revolution," cites a portion of a letter by him to Captain Mon-trefor, chief engineer of Gage's army at Bofton, dated New York, April, 1775, in which he fays : "We have lately been plagued with a rafcally Whig mob here, but they have effected nothing, only Sears, the king, was refcued at the jail-door." Auchmuty died in New York, in 1777.

Myles Cooper, alluded to in the fame paragraph, was the loyalift Prefident of King's College, New York, who, rendering himfelf obnoxious to the citizens by his advocacy of the royal caufe, was driven from the city in a popular commotion on the night of the 10th of May, 1775. He took refuge on board of a fhip-of-war in the harbor, in which he returned to England. The poet Trumbull, in his "M'Fingal," includes both thefe worthies in his enumeration of the "High Church Clergy" who were on the fide of the king :—

> " What warnings had ye of your duty
> From our old Rev'rend Sam. Auchmuty !
> *   *   *   *   *
> Have not our Cooper and our Seabury
> Sung hymns, like Barak and old Deborah !"

And frown'd at a diftance; but when he came near
Look'd pleafant and faid—" *What, Hugh, are you here!*

"*Your heart, I am certain, is horribly harden'd,*
"*But if you confefs—your fin will be pardon'd;*
"*In fpite of my preachments, and all I could fay,*
"*Like the prodigal fon, you wander'd away,*
"*Now tell me, dear penitent, which is the beft,*
"*To be with the rebels, purfu'd and diftreft,*
"*Devoid of all comfort, all hopes of relief,*
"*Or elfe to be here, and partake the king's beef?*

"*More people refemble the fnake than the dove,*
"*And more are converted by terror than love:*
"*Like a fheep on the mountains, or rather a fwine,*
"*You wander'd away from the ninety and nine;*
"*Awhile at the offers of mercy you fpurn'd,*
"*But your error you faw, and at length have return'd;*
"*Our mafter will therefore confider your cafe,*
"*And reftore you again to favour and grace,*
"*Great light fhall arife from utter confufion,*
"*And rebels fhall live to lament their delufion.*"

"Ah, rebels! (faid I) they are rebels *indeed*—
"Chaftifement, I hope, by the king is decreed:
"They have hung up *his fubjects* with bed-cords and halters,
"And banifh'd his *Prophets*, and thrown down his *altars.*
"And I—even I—while I ventur'd to ftay,
"They fought for my life—to take it away!
"I therefore propofe to come under your wing,
"A foe to REBELLION—a flave to the KING."

VII.

SUCH folemn confeffion, in fcriptural ftyle,
Work'd out my falvation, at leaft for a while ;
The parfon pronounc'd me deferving of grace,
And fo *they* reftor'd me to *Printing* and *Place.*

VIII.

BUT days, fuch as thefe, were too happy to laft ;
The fand of felicity fettled too faft !
When I fwore and protefted I honour'd the throne
The leaft they could do was to let me alone :
Though *George* I compar'd to an angel above,
They wanted fome folider proofs of my love ;
And fo they oblig'd me each morning to come
And turn in the ranks at the beat of the drum,
While often, too often (I tell it with pain)
They menac'd my head with a hickory cane,
While others, my betters, as much were oppreft—
But fhame and confufion fhall cover the reft.
  You, doubtlefs, will think I am dealing in fable
When I tell you I *guard an officer's ftable*—
With ufage like this my feelings are ftung ;
The next thing will be, I muft heave out the dung !
Six hours in the day is duty too hard,
And RIVINGTON fneers whene'er I mount guard,
And laughs till his fides are ready to fplit
With his jefts, and his fatires, and fayings of wit :
Becaufe he's excus'd, on account of his poft,

He cannot go by without making his boaſt,
As if I was all that is ſervile and mean—
But fortune, perhaps, may alter the ſcene,
And give him his turn to ſtand in the ſtreet,
Burnt Brandy ſupporting his *radical heat*—
But what for the king or the cauſe has he done
That we muſt be toiling while he can look on?
Great conqueſts he gave them *on paper*--'tis true,
When Howe was *retreating*, he made him *purſue:*
Alack! its too plain that Britons muſt fall—
When, *loaded with laurels*—they go to the wall.

From hence you may gueſs I do nothing but grieve,
And where we are going I cannot conceive—
The wiſeſt among us a CHANGE are expecting,
It is not for nothing, theſe ſhips are collecting;
It is not for nothing, that MATHEWS, the mayor,
And legions of Tories, for ſailing prepare;
It is not for nothing, that JOHN COGHILL KNAP
Is filing his papers, and plugging his tap;
See SKINNER* himſelf, the fighting attorney,
Is boiling potatoes to ſerve a long journey;
But where they are going, or meaning to travel
Would puzzle John Fauſtus, himſelf, to unravel;—
Perhaps to Penobſcot, to ſtarve in the barrens,

---

* Cortlandt Skinner, the laſt royal Attorney-General of New Jerſey, was author-
ized, early in the war, to raiſe a corps of Loyaliſts. Three battalions were organ-
ized and officered, and called the New Jerſey volunteers; but the enliſtments
were little over a thouſand men. He continued in command of the corps, with
the rank of Brigadier-General. After the war he returned to England.—SABINE's
Loyaliſts, ii. 306.

Perhaps to St. John's, in the gulph of St. Lawrence ;
Perhaps to New Scotland, to perifh with cold,
Perhaps to Jamaica, like flaves to be fold ;
Where, fcorch'd by the fummer, all nature repines,
Where Phœbus, great Phœbus, too glaringly fhines,
And fierce from the zenith diverging his ray
Diftreffes the ifle with a torrent of day.
   Since matters are thus, with proper fubmiffion
Permit me to offer my humble PETITION ;
(Though the *form* is uncommon, and lawyers may fneer,
With truth I can tell you, the fcribe is fincere) :

IX.

That, fince it is plain we are going away,
You will suffer *Hugh Gaine* unmolefted to ftay,
His fand is near run (life itfelf is a fpan)
So leave him to manage the beft that he can :
Whoe'er are his mafters, or monarchs, or regents,
For the future he's ready to fwear them allegiance ;
The CROWN he will promife to hold in difgrace :
The BIBLE—allow him to ftick in its place,
'Till THAT, in due feafon, you wifh to put down,
And bid him keep fhop at the fign of the CROWN.
If the Turk with his turban fhould fet up at laft here
While he gives him protection, he'll own him his mafter,
And yield due obedience (when Britain is gone)
Though rul'd by the fceptre of PRESBYTER JOHN.
   My prefs, that has call'd you (as tyranny drove her)
Rogues, rebels, and rafcals, a thoufand times over,

Shall be at your fervice by day and by night,
To publifh whate'er you think proper to write;
Thofe *types* which have rais'd George the third to a level
With angels—fhall prove him as black as the devil,
To HIM that contriv'd him, a fhame and difgrace,
Nor bleft with one virtue to honour his race!

Who knows but, in time, I may rife to be great,
And have the good fortune to *manage* a STATE?
Great noife among people great changes denotes,
And I fhall have money to purchafe their votes—
The time is approaching, I'll venture to fay,
When folks worfe than me will come into play,
When your double fac'd people fhall give themfelves airs,
And AIM to take hold of the helm of affairs,
While the honeft bold SOLDIER, that fought your renown,
Like a dog in the dirt, fhall be crufh'd and held down.

Of honours and profits allow me a fhare!
I frequently dream of a prefident's chair!
And vifions full often intrude on my brain,
That for me to interpret, would rather be vain.

Bleft feafons advance, when Britons fhall find
That they can be happy, and you can be kind,
When *Rebels* no longer at Traitors fhall fpurn,
When ARNOLD himfelf fhall in triumph return!

X.

But my *paper* informs me it's time to conclude;
I fear my Addrefs has been rather too rude—

If it has—for my boldnefs your pardon I pray,
And further, at prefent, prefume not to fay,
Except that (for form's fake) in *hafte* I remain
Your humble Petitioner—honeft—HUGH GAINE.

ON THE DEATH OF COLONEL LAURENS.*

SINCE on her plains this generous chief expir'd,
  Whom fages honour'd, and whom France admir'd;
Does Fame no ftatues to his memory raife,
Nor fwells one column to record his praife
Where her palmetto fhades the adjacent deeps,
Affection fighs, and Carolina weeps!

  Thou, who fhalt ftray where death this chief confines,
Revere the patriot, fubject of thefe lines:
Not from the duft the mufe tranfcribes his name,
And more than marble fhall declare his fame
Where fcenes more glorious his great foul engage,
Confeft thrice worthy in that clofing page

---

*   * Lieutenant-Colonel John Laurens was the fon of the eminent minifter, Henry Laurens, of South Carolina. He was educated in England; had ferved as aide to Wafhington, and diftinguifhed himfelf in the Maryland, Pennfylvania, and Rhode Ifland campaigns. He fubfequently ferved with General Moultrie in South Carolina. In 1780, he was employed on a miffion to the French Court for a loan and fupplies, in which he was fuccefsful. On his return, he gained frefh laurels at the fiege of Yorktown. Returning to his native South Carolina, he fell gallantly, at the early age of twenty-feven, in an engagement with a detachment of the Britifh garrifon from Charlefton, at the River Combahee, in Auguft, 1782. Alexander Hamilton was his intimate friend, and Wafhington greatly admired him.

16

When conquering Time to dark oblivion calls,
The marble totters, and the column falls.

    LAURENS! thy tomb while kindred hands adorn,
Let northern mufes, too, infcribe your urn.—
Of all, whofe names on death's black lift appear,
No chief, that perifh'd, claim'd more grief fincere,
Not one, Columbia, that thy bofom bore,
More tears commanded, or deferv'd them more!—
Grief at his tomb fhall heave the unwearied figh,
And honour lift the mantle to her eye :
Fame thro' the world his patriot name fhall fpread,
By heroes envied and by monarchs read :
Juft, generous, brave—to each true heart allied :
The Briton's terror, and his country's pride ;
For him the tears of war-worn foldiers ran,
The friend of freedom, and the friend of man.

    Then what is death, compar'd with fuch a tomb,
Where honour fades not, and fair virtues bloom,
When filent grief on every face appears,
The tender tribute of a nation's tears ;
Ah! what is death, when deeds like his thus claim
The brave man's homage, and immortal fame!

ON THE DEPARTURE OF THE BRITISH FROM CHARLESTON.

(*December* 14, 1782.)

HIS triumphs of a moment done;
　　His race of defolation run,
The Briton, yielding to his fears,
To other fhores with forrow fteers:

To other fhores—and coarfer climes
He goes, reflecting on his crimes,
His broken oaths, a murder'd HAYNE,
And blood of thoufands, fpilt in vain.

To *Cooper's* ftream, advancing flow,
Afhley no longer tells his woe,
No longer mourns his limpid flood
Difcolour'd deep with human blood.

Lo! where thofe focial ftreams combine
Again the friends of Freedom join;
And, while they ftray where once they bled,
Rejoice to find their tyrants fled.

Since memory paints that difmal day
When Britifh fquadrons held the fway,
And circling clofe on every fide,
By fea and land retreat deny'd—

Shall fhe recall that mournful fcene,
And not the virtues of a GREENE,
Who great in war—in danger try'd,
Has won the day, and crufh'd their pride.

Through barren waftes and ravag'd lands
He led his bold undaunted bands,
Through fickly climes his ftandard bore
Where never army march'd before :

By fortitude, with patience join'd,
(The virtues of a noble mind)
He fpread, where'er our wars are known,
His country's honour and his own.

Like Hercules, his generous plan
Was to redrefs the wrongs of men ;
Like him, accuftom'd to fubdue,
He freed a world from *monfters* too.

Through every want and every ill
We faw him perfevering ftill,
Through Autumn's damps and Summer's heat,
'Till his great purpofe was complete.

Like the bold eagle, from the fkies
That ftoops, to feize his trembling prize,
He darted on the flaves of kings
At Camden heights and Eutaw Springs.

Ah! had our friends that led the fray
Surviv'd the ruins of that day,
We fhould not damp our joy with pain,
Nor, fympathifing, now complain.

Strange! that of thofe who nobly dare
Death always claims fo large a fhare,
That thofe of virtue moft refin'd
Are fooneft to the grave confign'd!——

But fame is theirs—and future days
On pillar'd brafs fhall tell their praife;
Shall tell—when cold neglect is dead—
" *Thefe* for their country fought and bled."

ON THE BRITISH KING'S SPEECH,

RECOMMENDING PEACE WITH THE AMERICAN STATES.

GROWN fick of war, and war's alarms,
   Good GEORGE has chang'd his note at laft—
Conqueft and Death have loft their charms;
   He and his nation ftand aghaft
To fee what horrid lengths they've gone,
And what a brink they ftand upon.

Old BUTE and NORTH! twin fons of hell,
   If you advis'd him to retreat
Before our vanquifh'd thoufands fell
   Proftrate, fubmiffive at his feet;
Awake once more his latent flame
And bid us yield you all you CLAIM.

The Macedonian wept and figh'd
   Becaufe no other world was found
Where he might glut his rage and pride,
   And by its ruin be renown'd;
The *world* that *Sawny* wifh'd to view
George fairly had—and loft it too!

Let jarring powers make war or peace,
    Monfter !—no peace fhall greet thy breaft :
Our murder'd friends fhall never ceafe
    To hover round and break your reft !
The Furies fhall your bofom tear,
Remorfe, diftraction, and defpair
And hell, with all its fiends, be there !

Curs'd be the fhip that e'er fets fail
    Hence, freighted for thy odious fhore ;
May tempefts o'er her ftrength prevail,
    Deftruction round her roar !
May Nature all her *aids* deny,
    The fun refufe his light,
The needle from its object fly,
    No ftar appear by night ;
'Till the bafe pilot, confcious of his crime,
Directs the prow to fome more CHRISTIAN clime.

Genius ! that firft our race defign'd,
    To other kings impart
The finer feelings of the mind,
    The virtues of the heart ;
Whene'er the honours of a throne
    Fall to the bloody and the bafe,
Like Britain's monfter, pull them down,
    Like his, be their difgrace !

Hibernia, feize each native right !
    Neptune, exclude him from the main ;

Like *her* that funk with all her freight,
The *Royal George*, take all his fleet,
 And never let them rife again :
Confine him to his gloomy ifle,
 Let Scotland rule her half,
Spare him to curfe his fate awhile,
 And WHITEHEAD,* thou, to write his Epitaph.—
  [1783.]

---

* At that time Poet-Laureat to the king of Great Britain—author of the exe
crable Birth-day Odes.—*Author's note.*

MANHATTAN CITY.

A PICTURE.

FAIR miſtreſs of a warlike STATE,
  What crime of thine deſerves this fate?
While other ports to FREEDOM riſe,
In thee that flame of honour dies.

With wars and horrors overſpread,
Seven years, and more, we fought and bled:
Seiz'd Britiſh hoſts and Heſſian bands,
And all—to leave thee in their hands.

While Britiſh tribes forſake our plains,
In you, a ghaſtly herd remains:
Muſt vipers to your halls repair;
Muſt poiſon taint that pureſt air?

Ah! what a ſcene torments the eye;
In thee what putrid monſters lie!
What dirt, and mud, and mouldering walls,
Burnt domes, dead dogs, and funerals!

Thoſe graſſy banks, where oft I ſtood,
And fondly view'd the paſſing flood;

There owls obfcene, that day-light fhun,
Pollute the waters, as they run.

Thus in the eaft—once Afia's queen—
PALMYRA's tottering towers are feen ;
While through her ftreets the ferpent feeds,
Thus fhe puts on her mourning weeds !

Lo ! SKINNER there for *Scotia* hails
The fweepings of Cefarean jails :
While, to receive the odious freight,
A thoufand fable *tranfports* wait.

Had he been born in days of old
When men with gods their 'fquires enroll'd,
Hermes had claim'd his aid above,
Arch-quibbler in the courts of Jove.

O chief, that wrangled at the bar—
Grown old in *lefs fuccefsful war ;*
What crowds of mifcreants round you ftand,
What vagrants bow to thy command !

Long, much too long in YORK refide
A race, that mortifies our pride—
A race, that all mankind defames,
And NOVA-SCOTIA only claims.
          [1783.]

A NEW-YORK TORY'S EPISTLE TO ONE OF HIS FRIENDS IN PENNSYLVANIA.

WRITTEN PREVIOUS TO HIS DEPARTURE FOR NOVA SCOTIA.

DARK glooms the day that fees me leave this fhore,
    To which fate whifpers I muft come no more :
From civil broils what dire difafters flow—
Thofe broils condemn me to a land of woe
Where barren pine trees fhade the dreary fteep,
Frown o'er the foil or murmur to the deep,
Where fullen fogs their heavy wings expand,
And nine months winter chills the difmal land !
Could no kind ftars have mark'd a different way,
Stars, that prefided on my natal day ?—
Why is not man endued with power to know
The ends and meanings of events below !
Why did not heaven (all other fenfe deny'd)
Teach me to take the true-born BUCKSKIN fide,
Show me the balance of the wavering fates
And fortune fmiling on thefe new-born STATES !
    Friend of my heart !—my refuge and relief,
Who help'd me on through feven long years of grief,
Whofe better genius taught you to remain

In the foft quiet of your rural reign,
Who ftill defpis'd the *Rebels* and their caufe,
And, while you paid the taxes, damn'd their laws,
And wifely ftood fpectator of the fray
Nor trufted GEORGE, whate'er he chofe to fay;
Thrice happy thou, who wore a double face,
And as the balance turn'd, could *each* embrace;
Too happy JANUS! had I fhar'd thy art,
To fpeak a language foreign to my heart,
And ftoop'd from pomp and dreams of regal ftate
To court the friendfhip of the *men* I hate,
Thefe ftrains of woe had not been penn'd to-day,
Nor I to foreign climes been forc'd away:
　　Ah! GEORGE—that name provokes my keeneft rage:
Did he not fwear, and promife, and engage
His loyal fons to nurture and defend,
To be their god, their father, and their friend—
Yet bafely quits us on a hoftile coaft
And leaves us wretched, where we need him moft.
His was the part to promife and deceive,
By him we wander and by him we grieve;
Since the firft day, that thefe diffentions grew
When Gage to Bofton brought his blackguard crew,
Amus'd with conquefts, honours, riches, fame,
Pofts, titles, earldoms—and a deathlefs name,
From place to place we urge our vagrant flight
To follow ftill thefe vapours of the night,
From town to town have run our various race,
And acted all that's mean, and all that's bafe—

Yes—from that day until this hour we roam,
Vagrants forever from our native home!
 And yet, perhaps, fate fees the golden hour
When happier hands fhall crufh rebellious power,
When hoftile tribes their plighted faith fhall own
And fwear fubjection to the Britifh throne,
When *George the fourth* fhall their petitions fpurn,
And banifh'd thoufands to their fields return.
 From dreams of conqueft, worlds, and empires won,
Britain awaking, mourns her fetting fun,
No rays of joy her evening hour illume,
'Tis one fad chaos, one unmingled gloom!
Too foon fhe finks unheeded to the grave,
No eye to pity, and no hand to fave:
What are her crimes that fhe alone muft bend?
Where are her hofts to conquer and defend—
Muft fhe alone with thefe new regions part,
Thefe realms that lay the neareft to her heart,
But foar'd at once to independent power,
Not funk, like Scotland, in the trying hour?—-
See, flothful Spaniards golden empires keep,
And rule vaft realms beyond the Atlantic deep;
Must *we* alone furrender half *our* reign,
And they their empires and their worlds retain?—
Britannia rife—fend JOHNSTONE to PERU,
Seize thy bold thunders and the war renew,
Conqueft or *ruin*—one muft be thy doom,
Strike—and fecure a triumph or a tomb!
 But we, fad outcafts from our native reign,

Driven from thefe fhores, a poor deluded train,
In diftant wilds, conducted by defpair,
Seek, vainly feek, a hiding place from care!
Even now yon' tribes, the foremoft of the band,
Crowd to the fhips and cover all the ftrand ;
Forc'd from their friends, their country, and their GOD,
I fee the unhappy mifcreants leave the fod!
Matrons and men walk forrowing fide by fide,
And virgin grief, and poverty, and pride ;
All, all with aching hearts prepare to fail,
And late repentance, that has no avail!
While yet I ftand on this forbidden ground
I hear the death-bell of deftruction found,
And threatening hofts, with vengeance on their brow
Cry " where are Britain's bafe adherents now ?"
Thefe, hot for vengeance, by refentment led,
Blame on our hearts the failings of the head ;
To us no peace, no favours they extend,
Their rage no bounds, their hatred knows no end ;
In one firm league I fee them all combin'd,
We, like the damn'd, can no forgivenefs find—
As foon might Satan from perdition rife,
And the loft angels gain their vanifh'd fkies,
As malice ceafe in their dark fouls to burn,
Or we, once fled, be fuffer'd to return.

  Curs'd be the UNION that was form'd with France,
I fee their *lillies*, and the *ftars*, advance!
Did they not turn our triumphs to retreats,
And prove our CONQUESTS nothing but DEFEATS ?—

My heart mifgives me, as their chiefs draw near,
I feel the influence of all-potent fear :
Henceforth muft I, abandon'd and diftreft,
Knock at the door of pride, a beggar gueft,
And learn from years of mifery and pain
Not to oppofe fair Freedom's caufe again !—
    One truth is clear from Nature, conftant ftill,
Kings hold not worlds, or empires, at their will :—
Nor *rebels* they, who native *freedom* claim,
Conqueft alone can ratify the name—
But great the tafk, refiftance to controul
When genuine VIRTUE fires the ftubborn foul ;
The warlike beaft, in Lybian deferts plac'd
To reign the mafter of the fun-burnt wafte,
Not tamely yields to wear a fervile chain :
Force may attempt it, and attempt in vain——
Nervous and bold, by native valour led :
His prowefs ftrikes the proud invader dead,
By force nor fraud from Freedom's charms beguil'd,
He reigns fecure the monarch of the wild.

                                    TANTALUS.

    [*May,* 1783.]

RIVINGTON'S CONFESSIONS.

ADDRESSED TO THE WHIGS OF NEW-YORK.

I.

LONG life and low spirits were never my choice,
   As long as I live I intend to rejoice ;
When life is worn out, and no wine's to be had,
'Tis time enough then to be serious and sad.

'Tis time enough then to reflect and repent
When our liquor is gone, and our money is spent,
But I cannot endure what is practis'd by some
This anticipating of mischiefs to come ;

A debt must be paid, I am sorry to say,
Alike, in their turns, by the grave and the gay.
And due to a despot that none can deceive
Who grants us no respite and signs no reprieve.

Thrice happy is he that from care can retreat,
And its plagues and vexations put under his feet ;
Blow the storm as it may, he is always in trim,
And the sun's in the zenith forever to him.

Since the world then, in earneſt, is nothing but care,
(And the world will allow I have alſo my ſhare)
Yet, toſs'd as I am in the ſtormy expanſe,
The beſt way, I find, is to leave it to chance.

Look round, if you pleaſe, and ſurvey the wide ball
And CHANCE, you will find, has direction of all :
'Twas owing to *chance* that I firſt ſaw the light,
And chance may deſtroy me before it is night !

'Twas a chance, a mere chance, that your arms gain'd the day,
'Twas a chance that the Britons ſo ſoon went away,
To chance by their leaders the nation is caſt
And chance to perdition will ſend them at laſt.

Now becauſe I remain when the puppies are gone
You would willingly ſee me hang'd, quarter'd, and drawn,
Though I think I have logic ſufficient to prove
That the *chance* of my ſtay—is a proof of my love.

For deeds of deſtruction ſome hundreds are ripe,
But the worſt of my foes are your lads of the type :
Becauſe they have nothing to put on their ſhelves
They are ſtriving to make me as poor as themſelves.

There's LOUDON, and KOLLOCK, thoſe ſtrong bulls of Baſhan,
Are ſtriving to *hook* me away from my ſtation,
And HOLT, all at once, is as wonderful great
As if none but himſelf was to print for the STATE.

17

Ye all are convinc'd I'd a right to expect
That a finner returning you would not reject—
Quite fick of the fcarlet and flaves of the throne,
'Tis now at your option to make me your own.

Suppofe I had gone with the Tories and rabble,
To ftarve or be drown'd on the fhoals of cape *Sable*,
I had fuffer'd, 'tis true—but I'll have you to know,
You nothing had gain'd by my trouble and woe.

You fay that with grief and dejection of heart
I pack'd up my awls, with a view to depart,
That my fhelves were difmantled, my cellars unftor'd,
My boxes afloat, and my hampers on board:

And hence you infer (I am fure without reafon)
That a right you poffefs to entangle my weazon—
Yet your barns I ne'er burnt, nor your blood have I fpilt,
And my *terror* alone was no proof of my guilt.

The charge may be true—for I found it in vain
To lean on a ftaff that was broken in twain,
And ere I had gone at Port Rofeway to fix,
I had chofe to fell drams on the fouth fide of Styx

I confefs, that, with fhame and contrition oppreft,
I fign'd an agreement to go with the reft,
But ere they weigh'd anchor to fail their laft trip,
I faw they were vermin, and gave them the flip:

Now, why you ſhould call me the worſt man alive,
On the word of a convert, I cannot contrive,
Though turn'd a plain honeſt republican, ſtill
You own me no proſelyte, do what I will.

My paper is alter'd—good people, don't fret ;
I call it no longer the ROYAL GAZETTE ;
To me a great monarch has loſt all his charms,
I have pull'd down his LION, and trampled his ARMS.

While fate was propitious, I thought they might ſtand,
(You know I was zealous for George's command)
But ſince he diſgrac'd it, and left us behind,
If I thought him an angel—I've alter'd my mind.

On the very ſame day that his army went hence
I ceas'd to tell lies for the ſake of his pence ;
And what was the reaſon ?—the true one is beſt—
I worſhip no ſuns when they hang to the weſt :

In this I reſemble a Turk or a Moor,
Bright Phœbus aſcending, I proſtrate adore ;
And, therefore, excuſe me for printing ſome lays,
An ode or a ſonnet in Waſhington's praiſe.

His prudence, and caution has ſav'd your dominions,
This chief of all chiefs, and the pride of Virginians !
And when he is gone—I pronounce it with pain—
We ſcarcely ſhall meet with his equal again.

The gods for that hero did trouble prepare,
But gave him a mind that could feed upon care,
They gave him a fpirit, ferene but fevere,
Above all diforder, confufion, and fear;
In him it was fortune where others would fail:
He was born for the tempeft, and weather'd the gale.*

Old Plato afferted that life is a dream
And man but a fhadow, a cloud, or a ftream;
By which it is plain he intended to fay
That man, like a fhadow, muft vanifh away:

If this be the fact, in relation to man,
And if each one is ftriving to get what he can,
I hope, while I live, you will all think it beft,
To allow me to buftle along with the reft.

A view of my life, though fome parts might be folemn,
Would make, on the whole, a ridiculous volume;
In the life that's hereafter (to fpeak with fubmiffion)
I hope I fhall publifh a better edition:

Even fwine you permit to fubfift in the ftreet;—
You pity a dog that lies down to be beat—
Then forget what is paft, for the year's at a clofe—
And men of my age have fome need of repofe.

* This ftanza is added in the edition of 1809.

II.

BUT as to the Tories that yet may remain,
They fcarcely need give you a moment of pain:
What dare they attempt when their mafters are fled;—
When the foul is departed, who wars with the dead?

On the waves of the Styx had they rode quarantine,
They could not have look'd more infernally lean
Than the day, when repenting, difmay'd and diftreft,
Like the doves to their windows, they ftuck to their neft.

Poor fouls! for the love of the king and his nation
They have had their full quota of mortification;
Wherever they fought, or whatever they won
The dream's at an end—the delufion is done.

The TEMPLE you rais'd was fo wonderful large
Not one of them thought you could anfwer the charge,
It feem'd a mere caftle conftructed of vapour,
Surrounded with gibbets, and founded on PAPER.

On the bafis of freedom you built it too ftrong!
And CARLETON confefs'd, when you held it fo long,
That if any thing human the fabric could fhatter,
The ROYAL GAZETTE muft accomplifh the matter.

An engine like that, in fuch hands as my own
Had fhaken king CUDJOE* himfelf from his throne,

* The negro king in Jamaica; whom the Englifh declared Independent in
1739.

In another rebellion had ruin'd the Scot,
While the Pope and Pretender had both gone to pot.

If you ſtood my attacks, I have nothing to ſay—
I fought, like the Swiſs, for the ſake of my pay ;
But while I was proving your fabric unſound
Our veſſel *miſſ'd ſtay*, and we all went aground.

Thus ended in ruin what madneſs begun,
And thus was our nation diſgrac'd and undone,
Renown'd as we were, and the lords of the deep,
If our outſet was folly, our exit was ſleep.

A dominion like THIS, that ſome millions had coſt !—
The king might have wept when he ſaw it was loſt ;—
This jewel—whoſe value I cannot deſcribe ;
This pearl—that *was richer than all his Dutch tribe.*

When the war came upon us, you very well knew
My income was ſmall and my riches were few—
If your money was ſcarce, and your proſpeċts were bad,
Why hinder me printing for people that had ?

'Twou'd have pleas'd you, no doubt, had I gone with a few
        ſetts
Of books, to exiſt in your cold Maſſachuſetts ;
Or to wander at *Newark*, like ill fated HUGH,
Not a ſhirt to my back, or a ſoal to my ſhoe :

Now, if we miſtook (as we did, it is plain)
Our error was owing to wicked HUGH GAINE,

For he gave fuch accounts of your ftarving and ftrife
As prov'd that his pictures were drawn from the life.

The part that I acted, by fome men of fenfe
Was wrongfully held to be malice propenfe,
When to all the world elfe it was perfectly plain,
One principle rul'd me—a paffion for gain.

You pretend I have fuffer'd no lofs in the caufe,
And have, therefore, no right to partake of your laws :——
Some people love talking—I find to my coft,
I too am a lofer—my PENSION is loft!

Nay, did not your printers repeatedly ftoop
To defcant and reflect on my PORTABLE SOUP?
At me have your porcupines darted the quill,
You have plunder'd my Office and publifh'd my *Will.*

Refolv'd upon mifchief, you held it no crime
To fteal my *Reflections,* and print them in rhyme,
When all the town knew (and a number confefs'd)
That papers, like thefe, were no caufe of arreft.

You never confider'd my ftruggles and ftrife ;
That my lot is to toil and to worry through life ;
My windows you broke—not a pane did you fpare—
And my houfe you have made a mere old *man of war.*

And ftill you infift I've no right to complain !—
Indeed if I do, I'm afraid it's in vain—

Yet am willing to hope you're too learnedly read
To hang up a printer for being misled.

If this be your aim, I must think of a flight—
In less than a month I must bid you good night,
And hurry away to that *whelp*-ridden shore
Where CLINTON and CARLETON retreated before.

From signs in the sky, and from tokens on land
I'm inclin'd to suspect my departure's at hand :
Old Argo* the ship,—in a peep at her star,
I found they were scraping her bottom for TAR :

For many nights past, as the house can attest,
A boy with a feather-bed troubled my rest :
My shop, the last evening, seem'd all in a blaze,
And a HEN crow'd at midnight, my waiting man says ;

Even then, as I lay with strange whims in my head,
A ghost hove in sight, not a yard from my bed,
It seem'd General ROBERTSON, *brawly* array'd,
But I grasp'd at the substance, and found him a shade !

He appear'd as of old, when head of the throng,
And loaded with laurels, he waddled along—
He seem'd at the foot of my bedstead to stand
And cry'd—"Jamie Rivington, reach me your hand,

* A southern Constellation consisting of 24 stars.

" And Jamie, (faid he) I am forry to find

" Some demon advis'd you to loiter behind;

" The country is hoftile—you had better get off it,

" Here's nothing but fquabbles, all plague, and no profit !

" Since the day that Sir William came here with his throng

" He manag'd things fo, that they always went wrong;

" And tho' for his knighthood, he kept MESCHIANZA,

" I think he was nothing but mere Sancho Panza :

" That famous conductor of *moon-light* retreats,

" Sir HARRY, came next with his armies and fleets,

" But, finding '*the Rebels were dying and dead,*'

" He grounded his arms and retreated—to bed.

" Other luck we had once at the battle of *Boyne !*

" But *here* they have ruin'd Earl *Charles* and *Burgoyne*,

" Here brave Colonel *Monckton* was thrown on his back,

" And here lies poor *Andre !* the beft of the pack."

So faying, he flitted away in a trice,

Juft adding, " he hop'd I would take his advice "—

Which I furely fhall do, if you pufh me too hard—

And fo I remain, with eternal regard,

JAMES RIVINGTON, Printer, of late to the king,

But now a republican, under your wing—

Let him ftand where he is—don't pufh him down hill,

And he'll turn a true *Blue-Skin*, or juft what you will.——

　　[*December* 31, 1783.]

OCCASIONED BY GENERAL WASHINGTON'S

ARRIVAL IN PHILADELPHIA, ON HIS WAY TO HIS RESIDENCE IN VIRGINIA.

(December, 1783.)

THE great, unequal conflict paſt,
   The Briton baniſh'd from our ſhore,
Peace, heaven-deſcended, comes at laſt,
   And hoſtile nations rage no more;
     From fields of death the weary ſwain
     Returning, ſeeks his native plain.

In every vale ſhe ſmiles ſerene,
   Freedom's bright ſtars more radiant riſe,
New charms ſhe adds to every ſcene,
   Her brighter ſun illumes our ſkies:
     Remoteſt realms admiring ſtand,
     And hail the *Hero* of our land:

He comes!—the Genius of theſe lands—
   Fame's thouſand tongues his worth confeſs,
Who conquer'd with his ſuffering bands,
   And grew immortal by diſtreſs:

Thus calms fucceed the ftormy blaft,
And valour is repaid at laft.

O WASHINGTON!—thrice glorious name,
What due rewards can man decree—
Empires are far below thy aim,
And fceptres have no charms for thee;
Virtue alone has your regard,
And fhe muft be your great reward.

Encircled by extorted power,
Monarchs muft envy your *Retreat*
Who caft, in fome ill fated hour,
Their country's freedom at their feet;
'Twas yours to act a nobler part,
For injur'd Freedom had your heart.

For ravag'd realms and conquer'd feas
Rome gave the great imperial prize,
And, fwell'd with pride, for feats like thefe,
Transferr'd her heroes to the fkies:—
A brighter fcene your deeds difplay,
You gain thofe heights a different way.

When *Faction* rear'd her briftly head,
And join'd with tyrants to deftroy,
Where'er you march'd the monfter fled,
Timorous her arrows to employ:
Hofts catch'd from you a bolder flame,
And defpots trembled at your name.

Ere war's dread horrors ceas'd to reign,
  What leader could your place fupply ?—
Chiefs crowded to the embattled plain,
  Prepar'd to conquer or to die—
    Heroes arofe—but none, like you,
    Could fave our lives and freedom too.

In fwelling verfe let kings be read,
  And princes fhine in polifh'd profe ;
Without fuch aid your triumphs fpread
  Where'er the convex ocean flows,
    To Indian worlds by feas embrac'd,
    And Tartar, tyrant of the wafte.

Throughout the eaft you gain applaufe,
  And foon the *Old World*, taught by you,
Shall blufh to own her barbarous laws,
  Shall learn inftruction from the *New :*
    Monarchs fhall hear the humble plea,
    Nor urge too far the proud decree.

Defpifing pomp and vain parade,
  At home you ftay, while France and Spain
The fecret, ardent wifh convey'd,
  And hail'd you to their fhores in vain :
    In *Vernon's* groves you fhun the throne,
    Admir'd by kings, but feen by none.

Your fame, thus fpread to diftant lands,
  May envy's fierceft blafts endure,

Like Egypt's pyramids it ſtands,
   Built on a baſis more ſecure;
      Time's lateſt age ſhall own in you
      The patriot and the ſtateſman too.

Now hurrying from the buſy ſcene,
   Where thy *Potowmack's* waters flow,
May'ſt thou enjoy thy rural reign,
   And every earthly bleſſing know;
      Thus HE,* who Rome's proud legions ſway'd,
      Return'd, and ſought his ſylvan ſhade.

Not leſs in wiſdom than in war
   Freedom ſhall ſtill employ your mind,
Slavery muſt vaniſh, wide and far,
   'Till not a trace is left behind;
      Your counſels not beſtow'd in vain,
      Shall ſtill protect this infant reign.

So, when the bright, all-cheering ſun
   From our contracted view retires,
Though folly deems his race is run,
   On other worlds he lights his fires:
      Cold climes beneath his influence glow,
      And frozen rivers learn to flow.

O ſay, thou great, exalted name!
   What Muſe can boaſt of equal lays,

* Cincinnatus.

Thy worth difdains all vulgar fame,
  Tranfcends the nobleft poet's praife :
    Art foars, unequal to the flight,
    And genius fickens at the height.

For States redeem'd—our weftern reign
  Reftor'd by thee to milder fway,
Thy confcious glory fhall remain
  When this great globe is fwept away,
    And *all* is loft that pride admires,
    And all the pageant fcene expires.

THE TRIUMPHAL ARCH.

Occafioned by rejoicings in Philadelphia on the acknowledgment of the National
Independence.

TOWARD the ſkies
　　What columns riſe
　In Roman ſtyle, profuſely great!
　　What lamps aſcend,
　　What arches bend,
　And ſwell with more than Roman ſtate!
High o'er the central arch diſplay'd,
　Old Janus ſhuts his temple door,
And ſhackles war in darkeſt ſhade—
　Saturnian times in view once more.

Pride of the human race, behold
　In Gallia's prince the virtues glow,
Whoſe conduct prov'd, whoſe goodneſs told
　That kings can feel for human woe.
Thrice happy France, in Louis bleſt,
Thy genius droops her head no more;
　In the calm virtues of the mind
　Equal to him no Titus ſhin'd—
No Trajan—whom mankind adore.

Another fcene too foon difplays!
    Griefs have their fhare, and claim their part,
They monuments to ruin raife,
    And fhed keen anguifh o'er the heart:
Thofe heroes that in battle fell
    Demand a fympathetic tear,
Who fought, our tyrants to repell—
    Memory preferves their laurels here.
        In vernal fkies
        Thus tempefts rife,
And clouds obfcure the brighteft fun—
        Few wreathes are gain'd
        With blood unftain'd—
No honours without ruin won.

The arms of France three lillies mark—.
    In honour's dome with thefe enroll'd
The plough, the fheaf, the gliding barque
    The riches of our State unfold.

Ally'd in heaven, a fun and ftars
    Friendfhip and peace with France declare—
The *branch* fucceeds the fpear of Mars,
    Commerce repairs the waftes of war;
        In ties of *concord* ancient foes engage,
        Proving the day-fpring of a brighter age.
Thefe STATES defended by the brave,
    Their military trophies, fee!
The virtue that of old did fave
    Shall ftill maintain them, *great* and *free*;

Arts fhall pervade the weftern wild,
And favage hearts become more mild.

Of fcience proud, the fource of fway,
  Lo! emblematic figures fhine;
The arts their kindred forms difplay,
  Manners to foften and refine:
A ftately Tree to heav'n its fummit fends,
And clufter'd fruit from thirteen boughs depends.

      With laurel crown'd
      A chief renown'd
(His country fav'd) his faulchion fheathes;
      Neglects his fpoils
      For rural toils,
And crowns his plough with laurel wreaths:—
While we this Roman chief furvey,
  What apt refemblance ftrikes the eye!
Thofe features to the foul convey
  A WASHINGTON, in fame as high,
    Whofe prudent, perfevering mind
    Patience with manly courage join'd,
And when difgrace and death were near,
  Look'd through the dark diftreffing fhade,
Struck hoftile Britons with unwonted fear,
  And blafted their beft hopes, and pride in ruin laid!

Victorious Virtue! aid me to purfue
The tributary verfe, to triumphs due—

18

Behold the peafant leave his lowly fhed,
  Where tufted forefts round him grow ;—
Though clouds the dark fky overfpread,
    War's dreadful art his arm effays,
    He meets the hoftile cannon's blaze,
  And pours redoubled vengeance on the foe.

Born to protect and guard our native land,
  Victorious Virtue ! ftill preferve us free ;
PLENTY—gay child of peace, thy horn expand,
  And, CONCORD, teach us to agree !
May every virtue that adorns the foul
  Be here advanc'd to heights unknown before ;
Pacific ages in fucceffion roll
    'Till Nature blots the fcene,
    Chaos refumes her reign
  And heaven with pleafure views its works no more.
    [*Philadelphia, May* 10. 1784.]

ON THE DEATH OF A REPUBLICAN PATRIOT AND STATESMAN.*

SOON to the grave defcends each honour'd name
　　That rais'd their country to this blaze of fame:
Sages, that plann'd, and chiefs that led the way
To Freedom's temple, all too foon decay,
Alike fubmit to one impartial doom,
Their glories clofing in perpetual gloom,
Like the bright fplendours of the evening, fade,
While night advances, to complete the fhade.

　　REED, 'tis for thee we fhed the unpurchas'd tear,
Bend o'er thy tomb, and plant our laurels there:
Your acts, your life, the nobleft pile tranfcend,
And Virtue, patriot Virtue, mourns her friend,
Gone to thofe realms, where worth may claim regard,
And gone where virtue meets her beft reward.

---

* General Jofeph Reed died in Philadelphia, March 5, 1785. Educated at
the College of New Jerfey, he was bred to the law, paffed much of his youth
and early manhood in England, returned home previous to the breaking out of the
war for independence, and took part in the preliminary civil proceedings as a dele-
gate to the old Continental Congrefs, and in other capacities. He was aide and
fecretary to Wafhington, and fubfequently adjutant-general. Refigning this
office, he continued to ferve in the army as a volunteer. He was a member of
Congrefs in 1778.

No fingle art engag'd his vigorous mind,
In every fcene his active genius fhin'd :
Nature in him, in honour to our age,
At once compos'd the foldier and the fage—
Firm to his purpofe, vigilant and bold,
Detefting traitors, and defpifing gold,
He fcorn'd all bribes from Britain's hoftile throne,
For all his country's wrongs he held his own.

    REED, reft in peace : for time's impartial page
Shall raife the blufh on this ungrateful age :
Long in thefe climes thy name fhall flourifh fair,
The ftatefman's pattern and the poet's care ;
Long in thefe climes thy memory fhall remain,
And ftill new tributes from new ages gain,
Fair to the eye that injur'd honour rife—
Nor traitors triumph while the patriot dies.

A RENEGADO EPISTLE TO THE INDEPENDENT AMERICANS.

WE Tories, who lately were frighten'd away,
    When you march'd into York all in battle array,
Dear whigs, in our exile have fomewhat to fay.

From the clime of New Scotland we wifh you to know
We ftill are in being—mere fpectres of woe,
Our dignity high, but our fpirits are low.

Great people we are, and are call'd the king's friends—
But on friendfhips like thefe what advantage attends?
We may ftay and be ftarv'd when we've anfwer'd his ends!

The Indians themfelves, whom no treaties can bind,
We have reafon to think are perverfely inclin'd—
And where we have friends is not eafy to find.

From the day we arriv'd on this defolate fhore
We ftill have been wifhing to fee you once more,
And your freedom enjoy, now the danger is o'er.

Although we be-rebel'd you up hill and down,
It was all for your good—and to honour a crown
Whofe fplendors have fpoil'd better eyes than our own.

That villains we are, is no more than our due,
And so may remain for a century through,
Unless we return, and be tutor'd by you.

Although with the dregs of the world we are class'd,
We hope your resentment will soften at last,
Now your toils are repaid, and our triumphs are past.

When a matter is done, 'tis a folly to fret—
But your market-day mornings we cannot forget,
With your coaches to lend, and your horses to let,

Your dinners of beef, and your breakfasts of *toast* !
But we have no longer such blessings to boast,
No cattle to steal, and no turkies to roast.

Such enjoyments as these, we must tell you with pain,
'Tis odds we shall only be wishing in vain
Unless we return and be brothers again.

We burnt up your mills and your meetings, 'tis true,
And many bold fellows we crippled and slew—
(Aye ! we were the boys that had something to do !)

Old HUDDY we hung on the Neversink shore—
But, Sirs, had we hung up a thousand men more,
They had all been aveng'd in the torments we bore,

When ASGILL to Jersey you foolishly fetch'd,
And each of us fear'd that his neck would be stretch'd,
When you were be-rebel'd, and we were be-wretch'd.

In the book of deſtruction it ſeems to be written
The Tories muſt ſtill be dependent on Britain—
The worſt of dependence that ever was hit on.

Now their work is concluded—that pitiful job—
They ſend over convicts to ſtrengthen our mob—
And ſo we do nothing but ſnivel and ſob

The worſt of all countries has fall'n to our ſhare,
Where winter and famine provoke our deſpair,
And fogs are forever obſcuring the air.·

Although there be nothing but ſea dogs to feed on,
Our friend Jemmy Rivington made it an Eden—
But, alas! he had nothing but lies to proceed on.

Deceiv'd we were all by his damnable ſchemes—
When he colour'd it over with gardens and ſtreams,
And grottoes and groves, and the reſt of his dreams.

Our heads were ſo turn'd by that conjurer's ſpell,
We ſwallow'd the lies he was order'd to tell—
But his "happy retreats" were the viſions of hell.

We feel ſo enrag'd we could rip up his weazon,
When we think of the ſoil he deſcrib'd with its trees on,
And the plenty that reign'd, and the charms of each ſeaſon.

Like a parſon that tells of the joys of the bleſt
To a man to be hang'd—he himſelf thought it beſt
To remain where he was, in his haven of reſt.

Since he help'd us away by the means of his types,
His precepts fhould only have lighted our pipes,
His example was rather to honour your ftripes.

Now, if we return, as we're bone of your bone,
We'll renounce all allegiance to George and his throne
And be the beft fubjects that ever were known.

In a fhip, you have feen (where the duty is hard)
The cook and the fcullion may claim fome regard,
Tho' it takes a good fellow to brace the main yard.

Howe'er you defpife us, becaufe you are free,
The world's at a lofs for fuch people as we,
Who can pillage on land, and can plunder at fea.

So long for our rations they keep us in waiting—
The lords and the commons, perhaps, are debating
If Tories can live without drinking or eating.

So we think it is better to fee you by far—
And have hinted our meaning to governor PARR—*
The worft that can happen is—*feathers and tar.*
     [*Nova Scotia, Feb.* 1784.]

         * Then Governor of Nova Scotia.

ON THE LEGISLATURE OF GREAT BRITAIN PROHIBITING THE SALE OF

DOCT. DAVID RAMSAY'S "HISTORY OF THE REVOLUTION OF SOUTH-CAROLINA," IN LONDON.—*

SOME bold bully *Dawſon*, expert in abuſing,
  Having paſs'd all his life in the practice of bruiſing,
At laſt, when he thinks to reform and repent,
And wiſhes his days had been ſoberly ſpent,
Though a courſe of contrition in earneſt begins,
He ſcarcely can bear to be told of his ſins.

  So, the Britiſh, worn out with their wars in the weſt,
(Where burning and murder their proweſs confeſt,)
When at laſt they agreed 'twas in vain to contend,
(For the days of their thieving were come to an end)
They got *their hiſtorians* to ſcribble and flatter,
And fooliſhly thought they could huſh up the matter.

  But RAMSAY aroſe, and with TRUTH on his ſide,
Has told to the world what they labour'd to hide,
With his pen of diſſection, and pointed with ſteel,
If they ne'er before felt—he has taught them to feel,

---

* David Ramſay's "Hiſtory of the Revolution in South Carolina," was publiſhed at Trenton, New Jerſey, in 1785.

Themfelves and their projects has truly defin'd,
And drag'd them to blufh at the bar of mankind.

    As the author, his friends, and the world might expect,
They find that the work has a damning effect ;
In reply to his facts they abufe him and rail,
And, prompted by malice, prohibit the fale.

    But, we truft, their chaftifement is only begun—
Thirteen are the ftates—and he writes but of *one;*
Ere the twelve that are filent their ftory have told,
THE KING WILL RUN MAD—AND THE BOOK WILL BE SOLD.

THE

P Y R A M I D

OF THE

FIFTEEN AMERICAN STATES.

BARBARA Pyramidum fileat miracula Memphis ;*
  Heu, male fervili marmora ſtructa manu !
Libera jam, ruptis, Atlantias ora, catenis,
  Jactat opus Phario marmore nobilius :
Namque Columbiadæ, facti monumenta parantes,
  Vulgarem ſpernunt ſumere materiam ;
Magnanimi cœlum ſcandunt, perituraque ſaxa
  Quod vincat, celſa de Jovis arce petunt.
Audax inde cohors ſtellis *E Pluribus Unum*
  Ardua Pyramidos tollit ad aſtra caput.
Ergo, Tempus edax, quamvis duriſſima ſævo
  Saxa domas morſu, nil ibi juris habes :
Dumque polo ſolitis cognata nitoribus ardent
  Sidera fulgebit Pyramis illa ſuis !

[*TRANSLATION.*]

NO more let barbarous MEMPHIS boaſt
  Huge ſtructures rear'd by ſervile hands—
A nation on the Atlantic coaſt
  Fetter'd no more in foreign bands,

---

* The Latin verſes were written by Mr. JOHN CAREY, formerly of Philadelphia

A nobler PYRAMID diſplays
Than Egypt's marble e'er could raiſe.

COLUMBIA'S ſons, to extend the fame
  Of their bold deeds to future years
No marble from the quarry claim,
  But, ſoaring to the ſtarry ſpheres,
Materials ſeek in Jove's blue ſky
To endure when braſs and marble die!

Arriv'd among the ſhining hoſt,
  Fearleſs, the proud invaders ſpoil
From countleſs gems, in æther loft,
  THESE STARS, to crown their mighty toil:
To heaven a PYRAMID they rear
And point the ſummit with a ſtar.

Old waſteful TIME! though ſtill you gain
  Dominion o'er the brazen tower,
On THIS your teeth ſhall gnaw in vain,
  Finding its ſtrength beyond their power:
While kindred ſtars in æther glow,
THIS PYRAMID WILL SHINE BELOW!

INDEX OF NAMES.

THE END.

www.ingramcontent.com/pod-product-compliance
Lightning Source LLC
Chambersburg PA
CBHW060520030726
47498CB00004B/1014

* 9 7 8 3 7 4 3 3 0 5 1 5 1 *